PENGUIN

THE CREATO

Emilio Calderón is a historian, editor, and author. He is the founder of Editorial Cirene, a publishing house in Spain. In 1995 he began writing young adult fiction. In 2003, Calderón received the Valle-Inclán Fellowship of the Spanish Royal Academy in Rome. The result was *The Creator's Map*, his first novel for adults, the translation rights to which have been sold in more than twenty countries. His latest novel, *The Jew from Shanghai*, won the 2008 Fernando Lara Prize in his native Spain. He lives in Málaga.

THE · CREATOR'S · MAP

Emilio Calderón

PENGUIN BOOKS

PENGUIN BOOKS

Published by the Penguin Group

Penguin Group (USA) Inc., 375 Hudson Street, New York, New York 10014, U.S.A.

Penguin Group (Canada), 90 Eglinton Avenue East, Suite 700, Toronto,
Ontario, Canada M4P 2Y3 (a division of Pearson Penguin Canada Inc.)

Penguin Books Ltd, 80 Strand, London WC2R 0RL, England

Penguin Ireland, 25 St Stephen's Green, Dublin 2, Ireland (a division of Penguin Books Ltd)

Penguin Group (Australia), 250 Camberwell Road, Camberwell,
Victoria 3124, Australia (a division of Pearson Australia Group Pty Ltd)

Penguin Books India Pvt Ltd, 11 Community Centre, Panchsheel Park, New Delhi – 110 017, India

Penguin Group (NZ), 67 Apollo Drive, Rosedale, North Shore 0632,
New Zealand (a division of Pearson New Zealand Ltd)

Penguin Books (South Africa) (Pty) Ltd, 24 Sturdee Avenue,
Rosebank, Johannesburg 2196, South Africa

Penguin Books Ltd, Registered Offices:
80 Strand, London WC2R 0RL, England

First published in the United States of America by The Penguin Press,
a member of Penguin Group (USA) Inc. 2008
Published in Penguin Books 2009

1 3 5 7 9 10 8 6 4 2

Originally published in Spanish as *El Mapa del Creador* by Roca Editorial de Libros,
S.L., Barcelona. This English-language edition published by arrangement with
Roca Editorial de Libros, S.L. All rights reserved.

Publisher's Note

This is a work of fiction. Names, characters, places, and incidents are either the product of
the author's imagination or are used fictitiously, and any resemblance to actual persons,
living or dead, business establishments, events, or locales is entirely coincidental.

ISBN 978-1-59420-181-3 (hc.)
ISBN 978-0-14-311550-2 (pbk.)
CIP data available

Printed in the United States of America
DESIGNED BY AMANDA DEWEY

To the real José María Hurtado de Mendoza, for lending me his name and his knowledge of Fascist architecture. To María Jesús Blasco, who told me about the Protestant Cemetery in Rome and "Liberty" style sculpture. And, of course, to Beatrice Cenci's ghost, who whispered this story in my ear one warm June night in Studio 18 of the Spanish Academy in Rome.

THE · CREATOR'S · MAP

PART · ONE

I.

Rome, October 1952

I FELT BOTH RELIEVED and uneasy when I read in the newspaper yesterday that Prince Junio Valerio Cima Vivarini had been found, decapitated, near the Schlegeis Glacier at the foot of Hochfeiler peak in a remote region of the Austrian Alps. Relieved because with his death the Second World War finally came to an end for me, even though Europe had already spent six years trying to rebuild itself; uneasy because the last time Junio spoke to Montse, my wife, back in March 1950, he had let her know that if he died under violent circumstances, we would receive certain documents, as well as instructions about what to do with them. And when Montse asked him about the nature of those documents, Junio had said only that they concerned a secret that he could not reveal "for your own safety." Junio had been an enthusiastic defender of the Third Reich during the war, so the last thing we wanted was to get ourselves entangled in his affairs. In addition to its personal ramifications for us, Junio's death was widely covered in the press, not only because he was a controversial figure but because another man, Emmanuel Werba, had also been found murdered a few months earlier in the same place and under the same circumstances. The decapitations of Junio and Mr. Werba, it seems, had revived the legend that the Nazis had hidden enough treasures in the Bavarian Alps to get the Fourth Reich off to a healthy start. These treasures were said to be guarded by members of the elite corps of the SS, faithful adherents of the esoteric beliefs to the Reichsführer-SS, Heinrich Himmler.

Masterpieces from all over Europe were discovered in a mine in Alt-aussee in the same region: 6,577 paintings, 230 watercolors and drawings, 954 prints and sketches, 137 sculptures, 78 pieces of furniture, 122 rugs, and 1,500 boxes of books. They included works by the Van Eyck brothers, Vermeer, Brueghel, Rembrandt, Halls, Rubens, Titian, Tintoretto, and many other great masters. Moreover, near the town of Redl-Zipf, an American soldier found jewels, gold, and 600 million counterfeit pounds sterling hidden in coffers and granary bins, treasures the Germans had planned to use to devastate the economy of Great Britain if the war had lasted any longer. The plan, baptized "Operation Bernhard," was conceived by the commander of the SS, Alfred Naujocks, and ratified by Hitler himself. In July 1944 the Nazis printed some 400,000 counterfeit bills they planned to throw out of planes while flying over English territory, an act that would have led to the immediate devaluation of the pound and the resulting collapse of the British economy. Subsequent unexpected circumstances (at that stage of the war the Luftwaffe needed every plane at its disposal to defend German airspace) prevented the operation, and the money was hidden in Austria. Thus, the deaths of Junio and Mr. Werba could have been interpreted as a warning to those who might still be tempted to search for still-undiscovered Nazi treasures.

As I sat in my study looking at the newspapers spread out on my desk, I could not help returning to the events of fifteen years earlier, when Montse first came into my life and the prince first came into ours.

2.

I T ALL BEGAN at the end of September 1937 at the Spanish Academy of History, Archeology, and Fine Arts in Rome, where I was living as a *pensionado*, or government-sponsored scholar studying Italian architecture.

The Spanish Civil War between the Republican government and the Nationalist rebels commanded by General Franco had broken out a year earlier, and life for us Spaniards in Rome was becoming more and more complicated. From the very outset of the conflict, the Spanish Embassy had sided with the Nationalists. The director of the academy, an appointee of the Republican government, had been immediately and summarily dismissed, and the embassy secretary, Olarra, had taken over. Thus we spent the first year of the war with him and his family, as well as the house butler, an Italian named Cesare Fontana.

The other three *pensionados*—José Ignacio Hervada, José Muñuz Molleda, and Enrique Pérez Comendador and his wife, Magdalena Lerroux—shared the Nationalists' aspirations; I, on the other hand, felt no affinity to either side. Because it was nearly impossible to receive firsthand news from Spain, the embassy decided to make use of the academy's privileged location on the Janiculum Hill, or the "Gianicolo," and installed a radiotelegraph station on one of its terraces. Three operators manned it around the clock.

Then, at the beginning of 1937, fifteen Catalonian families arrived on the academy's doorstep. Supporters of the Nationalist rebels and members of the bourgeoisie, they had escaped from Barcelona, fearing Republican reprisals and the anarchist hordes. Between the *pensionados*, the staff, the military personnel manning the radiotelegraph station, and these "refugees"—whom Olarra had welcomed with open arms—more than fifty of us were living at the Spanish Academy by the end of winter. With so many people to provide for, we were beginning to suffer real pangs of cold and hunger.

In desperation, we *pensionados*—with the support of most of the refugees—began to sell off some of the academy's assets for cash. Faced with ever-increasing hardships, Secretary Olarra himself was obliged to give his tacit approval. At first we made do selling random pieces of furniture, but we soon realized we could use that wood for fuel the following winter and instead turned our attention to the books. If there was anything of value in the academy, it was its library. The monks who had lived there since the sixteenth century had left countless volumes, to which was added a large endowment at the time of the academy's founding in 1881. Magdalena Lerroux, Pérez Comendador's wife, knew of an *antica libreria* on Via dell'Anima that bought books, so we decided to select a number of volumes and try our luck.

The person in charge of choosing the books we would try to sell was Montserrat, a young refugee who, on her own initiative and apparently for the sole purpose of keeping herself occupied, had taken charge of organizing the library. Always dressed in an off-white blouse and long skirt, with a matching scarf covering her hair, Montserrat—Montse—looked more like a nurse than an amateur librarian. She sometimes acted like a young nun, speaking rarely and then very modestly, especially in front of her elders. A few weeks after her arrival, Montse confided to me that her attire as well as her behavior was only a concession to her father's efforts to render her invisible. Those efforts, however, were doomed to fail, betrayed by Montse's astounding beauty. She had sea-green eyes, skin as white as Carrara marble, an incomparably long and delicate neck, a slender figure, and a poised and elegant bearing. This was the kind of beauty no clothes could hide, the kind that left men bewildered.

Pérez Comendador pulled names out of a hat to determine which *pensionado* would accompany Montse to the bookstore to carry out what everybody hoped would be a favorable transaction.

"You're it, José María," he said, turning to me.

I eagerly agreed, welcoming any activity that would break the routine, which at the time consisted almost entirely of waiting anxiously for news from Spain over the wireless. I must also admit that I had felt attracted to Montse from the first day I met her, maybe because I saw in her beauty a form of salvation, a way to free my thoughts from the cataclysm of the war.

"How much should I ask for them?" I inquired, fully aware of my ignorance of the business world.

"Double whatever they offer you. That way you can lower your price to somewhere in between what you asked and they offered," suggested Pérez Comendador, whose life as a married man had made it necessary for him to pay attention to numbers.

Like an enamored schoolboy on his first date, I carried the books, but it was Montse who took the lead. We descended through the academy's cool, lush gardens, emerging on Via Garibaldi through the *porta interdetto*, its use prohibited by Mussolini's police to prevent the nocturnal comings and goings of so-called anarchists and women of the night. As the order had not yet been enforced, we continued to use that door, more convenient than the one that led to the San Pietro in Montorio stairway, which was quite steep and difficult to climb.

Once we were out in the open air, the sun reminded us that it was still summer, the humid dog days so typical of Rome. A flock of starlings heading westward announced the imminent arrival of autumn. Montse's off-white garments made me think of an angel, and the swaying of her hips, the devil. This affirmation that her demeanor at the academy was nothing but a deliberate pretense was what initially drew me to her; looking back, I know that this was the precise moment I began to fall in love.

"Do you know the way?" she asked in a tone of voice that told me she had left her modesty within the walls of the academy.

"Yes, don't worry."

"This pavement is impossible," she said as she negotiated the cobblestones that covered most of the city streets.

I looked and saw that Montse was wearing high heels, shoes she might have worn to go out dancing.

"You could easily twist your ankle in those heels," I said.

"I thought they made me look more serious, more formal, and my father always says that when it comes to business, seriousness and formality are the most important things."

Not to mention in daily life, I thought, remembering Señor Fábregas's perpetually sullen and stern demeanor. An industrialist with a textile factory in Sabadell, Montse's father was obsessed by the events unfolding in Barcelona. He carried with him at all times an article by the British journalist George Orwell, a man of leftist tendencies who was sympathetic to the cause of the Popular Front and the Republican government. The article describes how Orwell felt when he arrived in Barcelona, his sense of having reached some strange continent where the moneyed classes had ceased to exist, the formal *usted* form of address was obsolete, and the hat and tie were considered fascist attire. Whenever someone asked Señor Fábregas why he had gone into exile, he would pull out Orwell's article, then proceed to read it aloud, clearly enunciating each word. And in case his interlocutor suggested that it was Franco who had broken the rule of law, Señor Fábregas would take out another newspaper article, this one from the Catalán Nationalist newspaper *La Nació*, dated June 9, 1934, in which he had underlined the following sentence: "We have never wanted to belong to the Spanish state because the smell of gypsies disgusts us"; after which he would add, "This is the prophecy of war. This is why Franco decided to call their bluff: the enemy was treacherous and harbored the basest instincts." Now in Rome he devoted himself to raising money to help liberate Catalonia from what he called "Bolshevist anarchy."

"Do you like Rome?" I asked Montse, still trying to break the ice.

"I like the buildings here more than the ones in Barcelona, but I prefer the streets of Barcelona. The streets of Rome are like in the Raval district, only here they are lined with palaces. And what wonderful palaces! And you," she asked me pointedly, "do you like Rome?"

"I plan to live here the rest of my life," I answered categorically.

This idea had been churning in my head for months, but this was the first time I had actually put it into words.

"At the academy?" Montse asked with interest.

"No, when the war is over the academy will also be done for. I'm planning to open up an architectural office here."

Oddly enough, it had been the former director of the academy, Ramón Valle-Inclán, who had invited me to study Fascist architecture in the hopes of finding out if there was anything about it that could be useful to our Republic. He had since died in his native Galicia, and the Republic itself was on the point of collapsing like a poorly designed building. Thanks to the subject of my studies, Secretary Olarra still trusted me, at least officially; one of his many duties was spying for the embassy, informing on those whose ideas or behavior were politically suspect.

"Why don't you want to return to Spain? I would love to go back to Barcelona. Anyway, if anything is going to be needed in Spain after the war it is architects."

Montse was right. If Franco won the war, he would need architects who had studied Fascist architecture. However, what Franco would need was one thing, and what I wished to do quite another.

"I have no family, nobody waiting for me in Spain," I said.

Montse scrutinized me silently, as if demanding that I provide more detailed information.

"My parents died, and my grandparents, too. I'm an only child."

"You must have an aunt or uncle, a cousin. . . . Everybody has cousins."

"I do, but they live in Santander and I never see them. I met my aunts and uncles a couple of times in Madrid, when they came to settle my grandparents' estate. But things got ugly, and the relationship between them and my parents soured. As for my cousins, we are strangers. . . ."

"Families are like miniature countries; there can also be traitors within," Montse blurted out, then sighed.

I looked at her, surprised.

"That's what my father says. My Uncle Jaime is a Red. We are not allowed to mention his name," she added.

"But you just did," I said.

"I don't want my father and my uncle to end up like Cain and Abel."

I was about to ask her who was who, but I was afraid to initiate a conversation on a topic that might prove sensitive. If I had learned anything in the past few months, it was that during a war, words could easily lead to misunderstandings. "Deep down, your father is right," I said. "Countries are like families. Once their members declare war on each other, the only thing they care about is building up their forces; they don't stop to consider the damage they are causing."

We crossed the Tiber over the Ponte Sisto, holding our noses to avoid smelling the thick, putrid air rising from the water. The river looked like a purulent scar across the face of the city. On one end of the bridge somebody had painted a fasces—an ax nestled in a bundle of rods—the symbol of the consuls and lectors of ancient Rome, adopted by Mussolini as the emblem of his movement.

When we got to Piazza Navona we stopped in front of Fontana dei Fiumi, Bernini's most famous fountain.

"They say that the giants who represent the Nile and the Río de la Plata are shielding their eyes so as not to see Borromini's church of Sant'Angese in Agone," Montse said, repeating a popular legend. "Apparently, there was great enmity between those two great artists."

"Everybody tells that story, but it's not true," I said. "The fountain was built before the church. The giant who represents the Nile is covering his face because he doesn't know where he comes from. Rome is full of similar legends that exalt its past. Maybe this old city doubted its own beauty and needed such tall tales to keep itself alive."

When we got to the bookshop—a small and ancient establishment, its walls lined with shelves stuffed with antique and secondhand books and decorated with prints of the famous *Vedute di Roma* by Piranesi—we were greeted by a vivacious, cheerful man in his fifties. He had a wide, round face; bright red cheeks; bulging, bloodshot eyes; a long nose; and thick, full lips.

"I am Marcello Tasso," he introduced himself. "I understand you have been sent here by Signora Pérez Comendador. I have been expecting you."

As he ushered us in, we noticed a small inlaid wood table under the counter; resting on it was an opened antique book and several metallic objects that resembled medical instruments. Signor Tasso noticed our interest and proceeded to explain.

"In addition to buying and selling books, I also restore them, even resurrect them from the dead," he said. "Many of my clients call me the book doctor of Rome, a title that gives me great pride. I am thinking of opening a museum for ill-treated books to show that the greatest threat to them is not insects or fire or sunlight or humidity or even the passage of time, but rather man. Doubtless a strange paradox if one considers that the book is a human artifact. It would be like saying that the greatest danger to man is God, his creator. . . . Though perhaps God deplores mankind to the same extent that man deplores books. . . . But we will be more comfortable in my office. Follow me."

Before I even realized what was happening, Signor Tasso had taken the books from my arms, an unequivocal sign that they belonged to his domain.

I don't know why, but the smell of mildewed, moth-eaten paper that permeated the bookshop, along with the proprietor's enthusiasm, gave me confidence. It was like going back to a time before the war, a world where there was no place for confrontations. The moment I stepped foot in his office, however, I was overcome with a strong feeling of aversion. On the walls were hanging prints from a series called *Carceri d'Invenzione*, or "Imaginary Prisons," sixteen etchings signed by Piranesi himself in 1762, in which the artist re-created an unreal architecture of passageways and staircases leading to an underground and anguished world, perhaps Hell itself, a work created in the middle of the Enlightenment in which shadows and chiaroscuros predominated. On one of the prints I read the words of the historian Livy referring to Ancus Marcius, the first king who ordered the construction of a jail in Rome: "*ad terrors increscentis audacie.*"

"How do you like Piranesi's prisons?" Signor Tasso asked when he saw me staring at them.

"Not very much," I answered. "I find them quite bleak."

"Yes, indeed, they are. In Piranesi's prisons we see everything that enslaves the human being: fear and the torment of knowing we are mortal; the enormity of space, which reminds us of our own smallness; man transformed into Sisyphus, conscious that his battle with life is lost. . . . Please," he said, remembering himself, "make yourselves comfortable."

Both chairs on our side of the desk were piled high with dusty books, so we remained standing.

"Would you like something to drink?" he asked us.

Montse and I both shook our heads even though our throats were dry from the walk there and our excitement.

"Let's see what you have brought me."

Signor Tasso scrutinized the books diligently, with an ease earned through vast experience. He quickly examined the covers, the tables of contents, the quality of the paper; he then checked the bindings to see what kind of shape they were in.

"Where did you get this book?" he asked finally, holding one up and arching his eyebrows.

"They all come from the Spanish Academy library," Montse answered, speaking in such impeccable Italian that I was quite taken aback.

Signor Tasso hesitated a few moments before responding.

"This book is extremely valuable. Have you ever heard of Pierus Valerianus?"

Montse and I shook our heads again.

"He was a Prothonotary Apostolic of Pope Clement VII. He wrote a book called *Hieroglyphica, or a Commentary on the Sacred Alphabet of the Egyptians and Other Peoples*. It was first published in 1556 in Basel and had fifty-eight chapters. Valerianus was one of the first writers to attempt to decipher Egyptian hieroglyphics, and he was particularly concerned with animal symbolism in relation to natural history. Certainly a difficult labor considering that the Counter-Reformation was in full swing."

"So?" Montse asked.

"The volume you have brought me is from that first edition of 1556."

"You are interested then," I said.

Signor Tasso showed the beginning of a wide smile, and a crimson tongue showed between his teeth.

"Let us say that I have a buyer for this book, someone who would be willing to pay a very handsome price for it."

"And what about the others?" I asked, eager to go as far as I could with the deal.

"I'll buy the rest from you. Now that Spain is at war, interest in Spanish literature has grown among Italian readers. As for Valerianus, come back here tomorrow at the same time."

Once we had agreed on a sum and the money for the other books was in our hands, I picked up the Valerianus. As we turned to leave, Signor Tasso said, "It would be better for that book to stay here, among books. I will know how best to take care of it." I looked at the bookseller suspiciously, then quickly understood that he was right. After all, his business would still be there the next day, as it had been during the previous thirty years.

"Agreed, but please give me a receipt. And promise me that if the book is stolen or suffers any kind of mishap while in your care, we will receive fair compensation."

I surprised myself with my business acumen, especially when Signor Tasso picked up a pen without hesitating.

"Tell me your name."

"José María Hurtado de Mendoza."

When Montse and I got outside, we were brimming with pride and satisfaction. Our pockets were full of money, and there was the promise of much more the following day. Not to mention all the other books still at the academy. With a little luck we would spend the coming winter warm and well fed. What we couldn't have imagined was how profoundly our lives were about to change.

3.

INSOMNIA DROVE ME out of bed around midnight, and I decided to go up to the terrace to catch some direct news from Spain. Any news we were offered about the war was already sifted through by our de facto censor, Secretary Olarra, who was playing the part of political commissar. He took it upon himself to relay to us the successes of the Nationalist troops, while relentlessly criticizing the Republic and scorning the behavior of soldiers who defended it, whom he disdainfully called "the faceless rabble."

Rubiños, the youngest of the three radiotelegraph operators, was on duty. He wore earphones and his eyes were closed. In his right hand he held a pencil, and in his left a notebook, where he was supposed to write out the dispatches that arrived from the peninsula. Based on the expression on his face, one might have concluded he was in a trance, or on the verge of falling headlong into the arms of sleep.

"Any news?" I asked.

Rubiños jumped out of his chair like a sleeping hare startled by a hunter. His fine, delicate blond hair had bunched up around the crown of his head, and his blue eyes swirled in their sockets as they sought me as a focal point.

"Nothing special, *mi pensionado*, except the Reds keep killing priests by forcing them to eat crucifixes and rosary beads. They've cut off a nun's breasts and left her body on the beach in Sitges, and in Madrid they're throwing priests into the lion cages like the ancient Romans did to the early Christians."

Rubiños was one of those young men who doesn't leave anything unsaid and enjoys elaborating on the most appalling details, as if proof of his adversary's cruelty helped strengthen his own convictions.

"You don't need to give me quite so many details, Rubiños."

"Feel like a smoke?" he asked. "It's fine-cut tobacco from the Italian cartel. Worse than the chicken feed I used to smoke in my native Galicia. My father says that to wage war you need two arms, two legs, a pair of balls, good tobacco, and good coffee. If the tobacco and the coffee are no good, it demoralizes the troops."

It was curious that Rubiños spoke as if the front were on the opposite bank of the Tiber rather than two thousand kilometers away. I, on the other hand, would never feel I was living the war firsthand no matter how close I was to the action.

"Thank you, but I don't smoke."

"Is it true you sold a half-dozen books for a good price?" he inquired.

A gust of dense, warm air carrying a humid scent mixed with the sweet aroma of Rubiños's cigarette and made its way into my lungs.

"More or less," I responded laconically.

"My father always says that the most valuable things are those that look the least valuable. Like books, for instance."

I thought of Montse. I imagined her sleeping, her beauty discreetly hidden under the academy's striped sheets. Perhaps she disobeyed her father in this way as well, by exposing her bare legs and arms, her naked breasts, while she slept. I was suddenly overwhelmed by the desire to embrace her, possess her, make her mine. A shiver ran up and down my spine, as if I had actually felt the caress of her skin. It lasted only an instant, but I became flustered and felt vaguely ashamed.

"Your father's right. If people read more, things wouldn't be as they are," I observed.

The look Rubiños gave me clearly indicated that he was uncertain how to interpret my words.

"I really should be listening to the radiotelegraph, excuse me, *mi pensionado*," he concluded.

All my efforts to explain to Rubiños that the title of *pensionado* did not carry with it any military or academic rank had been futile. In this way he was as formal as the Romans, who called everybody "doctor" or "engineer" or "professor," even "commander," regardless of whether they held any such title.

I walked over to the balustrade to contemplate the view of Rome. The city was enjoying a dark, placid slumber, broken only by the sound of a far-off engine or the tenuous amber glow of a street lamp. Once my eyes grew accustomed to the darkness, there paraded before me a seemingly infinite number of spectral domes and towers. I began to identify them by name from right to left, as I always did whenever I stood there. Santi Bonifacio e Alessio, Santa Sabina, Santa Maria in Cosmedin, Il Palatino, San Giovanni in Laterano, Il Vittoriano, Il Gesù, Sant'Andrea della Valle, Il Pantheon, Sant'Ivo alla Sapienza, Trinità dei Monti, Villa Medici, and, finally, St. Peter's. No view in Rome compared to this one from the terrace of the Spanish Academy; even Stendhal wrote about this spot as unique. It gave one the sensation of contemplating the city from a cloud, over and above its inhabitants, its buildings, and even its own history. On a clear day one could make out the Alban Hills and Castel Gandolfo, the summer residence of the popes, just behind the city's sharp and majestic profile; the domes shone brightly, burnished by the sun's rays, and the black cobblestone streets were infused with a white, milky light. On stormy days, however, the low clouds spread a gray veil over the city—sometimes they were no more than shards of mist that managed to brush their fingers against the domes and towers—lending it a rather ethereal, unreal aspect. However good the view was, and whatever the weather or time of day, Mussolini's dream of a new Rome—a vast city, both orderly and powerful, as it had been during the time of the first Emperor Augustus—was nowhere in view. The order the Duce had given to architects, urban planners, and archeologists was to "liberate the trunk of the great oak from all that hid it, from all that had grown around it throughout centuries of decadence." While the historic center had become less congested with the opening of Via dei Fori Imperiali, Via della Consolazione, Via del Teatro di Marcello, and Corso del Rinascimento, and interesting projects such as the Palazzo Littorio and the reconstruction of the Mausoleum of Augustus—the work of the architect Antonio Muñoz—were under way, Rome still had a long way to go before it would resemble a modern metropolis.

As I turned around to head back to my room, I caught sight of a ghostly figure. Thin and gloomy, Secretary Olarra loomed in the semidarkness like a cypress in a cemetery. He observed me closely and in silence.

"What are you doing up here?" he asked gruffly when he sensed I had seen him.

Olarra suspected anybody who visited the radiotelegraph station of being a spy for the Republic. He habitually spoke in harsh, intimidating tones; deep down, he trusted nobody. This suspicious and vehement defender of the abstruse moral, social, and political tenets of Fascism only vaguely resembled the Olarra who had worked shoulder-to-shoulder with former director Valle-Inclán two and a half years earlier, when the Republic was still a beautiful dream.

"I couldn't sleep," I answered.

"I've always thought that people who sleep poorly must feel guilty."

"I don't feel guilty of anything," I answered sharply.

"Then perhaps you have a problem of conscience," he suggested.

For Olarra, the only possible state of mind was overflowing optimism, and the very act of exhibiting such faith forwarded the goal of reconstituting Spain's order and moral tradition. Being reserved or taciturn was a symptom of weakness, a lack of faith in the cause. Beneath the surface, the warrior zeal Olarra advocated was a simple case of excess, as if exaggerated enthusiasm were the highest expression of the ideas that he defended. And deep down, it was. He was stronger than his ideas.

"It's just the heat," I said.

"Autumn will come tomorrow, and soon thereafter the rains will start and the temperatures will drop. Best of all, there will be no winter this year. In three or four weeks, spring will have arrived. Franco is devouring the peninsula in huge gulps. Asturias is about to fall, and when that happens, the northern front will be in the hands of Nationalist troops. Without the weapons and heavy industry in the north, the Republic is lost. The next step will be for Queipo de Llano's army to spread its tentacles over Madrid. I think it's time for you to push ahead with your work, because soon, very soon, the nation will be in need of your services."

Sometimes I wondered where he had learned to speak in such a vacuous, demagogic way, but all I had to do was look around me to see that Olarra was a man well worthy of his times. A quick glance at the foyers, hallways, and rooms of the majestic architecture favored by Mussolini was enough to make one realize that only a grandiloquent style of oratory could fill such spaces with a human voice.

"In any case, even if there is no winter, I still think we should keep selling books, just to be safe," I said. The Italian press was reporting that there was no end in sight for the three battles being waged around Madrid. "It seems that Spanish books are all the rage in Italy."

"Thanks to our crusade," Olarra said, then pronounced, "God bless the Caudillo! God bless the Duce! Now go back to bed and don't go frightening the ladies."

"And you, don't you sleep?" I asked him.

"I, sleep? With everything that's going on? I am the captain of a ship navigating through a storm. I don't have a thought for sleep, not a thought. And as if I didn't have enough to worry about, I am determined to translate the Vatican Library rules of cataloging into Spanish; they are currently pure gibberish."

A *cum laude* graduate of the Vatican School of Library Sciences, Secretary Olarra devoted his time to creating a fully integrated, Spanish-language text, which could be used to assist in the cataloging of the enormous collections of the Vatican Apostolic Library. This labor had occupied him for the previous several years and, paradoxically, had led him to neglect the academy library.

4.

ONTSE SET OUT TO THE BOOKSHOP the next day oblivious to the
fact that she was about to meet her destiny. As soon as she stepped
onto Via Garibaldi she again became that vibrant and brazen young
woman of the day before. I noticed that she wore more perfume than usual
and hoped she had done so for me. She then began to question me closely,
which I attempted to reciprocate by asking her about her life in Barcelona
and her plans for the future.

Suddenly she blurted out, "As soon as they give you the money, give
it to me so I can hide it." Then, seeing how taken aback I was, she added,
"I brought a pouch just for that purpose."

"You don't trust me?" I asked her.

"Let's see. Are you an artist or an intellectual?"

If Montse had one virtue that stood out from all the rest it was her
ability to approach any subject in a totally natural way, call things by their
names, and never lose her friendly composure. Words didn't frighten her,
and this always gave her the advantage in any conversation.

"Why do you ask?"

"Just answer," she insisted.

I had never imagined I would have to take a stand on such a subjective
and imprecise issue.

"An artist?" I muttered, full of reservations.

"Artists are usually inept at business," she declared.

"What would you have said if I had chosen the other option?" I asked out of curiosity.

"The same. Intellectuals are also hopeless when it comes to money matters."

Her aplomb astounded me; her family's success in the business world had clearly given her great confidence. I suspected that she had probably often heard her father espousing that typically bourgeois dogma that categorizes people according to their occupations.

"I'm afraid twenty-year-old women from the Catalán bourgeoisie are, too," I countered.

"On January eleventh I turn twenty-one, and I've been helping my father in his office since I was eighteen. I have studied stenography, I know what a journal entry is, I know how to fill out forms for importing and exporting merchandise, I know what a liability and an asset are, and I speak five languages: English, French, Italian, Catalán, and Spanish."

Her words rendered me speechless.

"In 1931, when the Republic was proclaimed, my father and my Uncle Ernesto and Aunt Olga decided to make the life of my Uncle Jaime, whose name I am forbidden to utter, impossible, because he had gone over to the Popular Front and was involved in some kind of political-financial dealings," she continued. "After a difficult legal battle that lasted more than two and a half years, they managed to throw him out of the family business, which resulted in my uncle's total financial ruin. He was even forced to sell the gold watch he had inherited from my grandfather in order to survive. Half an hour after the transaction and just three hundred meters from the jewelry store, two unknown assailants gave him a vicious beating and stole his money. He almost died. I was the only one who went to visit him at the hospital, and I had to do it in secret."

I surmised from Montse's story that she held her father responsible for the beating, but I decided not to say anything.

"Signor Tasso does not appear to be that kind of man," I offered.

"Just in case, give me the money as soon as you get it, if possible without anybody seeing."

An Italian car was parked in front of the bookstore. Its license plate was a combination of letters and a number: SMOM 60. A chauffeur was dozing off inside, a peaked cap covering his face. I assumed it was an official vehicle of some kind.

"Our buyer? With a car like that, he must be a big shot," Montse speculated.

The big shot turned out to be a slender young man of about thirty, approximately six feet tall, with tanned skin. He was well proportioned; had a prominent cleft chin; dark eyes with a lively, insolent expression; and black, shiny hair combed flat against his skull with hair cream. He was wearing the black shirt and gray drill pants of the Italian Fascists, and he exuded a strong scent of expensive perfume.

"Allow me to introduce you to Prince Junio Valerio Cima Vivarini," Signor Tasso said. "He is a well-known paleographer, and he is very interested in acquiring your book."

Introducing this prince as a famous paleographer was as extravagant as presenting him as a highly efficient butcher. In fact, he looked less like a blue-blooded prince than a member of the *principi*, the shock troops used by the Fascists to break up strikes and repress anti-Fascist activities. Though he could also pass for a *bullo di quartiere*, or neighborhood bully, that violent and belligerent character right out of Roman comedy.

"*Piacere*," the young man said as he stood up even straighter and clicked his heels in the most perfect Teutonic tradition.

I had never witnessed such a ridiculous scene. A Fascist prince and paleographer offering a military salute inside a bookstore full of dusty, old books. Mussolini was right when he said, "All life is gesture."

"*Piacere*," Montse repeated, as she removed the scarf covering her head.

Just by the tone of her voice I knew that I had lost, that I could never compete in fascination with this character. I also knew that dazzling someone is relatively simple and takes only an instant, while the truly difficult task is maintaining that bright light for a long time without damaging the other's vision. Junio didn't appear to be the kind of man who would care much about a woman: I suspected he had such varied interests that he lacked the constancy a relationship requires. Months, even years, would pass before either Montse or I could complete the map of Junio's character, for he was a person of such extraordinary complexity that he ended up seeming simple. The cruelest but also the kindest of men, the most intolerant and at the same time the most understanding, the haughtiest and the humblest, the strongest and the most vulnerable. Like Montse, he was always playing a role, which varied according to the different circles he moved in—a kind of dissembling that led him to take on various identities. Now, looking back with the compassion his death has evoked in me, I can say that he was a victim of his times, an eccentric who happened to be born when Europe itself had gone crazy.

The truth is that if Junio stole Montse from me at that moment of their first meeting, the dangerous and inaccessible world that surrounded him slowly returned her to me. And it was only thanks to the fact that I was the link between her and Junio that she eventually ended up accepting me. I had only to wait. But let us proceed one step at a time, because Montse did not come back to me all at once, but sporadically and haphazardly, like the remains of a shipwreck that the sea spews up on the beach, a long process only the currents understand.

"The book is worth at least seven thousand lire, but I am prepared to pay up to fifteen thousand," Junio said.

My chagrin at observing Montse with the prince was magnified by this mockery he was making of Pérez Comendador's advice to me on how to conduct the negotiations.

"I don't understand," I said. "If the book is worth seven thousand lire, why would you want to pay fifteen thousand? It's absurd!"

Montse flashed me a fierce look of disapproval, as if she knew that the prince's generosity had everything to do with her.

"Let's just say that money is not a problem for me," Junio said with a proper dose of smugness.

"So, why not pay sixteen thousand or, even better, seventeen thousand?" I suggested.

"Okay, I'll give you seventeen thousand lire," he agreed.

It occurred to me that this entire dialogue had no purpose other than flaunting our egos.

"It's a deal," I said.

"You are forgetting my commission," interrupted Signor Tasso, who had so far remained silent.

"How much would that be?" the prince asked, obviously much more skilled at this game of buying and selling.

"One thousand lire from each party."

"That seems fair."

Both men looked at me, waiting for me to speak.

"Agreed," I said finally.

I interpreted this negotiation as a victory over Junio and as a way of vindicating myself in front of Montse. I had no way of knowing that, in addition to the book, he was buying us; it was still too soon and we too naive to realize it.

While the other two were distracted for a moment packing up the book, I gave Montse the money, as she had requested: my way of putting her to the test.

"No, you keep it," she said, lowering her voice.

"What if they attack us like they did your Uncle Jaime?" I asked her.

"Who's going to attack us, a prince with a chauffeur, a Fascist Robin Hood?"

Montse's words contained more than a simple dose of irony. Something within her had been set in motion, a process whereby one person begins to trust another unreservedly and without any basis other than physical attraction. Not being the repository of this trust, I saw it as foolish and unfair. I told myself that Montse was too young, and that there were probably as many dethroned princes as stray cats in Rome.

5.

THE SIXTEEN THOUSAND LIRE were enough to impress Secretary Olarra, who, after counting the money twice, exclaimed, "The Duce gave José Antonio Primo de Rivera fifteen thousand lire a month to support the Falangists in Spain! And you have managed to sell one book for sixteen thousand! The world has definitely gone mad!"

Everyone else was busy discussing an incident involving Doña Julia, one of the refugees most respected for her culinary arts. Apparently, the good woman had had an intense encounter during her siesta with the ghost of the academy. She had lain down to rest, as she did every afternoon, when suddenly she felt the long, transparent arms of a woman emerging from the mattress and wrapping themselves around her. After realizing that the embrace was so strong it prevented her from getting out of bed, she decided to close her eyes and recite the Our Father, the advised course of action, it would seem, in such a situation. The ghost vanished, and Doña Julia ran out of her room in terror.

For us *pensionados*, the story of the ghost was nothing new; on the contrary, it was an integral part of the academy's mysteries. According to some, this was the errant ghost of Beatrice Cenci, an aristocratic Roman lady beheaded for murdering her father, who had sexually abused her, and whose body was buried in the neighboring church of San Pietro in Montorio. The fact that her severed head had been kept in a silver urn, which had disappeared when the French troops entered Rome in 1798, had angered the deceased's ghost, who now wandered around the academy demanding that it be returned to her. Others claimed that the ghost was the spirit of one of the nuns who had lived in the building when it was a Franciscan convent. The refugees had been warned of the ghost's presence as soon as they set foot in the academy, so it was only a question of time before the power of suggestion would work its magic on one of them.

After listening patiently for more than an hour to the details of the incident and everybody's suggestions (someone even proposed that the academy be exorcised by a priest), I decided to take a walk through the Trastevere neighborhood to put my thoughts in order. I was overwhelmed by a sense of melancholy unease, and though it was difficult for me to admit it, I knew in my heart that Montse was the direct cause. There was something so unusual about her way of thinking, something that so far surpassed that of other girls her age and even my own (I was seven years older than she). She seemed always ready to enjoy every moment as if it were her last, and for this very reason she was extremely demanding of herself and others. It was as if Junio's mere appearance had helped me understand that even if I ever had the good fortune to make her mine, she would never give herself to me completely. That was her nature; freedom formed an intrinsic part of her most intimate self, and nothing, not even the deepest attachment, could change that. I saw clearly that to attempt to possess her completely would be like trying to lock a bird in a cage. Junio, it turned out, wasn't only a threat; he was also the touchstone that allowed me to apprehend Montse's true essence. Ultimately, I can see that my relationship with her would not have been possible without him, at least not on the same terms. Perhaps I would have managed some kind of temporary commitment, a teenage romance, but she never would have remained with me in Rome after the civil war and renounced her family, as she eventually did.

I descended the stairs that linked San Pietro in Montorio to Via Goffredo Mameli. From there I continued along Via Bertani, crossed Piazza di San Cosimato, continued along Via Natale del Grande, turned left on

San Francesco a Ripa, and, without consciously planning it, found myself in front of Frontoni, an old, ramshackle family-run café. I entered and ordered a *cappuccino freddo*. Signor Enrico, the proprietor, told me that it had taken its name from the brown and white habits of the Capuchin monks. It did not seem to matter to him that I had been coming to that café and ordering the same thing for two years, and that he told me that anecdote every single time.

For three-quarters of an hour I sat in silence, absorbed in my thoughts under the messianic gaze of the Duce, who stared down from a gigantic poster, until Signor Enrico approached and shook me out of my ruminations.

"A gentleman asked me to give you this note five minutes after he left."

I lifted my eyes and was surprised to see how much Signor Enrico resembled Mussolini. It was as if all Italians had decided to look like their leader, a strange mimetic phenomenon rather like the supposed resemblance between dogs and their owners.

"A gentleman?" I asked in surprise.

"A foreigner, like you."

"A regular customer?"

"No, he's never been here before. He looked like . . . a man from the north," Enrico added as his hand traced some figure in the air.

"A man from the north?"

"You know, blond hair, light eyes, face full of freckles. If we were in Sicily, I would say he was of Norman descent, but since we are not, I would say he was Norman. And where do the Normans live? In the north."

Signor Enrico's reasoning left me without retort. But when he handed me a twice-folded piece of paper, it took me a few moments to summon up the courage to read its contents. It said: "If you want information about SMOM 60, meet me tomorrow in the Protestant Cemetery at five in the afternoon. In front of the tomb of John Keats. Come with the girl."

I would have taken that message as a bad joke if not for the mention of Junio's license plate.

I had no idea who could have written that strange note or why, though clearly somebody else knew about the business we had just transacted with the prince. Even more surprising was that the anonymous correspondent appeared to take for granted that Montse and I would be interested in knowing more about Junio's secret life. Why would we, or I, at any rate, care who that second-rate prince really was and what his sins might be? I considered the possibility that this might be an attempt by a frustrated buyer to get the book at any cost.

As I began the rigorous climb through Trastevere first and then up the Gianicolo toward the academy, I was unaware that I was being watched, and that our lives were about to undergo an unexpected *capovolgimento*, or about-face—forcing us to render services to a cause, to spy on those who were spying on us, to pay heed to every word we uttered—and that this state of affairs would last until the Allied troops entered Rome seven years later.

6.

THE ACADEMY was in an uproar. Once the episode of the ghost had come to an end, the news of the sixteen thousand lire spread like wildfire, causing a riot of sorts in front of Secretary Olarra's office and leaving him no choice but to part with a certain amount of the money so that the women could buy meat after weeks of our going without. Having put the issue up for a vote, it was unanimously agreed that they would buy tripe and prepare *tripa a la madrileña*. Not even this innocent resolution was allowed to remain marginal to the political situation, for this dish was supposed to symbolize the imminent fall of the capital of Spain to the Nationalist troops.

"Pity the poor Reds when Franco enters Madrid!" exclaimed Señor Fábregas, already acting like Secretary Olarra's right-hand man.

I found Montse in the library. She had by now definitively discarded the nunlike head scarf and was wearing her hair pulled back with a headband.

"Why aren't you downstairs with the other women?" I asked her.

"Because I am not a slave to men," she answered matter-of-factly. "I'm going through the stacks to see if I can find a book about Egypt or some other subject related to paleography."

"To sell to Prince Cima Vivarini?"

I couldn't help posing the question in a rather captious tone; her stubbornness made me jealous, vexed, and eager to voice a protest.

"He has paid us sixteen thousand lire for a book. Maybe he is interested in continuing to acquire . . . our capital."

Montse may not have been a slave to men in general, but when it came to one in particular . . .

"I think you should read this," I said, handing her the note.

She glanced at it, then asked, "What does it mean?"

"I don't know. I was having a coffee at Frontoni and the owner gave it to me, apparently at the request of a man he'd never seen before, someone he said looked like a northerner, a foreigner. It's the license plate of your friend's car. I think it might be somebody who isn't happy that the prince bought the Pierus Valerianus, who now wants to talk us into pulling out of the deal."

Montse acted as if she hadn't understood my insinuation that she had already established a certain degree of intimacy with Junio. I, needless to say, had already decided that they belonged to each other.

"If that were the case, why didn't the man show himself? Why hasn't he spoken directly to you? And why should he ask to meet us in a cemetery and at that particular tomb?"

"I haven't the faintest idea. I guess the cemetery is quite large, and one needs to specify a meeting spot. Maybe the mystery man is English, like Keats."

"Come with the girl," Montse repeated.

"What do you think we should do?" I asked her.

Looking back, I realize that letting her make the decision was an act of cowardice on my part, especially now that I know the full extent of the consequences; deep down I wanted to find out how far she was willing to go and if my suspicions about her feelings for Junio were justified.

"If my father finds out I've gone to a Protestant cemetery, he'll kill me. On the other hand, maybe this man has something important to tell us," she said.

"How are we going to manage to go out together without your father getting suspicious?" I asked.

"Easy," she responded, pointing to the pile of books.

"Maybe we can fool your father, but I doubt we'll manage to fool Olarra. He has orders from the embassy to spy on all of us. I know two or three former *pensionados* in Spain who are being investigated because of his reports. He'll probably have us followed to the bookstore," I said.

"So, we'll go to Signor Tasso's bookstore before we go to the cemetery. We'll give him a new bunch of books, and we'll tell him we'd like to have another meeting with the prince, that we'd like him to visit the academy and take a look around the library, in case there are other volumes that might interest him. Olarra won't get suspicious because there wouldn't be any reason to."

I was a bit stunned by Montse's resourcefulness, as well as her determination to bring about another meeting with Junio.

Doña Julia's announcement that dinner was ready put an end to our conversation.

The *tripa a la madrileña* inspired unprecedented enthusiasm among the diners. They toasted Franco, Mussolini, Hitler, and the emperor of Japan, the four horsemen of the apocalypse who were going to free the world from the claws of the Communist bear. For the evening's grand finale, Olarra wound up the academy's gramophone, and several couples danced to the beat of a military march. Like the music, the scene was contrived and lifeless, except for several outbursts of nostalgia and a few tears shed when Pérez Comendador and his wife, Magdalena Lerroux, announced that they were going to take off on a long trip to Greece.

"Pérez Comendador is simply erasing himself from the map. I don't think it is the right moment to go on vacation anywhere," I heard Señor Fábregas say to Secretary Olarra.

"If there is one person in this house who is above suspicion, it is Pérez Comendador. He alone stood up to Valle-Inclán when he tried to convert the Academy into a den of anarchists and revolutionaries. And I can assure you that Don Ramón, whose character was worse than the devil himself, was no easy opponent." Olarra lowered his voice. "Perez Comendador's patron is, after all, the Duke del Infantado, so he has permission to go wherever he chooses. Let us also not forget that this means we will have two fewer mouths to feed."

"The day I leave here, it will be to go kill Reds," Señor Fábregas said.

"The day you leave here, it will be because the war has ended. If you wanted to kill Reds, you should have remained in Barcelona," Secretary Olarra corrected him.

After everybody went to their rooms, I climbed up to the terrace. I found Rubiños in the same position as the night before: his head bobbing like a boat as he navigated the turbulent waters of sleep. My arrival coincided with the tapping of the telegraph.

"Damn this machine," he exclaimed, recovering his composure.

Despite his attempt to maintain a military bearing, Rubiños had the air of a schoolboy rather than a soldier hungry for war.

I headed straight for the balustrade. This time I didn't count any towers or domes but immediately looked for the Cestius Pyramid, the tomb around which the Protestant Cemetery of Rome had been built. This pyramid-shaped mausoleum, commissioned by the praetor and plebeian tribune Cestius, who died in the year 12 BC, was built before the Porta San Paolo and the Testaccio had been incorporated into the city, and it was known for having inspired painters and poets of the Romantic movement. I happened to know that area well because its new post office was a distinguished example of Italian Rationalist architecture; it had never occurred to me to visit the neighboring cemetery.

A light rain, accompanied by a fresh breeze and heavy fog, announced the arrival of autumn; the city seemed to disappear before my eyes.

7.

DAWN FOUND ROME COVERED in a cloak of dead leaves that exuded a strong odor of fermentation, like that of overripe fruit. It seemed that summer had ended an eternity ago, and that a single night had sufficed to alter the city's aspect, now awash in shades of ocher, maroon, and yellow. This sudden change of season made me realize that nothing happens as we expect it to because our blind faith that things will turn out to our liking allows reality to catch us off guard. This is precisely what happened with our war: it had been gestating for so long yet nobody had been able to prevent it, always believing it was still a long way off. In the same way, I had convinced myself that autumn wouldn't come for ages, despite what the calendar said.

I met Montse after breakfast and together we went to Olarra's office to tell him we wanted to invite the buyer of the famous book to the Academy. The fact that I described Junio as a young Blackshirt, a member of the Italian nobility, and a well-known paleographer smoothed our way, for nothing pleased Olarra more than hobnobbing with leaders of the Fascist Party. His deepest desire was to meet someone who could introduce him to the Duce himself, a person for whom he felt limitless admiration.

"What did you say the prince's name was?" Olarra asked.

"Junio Valerio Cima Vivarini," I stated.

We left him savoring the name as if it were a delicacy.

"Now the secretary will go to my father to tell him about the Italian prince, and our hands will be freed," Montse said.

After lunch, we made our way to Signor Tasso's bookstore, carrying half a dozen *Don Quixotes*, every one we could find on the academy's bookshelves. Montse was particularly excited, as much for having thought up a clever strategy as for our mysterious appointment in the cemetery. She would see Junio again as soon as he accepted our invitation, and by then she would already know more about him, thanks to our secret meeting. Could she ask for anything more? As for me, I think I had begun to accept my bit part while awaiting further developments.

"If the mountain doesn't come to Muhammad, Muhammad must go to the mountain. It seems an excellent idea and I would like to be included in the invitation, if that would not inconvenience you," Signor Tasso said in response to our proposition.

The first part of our plan was turning out perfectly.

During our streetcar ride to Testaccio, a strong jolt threw Montse into my arms, and I had to use great restraint not to convert that fortuitous encounter into a deliberate embrace. I longed for our lives to be full of jolts like this one, but fortunately I realized that this wasn't the time or the place for expressing such emotions. We got off in front of the post office.

"An ugly building for an ugly world," Montse commented.

We walked down Via Caio Cestio along the cemetery wall until we found a locked iron gate. The sign invited us to ring the bell for entry.

Once inside, we stood facing one of the most spectacular sights in Rome: twenty to twenty-five thousand square meters dotted with elaborate tombstones, mausoleums, azaleas, hydrangeas, irises, oleander, wisteria, cypresses, and olive, laurel and pomegranate trees, all framed by the Aurelian Wall and the Cestius Pyramid. A place of astonishing beauty. Months later, when circumstances led me to the poetry of Keats and Shelley, I understood how the latter could write in his elegy dedicated to the former that "it might make one in love with death, to think that one should be buried in so sweet a place."

"Where is John Keats's grave?" I asked the guard.

"The graves of Percy Shelley and August von Goethe are straight ahead; John Keats's is on the left; and Antonio Gramsci's on the right," he said automatically.

Montse threaded her arm through mine in a gesture filled with apprehension and a certain gravitas, and we began walking in the direction the guard had indicated. Suddenly, the multicolored garden turned into an English landscape full of ancient trees with thick trunks and wide canopies and well-trimmed lawns dotted with solitary graves. Keats's was the last one, right at the foot of the pyramid. On the tombstone there was no name, only an epitaph that read:

HERE LIES ONE WHOSE NAME WAS WRIT IN WATER.

After we had been there for five minutes, a middle-aged man exactly fitting Signor Enrico's description approached. He had light eyes, red hair, milky-white skin, and freckles covering his face.

"I see you received my message. My name is Smith. John Smith," he said in Italian with a strong British accent.

"This is Montserrat Fábregas, and my name is José María Hurtado de Mendoza."

We all took turns shaking hands.

"I imagine you are wondering why I have asked you here. As it is not easy to explain in a few words, I hope you will have the patience to hear me out."

Smith, or whatever his name really was, remained silent, awaiting our response.

"Please, go ahead," Montse replied.

"I will divide my story into three chapters; though separated by time, they are, as you will soon see, all connected," he said.

"Then please proceed, before we do lose our patience," I said.

"This is the grave of John Keats, one of England's most important poets," Smith began. "And this one, next to it, contains the remains of the person who took care of him until his death, the painter Joseph Severn. They arrived in Rome in September 1820. Severn decided to come after having won a gold medal from the Royal Academy; Keats, on the other hand, came to Italy to find a healthier climate, for he was suffering from tuberculosis. The friends, who in fact had only met three days before the boat left England, moved into a small apartment at 26 Piazza di Spagna. Keats's health showed no signs of improvement; on the contrary, by the beginning of 1821 Severn had begun to look for an appropriate place to bury his friend. That place is where you are now standing. Of course at the time the cemetery was not fenced in or even tended, and goats as well as shepherds trampled the grass growing between the graves. It was, however, full of daisies, narcissus, hyacinth, and wild violets. Keats was thrilled with Severn's description of the place, so much so that he asked him to return several times. On one of those visits, Severn met a shepherd with whom he fell into friendly conversation; the shepherd confessed to him that he had discovered a strange document inside a trunk buried at the foot of the Cestius Pyramid. It was an Egyptian papyrus and Severn bought it from the shepherd to give to Keats, who was much in need of distraction. Keats enthusiastically accepted the gift and told the story of its discovery to his doctor, Dr. Clark, who in turn communicated the news to the British consul in Rome. Undoubtedly Keats's papyrus was the major topic of conversation at places like the Antico Caffè Greco, where all the foreign intellectuals met, and news of its discovery reached the ears of some members of the Roman Curia. Keats believed the papyrus contained the key to finding the treasure of some pharaoh in Egypt. Unfortunately, the poet died on February twenty-third of that year. But it didn't end there. Are you still with me?"

"Carry on," I said.

"As far as the Catholic Church was concerned, Keats was a Protestant, and in 1821 it was believed that his disease could cause an epidemic, so the order was given to burn everything inside his living quarters: furniture, clothes, books, papers, everything. Today we believe that the Vatican was, in fact, interested in taking possession of the papyrus that Severn had given him."

"For what purpose?" Montse asked.

"Because supposedly it contained a map, the so-called Creator's Map."

"And what is that?" Montse asked.

Smith hesitated for a moment before answering.

"It depends on how much of a believer you are. According to some, the map in question was drawn by God himself and in it are the keys to understanding the world from the time of its creation."

"Nothing of the kind can possibly exist," I objected.

"It would be best if we went on to the second chapter," Smith said, ignoring me. "I suppose you're wondering how and when the map found its way to the base of the Cestius Pyramid. Have you ever heard of Germanicus, the Roman general? He was one of the most important men of his time. He was the son of Nero Claudius Drusus, then was adopted by Emperor Tiberius and named as his heir. Tiberius, however, came to view Germanicus as a dangerous rival, and in the year 17 AD sent him to Antioch to put down rebellions. But Germanicus was not only a soldier; he was also a cultivated man who wrote and recited poetry, and he decided to take a trip to Egypt without Tiberius's permission. He arrived in the land of the Nile in the spring of the year 19 and remained there until the autumn. During those six months, Germanicus established contact with numerous sects that had preserved the culture and wisdom of the ancient Egyptians. It was in this way that he acquired the Creator's Map."

"How had the Egyptians gotten hold of it?" Montse asked.

"The map probably arrived in Egypt during the Persian occupation, five centuries earlier. The point is that Germanicus was poisoned upon his return to Antioch, and the map reached Rome with his belongings after his death. We don't know why somebody decided to hide it at that point, but it is very telling that they would choose to do so in such a typically Egyptian structure as the Cestius Pyramid."

Montse summed it up. "So, the map went from Persia to Egypt, and from the emperor Germanicus it passed into the hands of some unknown person, who hid it at the base of the Cestius Pyramid, where it was found by the shepherd who sold it to Severn; finally, the Vatican requisitioned it after John Keats's death."

"Exactly. But I have yet to tell you the third chapter, the most important of all and the reason you are here," said Smith, his increasing excitement lending color to his pale cheeks. "In 1918 a German nobleman named Rudolf von Sebottendorff founded an occult sect called the Thule Society, an offshoot of the German Order, an organization that had already consolidated half a dozen Nationalist organizations. The name Thule was chosen in memory of the legendary king of that name, who inspired Wagner, among others. Von Sebottendorff lived for a time in Cairo, where he joined a lodge of the Rite of Memphis and learned about the existence of the Creator's Map. A year later Anton Drexler, another member of Thule, founded in Munich the German Workers Party, which was in fact the political arm of the Thule Society. Adolf Hitler, at the time an informer for the military police, came to a party meeting and joined. A few months later he took over the leadership of the organization, which changed its name to the National Socialist German Workers Party and became the Nazi party we know today. Hitler's rise to power was accompanied at every stage by the Thule Society's collaboration and participation. Thule's objective was to push forward scientific research that would prove the superior qualities of the Aryan race. At this point a key actor, Karl Haushoffer, came on the scene. Professor of geopolitics and Orientalism, and a member of the Thule Society, he had developed the concept of 'blood and soil,' according to which the supremacy of the race depends on the conquest of what he calls lebensraum, or 'vital space.' In other words, for a nation, space would not be only a vehicle to power but power itself. To reinforce Haushoffer's theories, Thule has created the Deutsche Ahnenerbe, or the German Ancestral Heritage Society, dedicated to the study of ancient spiritual history, which includes a department of linguistics and another dedicated to researching the contents and symbols of popular traditions, again, with the goal of finding evidence that corroborates the supremacy of the Aryan race and its ancestral rights to occupy territories along Germany's borders. By now, Haushoffer's ideas have taken root in Hermann Göring, who has publicly articulated Germany's interest in controlling Austria and Czechoslovakia, as well as his desire for the Western powers to free them up to act in Eastern Europe. We also know that within the next few months, the Ahnenerbe will expand, adding departments for the study of German archeology and Esotericism. The Nazis are convinced that there exist in the world a dozen 'sacred objects' capable of granting unlimited power to those who possess them. The Creator's Map would be one of those supposedly magical objects."

"Are you trying to tell us that the Nazis want this map?" I asked him, by now fully assuming my role as skeptic.

"I am going to respond with a verse from John Keats: 'Fanatics have their dreams, wherewith they weave a paradise for a sect.' Not only do they wish to obtain the Creator's Map, but they also want the Ark of the Covenant, the Holy Grail, and the Holy Lance of Longinus, among other mystical objects. The Nazis believe in geomancy, and they are convinced that there is a sacred geography, that no nation is the result of secular, unplanned acts, and that behind every territory there exists a master plan. They believe the Creator's Map would reveal this plan to them."

"I still don't understand how," Montse insisted, prompting him to explain further.

"Throughout history many mountains have been thought of as the abodes of the gods. Take, for example, Mount Olympus for the Greeks, Mount Sinai for the Jews, Kanchenjunga for the Tibetan Buddhists, and Meru and Kailas for the Hindus. According to the geomancers, these sacred mountains are in fact energy centers that channel cosmic force through a series of holy, or ley, lines that extend to every corner of the earth. Temples, monasteries, and other sacred buildings are also points of confluence of these terrestrial forces, capable of exerting powerful influence upon the psychic body of nations. Whoever dominates this psychic body will have total control over its political power. This would explain the enormous success religion has had in all corners of the globe. All of these lines carrying this energy would be revealed in the Creator's Map."

The idea of a map with these features seemed to me about as absurd as our presence in that cemetery.

"I am an architect," I said, "and I can assure you that nobody has ever been able to show that the location of a building can influence the psyche of those inside it."

"The Chinese call it 'feng shui,'" Smith said.

"All superstitions have a name. Anyway, what have we got to do with all this?"

"The Pierus Valerianus is the only book in the world that mentions the Creator's Map in one of its appendices. In fact, the edition of 1556, the one that is known today, is not the first edition. There was another edition, published the same year, that was withdrawn precisely because it mentions the Creator's Map, and the Church has never admitted to its existence. This *princeps* edition was ordered to be burned in Basel, but as often occurs, not all copies of this special edition were destroyed. It was always believed that three or four copies were spared from the flames, but nobody knew where they were. Your book is one of these."

"And now you think Prince Cima Vivarini wants to sell it to the Nazis," I ventured.

For the first time, Smith cracked a smile.

"I don't think; I know. Prince Cima Vivarini is *the* representative of the Thule Society in Rome. Although his father is Venetian, his mother is an Austrian aristocrat with strong ties to the German nobility. Oddly enough, in spite of his origins he carries a passport from the Sovereign Military Order of Malta, the smallest country in the world."

"Are you talking about the island of Malta?" Montse asked.

"The knights of the Sovereign Order of Malta lost the island during the first third of the last century, at which point they settled in Rome, where they created an independent state whose territory includes the Palazzo di Malta on Via Condotti, and Villa Malta on the Aventine Hill. The Grand Master resides in the palace and the government bodies meet there; at the Aventine villa the priories of the order have their headquarters as well as their embassies to the Holy See and the Kingdom of Italy. The order has its own government, an independent magistrate, issues its own passports, mints money, and prints stamps like any other sovereign state. The license plates of the cars of this country contain the letters SMOM: Sovereign Military Order of Malta."

Montse and I looked at each other incredulously.

"Are you serious?" I asked.

"It was difficult for me to believe it at first as well, but Rome is the only city in the world that is the seat of three independent nations: the Kingdom of Italy, the Vatican City State, and the Sovereign Order of Malta. Its members belong to the highest European nobility, politicians and businessmen with deep Catholic beliefs. The most influential group includes the Hapsburgs, the Hohenzollern, and the Luxemburgs, families belonging to the oldest German aristocracy with ties to the Holy See. In theory, the mission of the order is to give humanitarian assistance to the most needy through clinics, hospitals, ambulances, and aid to refugees; but in fact it functions as a bridge between the reigning political and economic powers and the Vatican. We are afraid that now that Thule has in its power proof of the existence of the Creator's Map, they will attempt to remove it from the Vatican Library—where we believe it is kept hidden under conditions of the greatest secrecy."

"You still haven't informed us why you are telling us all of this," I pointed out.

"Let's just say that I need your help," Smith said, with the utmost gravity.

"What kind of help?" I asked.

"I want you to cultivate your relationship with Prince Cima Vivarini and keep abreast of his plans."

I wasn't one to believe in coincidences, but it was eerie how Montse seemed to have anticipated Smith's proposition by inviting Junio to visit the academy. Until that moment my idea of a spy was someone who listened in on other people's conversations with his ear pressed against the bedroom door. That there could be any other kind, or that Montse and I would ever dream of agreeing to Smith's proposal, was preposterous. "I'll do it," she said, before I had a chance to open my mouth. "I've hated the Nazis ever since they started burning books in 1933." I felt sure that for Montse this conversation was as thrilling as reading a suspense novel, and she seemed wholly oblivious to one important difference: here we would not enjoy the reader's impunity.

"We don't even know if he's telling the truth; he hasn't given us one convincing reason why we should do what he's asking of us," I said to her, hoping to make her reconsider.

"You're right," Smith admitted. "But for now it is in your interest to know only that I represent a group of persons who are defending the survival of democracy in Europe, and that the lives of many people could be in danger."

"I'll do it," Montse insisted.

I didn't understand Montse's obstinacy and it even offended me. Neither she nor I belonged to the world of espionage; we were ordinary, everyday people.

"Very good," Smith pronounced. He turned and addressed Montse. "Whenever you have something to report about the prince, go to a pizzeria named Pollarolo on Via di Ripetta next to the Piazza del Popolo. Ask for Marco and give your code name: 'Liberty.' He will tell you that the best pizza is the margarita. You will answer that you want yours with a basil leaf on top. You will eat calmly, pay, then come here at five in the afternoon, just like today. Don't write down anything the prince tells you, and don't talk to anybody. Not even José María."

Smith's instructions made it clear that what had at first seemed like a stupid game was actually quite serious, too serious for Montse to play at alone.

"I can accept Montse going out with the prince to get information from him," I said with feigned conviction, "but for her to then travel alone from one end of Rome to the other giving names and delivering secret reports seems too dangerous. Let her take care of the meetings, and I'll meet you here to pass on what she tells me."

I have to admit that at that point my motives had little to do with the survival of democracy in Western Europe. I was becoming a spy for purely sentimental reasons. "That sounds like a good idea," Smith declared approvingly.

Once Smith had left, Montse looked at me and smiled, as if expecting me to utter a disparaging comment. But night had begun to close in around us, and my only concern was to find a way out of the cemetery as quickly as possible.

8.

J UNIO WAS EXPECTED at the academy at four-thirty in the afternoon.
Twenty minutes before the appointed time Secretary Olarra, the butler
Fontana, and Señor Fábregas—representing the refugees—formed a welcoming committee, its numbers swelling with the arrival of their respec-
tive wives, as well as Montse and me. After discussing the proper way to
address a prince, we agreed that since he was not hereditary royalty, it was
best to use "Your Excellency," and nothing more. This was still being
discussed when Junio arrived, accompanied by Tasso, the bookseller, and
his chauffeur, who turned out to be a robust and ruddy young Hungarian
named Gabor. Olarra welcomed the prince with shouts of "Your Excellency! Believe! Obey! Fight!"; the prince, in turn, showed no signs of
being either impressed or flattered by such an extravagant welcome. Then
Olarra noticed one of the medals hanging from his chest.

"This award is . . . this award is . . ." the secretary stuttered, unable to
finish his sentence.

"The laureate cross of San Fernando," Junio offered. "I fought with
Queipo de Llano's troops on the Malaga front and was wounded."

"A hero! A hero!" Olarra exclaimed as if he were facing a miracle
rather than a man.

After the introductions—all carried out according to established pro-
tocol, which included Roman salutes and the kissing of hands—the visit
officially began. Olarra, in his role as cicerone, told Junio the history of

the institution from its founding until the present day, and I, as the resident architect, was the one to give him a tour of Bramante's celebrated *Tempietto* in the courtyard of San Pietro in Montorio Church. I must admit, I used the opportunity to show off my broad knowledge of the masterpiece to Montse, even though my exaggerated attempts to be helpful did not excite a general sense of admiration.

"The building is designed around a circular *cella,* which surrounds an opening in the rock, and it is here that Christian tradition situates the martyrdom of Saint Peter. This *cella* is surrounded in turn by a peristyle colonnade formed by sixteen Doric columns bearing an architrave and a frieze of triglyphs and metopes crowned by a balustrade. The superimposition of the lantern on the dome over the circular *cella* is Bramante's most noteworthy innovation," I elaborated.

"José María, this is not a university lecture," Secretary Olarra reminded me, giving me a look of strong disapproval.

"Is there a reason the building is circular?" the prince inquired.

"Yes, of course. It has to do with the *tholos,* or ancient Roman temples, which were circular for commemorative rather than practical reasons. During the Renaissance, a circular building symbolized the shape of the world as well as Plato's ideal city."

"Very interesting."

Olarra then took the initiative to show off his own prodigious knowledge by calling the prince's attention to the Pomarancio frescoes painted on the lunettes in the interior Renaissance cloister, which depicted the life and work of Saint Francis Xavier.

"I would now like to hear about the history of the book I bought. I can assure you, it is a true rarity," the prince said, thereby putting an end to the visit to the temple.

"It is impossible to know precisely when or how that book arrived at the academy, but the most probable answer is that it is one of the legacies of the convent," Olarra said, taking the floor again. "In the years immediately following the founding of the Society of Jesus in 1541, many monks, including Saint Francis Xavier himself, lived here before joining the order. Perhaps it was brought here by a Jesuit, or a Franciscan. Who knows? I'm ashamed to admit it, but until Miss Fábregas got here, the library was a bit chaotic. I didn't even know that we had such a book. Frankly, if I had known of its existence and importance, I never would have allowed it to be sold."

"Books have always suited Montse well," Señor Fábregas interjected. "As a little girl she preferred to read stories than to go out and play with her friends. And if you asked her what she wanted to be when she grew up, she would say, 'A librarian, so I can read all the books in the world.'"

"Papa, please!" Montse interrupted him, trying to hide her embarrassment.

When we got to the library, Montse abandoned her secondary role and took command. We were now in her domain, and she spoke in a composed and authoritative voice. Her attitude managed both to attract Junio's attention and to please her father. After five minutes, Señor Fábregas took me by the arm and told me that it would be best to leave Montse alone with the guests so she could show them the library without interruption; I thereby understood that he approved of the relationship between his daughter and the prince. Before withdrawing, I looked at the two of them, and despite the fact that at that moment Signor Tasso had begun speaking and Montse continued to pretend to be indifferent, I realized that something significant was going on between her and the prince. I felt confirmed in my view of the weakness of human beings: in spite of what Montse knew about her fairy-tale prince, she was allowing herself to be carried away by her fantasies. I even feared that she would forget her commitment to Mr. Smith and her newfound role as Mata Hari. For his part, Junio seemed not to care that Montse belonged to a social class far inferior to his own or that her physical characteristics did not fit the aesthetic ideals of the Aryan race (although, for that matter, neither did his).

Upon leaving the library, I found the prince's chauffeur, awaiting further orders. Although many years have passed since then, I can still see the young Gabor, like a member of the Sacred Battalion of Thebes, whose members fought in pairs and were always ready to give their lives for their comrades. I have heard that strong emotional, even homosexual, bonds united those warriors, and I still do not discount the possibility that this was the case between Junio and Gabor. I never had any proof, and I think Montse would disagree with me, claiming that women have a special intuition about such things, but the relationship between Junio and Gabor seemed to go beyond pure camaraderie or even loyalty. Whenever one spoke of the other he did so with great discretion and extreme caution, positioning himself like a shield to protect the other. This is what happened that afternoon when I attempted to coax information out of Gabor about the prince's activities. He withdrew, assuming the role of the humble servant. But clearly this was feigned humility; he was letting me know as politely as possible that I had no right to poke around in affairs that had nothing to do with me.

The visit ended with two fortunate events. First, both Junio and Signor Tasso selected books they were willing to buy for another sixteen thousand lire; second, the prince invited Montse for tea to thank her for services rendered. And although Señor Fábregas considered this first date a bit precipitous, Olarra reminded him that the prince was a hero of the civil war, something of which not a single Spaniard living in the academy could boast, not even himself. Not to mention the benefits that a relationship between Montse and a Blackshirt prince with contacts in the highest levels of the Fascist movement could confer on the academy. I must admit that I tried to get myself included in this tea by all means at my disposal, but Signor Tasso's presence left me without a seat in the car.

"The Italia has five seats, the fifth to be used only in cases of dire emergency. It would not be proper to force the young lady to sit between two gentlemen," Gabor explained.

After taking leave of the group in the courtyard of San Pietro in Montorio, and winking at Montse to remind her of the complicity between us, I took refuge on the terrace.

I found Rubiños listening to the Vatican Radio station. He seemed upset by something he had just heard.

"Do you understand the Church?" he asked me.

"Nobody understands the Church, Rubiños," I answered.

"That's what I always tell myself, but then I wonder if that's a good way for a Fascist to think. Guillén assures me that a Fascist has to have blind faith in authority and in the Church, because to wage war you must first believe and then obey."

Rubiños was referring to his immediate superior, Corporal José Guillén, a soldier with a religious vocation and outlandish ideas.

"Maybe you are not a Fascist. Have you ever considered that?"

Rubiños hesitated a few seconds. "If I'm not a Fascist, what am I?" he blurted out.

"We are all small in the face of great catastrophes, Rubiños. Right now none of us is anything, except a survivor."

"Guillén told me that individualism is our society's biggest cancer."

"Guillén's head is full of political slogans he repeats like a parrot. The problem with our society is not in our model of the State but rather in the lack of justice and fundamental rights."

"You've become a little like a Red, *mi pensionado*. If Olarra heard you say that, he'd have a fit. There's nothing he'd rather do than have some-one face the firing squad in the academy garden. He's dying to start a witch hunt so he can experience the war in person."

"Olarra is small, too," I added.

Rubiños gave me an impish smile, which made me think he agreed with me.

"It will probably turn out that I don't understand the Church because I don't understand human beings," he concluded.

I looked over the balustrade and proceeded with my ritual of counting the towers and domes etched against the violet-colored sky, though what I was really looking for was the place where Montse and Junio might be having tea, as if that were at all possible. It wasn't, of course, even though

I could imagine them in one place or another, sitting in one or another position, enjoying themselves with a happiness that burned a hole inside me. My bitter musings were interrupted by a shout from one of the buildings on Via Goffredo Mameli. Whatever that guttural rattle was, I heard it as a harmonious and taunting refrain repeated over and over: "*Ah! Com'è bello essere innamorati!*" *Indeed*, I thought bitterly, *how beautiful to be in love*.

9.

MONTSE RETURNED AT DINNERTIME. I had never seen her so happy; an unwitting happiness, almost childish, which made her act as if she were in a dream. More than talk, she smiled constantly; more than walk, she seemed to levitate. At first I chalked up her behavior to the excitement of danger overcome, but finally I had to admit that her mood was determined by the impetuousness of her heart. I have always wondered why happiness has such a strange effect. It is as if when we are happy we wish to live more intensely, more rapidly, when it seems the opposite should be true. Perhaps this is because we are conscious of how ephemeral happiness is and of the impossibility of pursuing it successfully throughout a lifetime, so we must enjoy it whenever we find it, however briefly. It was clear that Montse had walked right into it that afternoon, and now, as if that happiness were a horse, she was whipping it mercilessly to make it gallop faster and faster.

"So, how did it go?" I asked her.

Her eyes shone like fireflies, and like fireflies, I thought bitterly, her light was exclusively designed to attract her mate.

"It went brilliantly, because Junio is a wonderful person. But I have eaten so much I am ashamed of myself," she said.

I'd sensed that Montse accepted others without prejudice, shutting her eyes to their shadowy past, but she now seemed to be going overboard by characterizing a Fascist with strong ties to Nazism as a "wonderful person."

"I imagine you spoke to the prince about something even if your mouth was full."

"We had time to speak of many things. He told me all about the virtues of Fascism: steadfastness in one's work, extreme parsimony in word and gesture, moral and physical courage, decisiveness, absolute constancy to an oath once taken, and respect for tradition along with concern for the future. He also told me that freedom should never be a goal, but rather a means, and as a means should be controlled and dominated,and that in a society like Italy's it is of primary importance to fulfill one's duty before demanding one's rights. Did you know that Mussolini believes that youth is a divine disease one recovers from with each passing day?"

"To tell you the truth, I don't know a lot about Mussolini," I admitted, "but whenever I look at his cold face and angry scowl, I feel like I'm looking at a neighborhood thug."

"Of course the prince does not agree with Mussolini, at least not in everything. Junio is a Fascist with his own ideas. He's a modern man, even though he is a patriot. He reads poetry, Byron and Leopardi, and he likes abstract painting. And he doesn't have a girlfriend."

If Montse was attempting to provoke me, she was managing it quite well.

After hesitating a few moments, she added, "We also had a chance to talk about a certain map."

My jealousy had predisposed me to be critical of any subject she might have discussed with Junio, so I said to her with a certain uneasiness, "You talked to him about the Creator's Map?"

"Why shouldn't I have? That's what Mr. Smith asked me to do," Montse said.

"Yes, Smith asked you to, but it was assumed that the prince, not you, would be the one to bring it up, so as not to arouse suspicion and lose his trust."

"Think of it this way," said Montse. "I found the book and chose to sell it, so it would be normal for me to have glanced at its contents. Why shouldn't I discuss it with the person who bought it? I didn't, of course, refer to the map by the name Smith gave it. I simply said that in the book's last chapter there is mention of the existence of a strange map—"

"How did the prince react?" I interrupted her.

"Totally matter-of-factly. I don't know if that map has much value, but Junio doesn't seem to think it does. He told me it's like a blueprint for a myth, according to which God, with his own hand, drew a map of the world's main lines and points of power, and the sunken continents and underground cities where races of superior men reside. Something like the Ten Commandments, but related to the world's cartography. He also told me that he sent the book to Heinrich Himmler, head of the SS, because the Nazis are looking for proof that, quote, 'during the golden age gods dressed in air and walked among men,' unquote. He is now waiting for further instructions from Germany."

"What's that quotation from?"

"It's from Hesiod, the Greek mythologist. It refers to the myth of the lost continent, a land where men lived with gods. It seems the Nazis are convinced that they are the descendants of one of these imaginary civilizations. They believe that the Vatican not only has the Creator's Map but also a secret manuscript that tells the history of Atlantis, or Thule, the homeland of the great ancestors. They believe the Aryan peoples were taken out of Atlantis by the last of the Men-Gods, or Supermen, after the universal flood, then settled in Europe and Asia from the Gobi Desert to the Himalayas. There, on the highest peaks on earth, a Solar Oracle was established, from which the planet could be governed, and since then they have continually been reincarnated as leaders of the various peoples who survived the catastrophe."

I couldn't deny that Montse had done her work well, though I was not willing to admit it to her.

"Sounds like all the calamities in our world can be attributed to these superior beings. All you have to do is look at Hitler's face, or his sidekick

Himmler, to know without a doubt that they are anything but beings from a superior race. Frankly, I don't understand why Smith is wasting his time worrying about such harebrained ideas, much less having us waste ours. Thinking that a map has the power to change the world is the stupidest thing I've ever heard."

At the time I couldn't possibly have known how right I was, though I was mistaken in one very important aspect that later came to light: even if a map or a lance or a chalice could not change history, the fanaticism of those who allow themselves to be deceived by such apocalyptic and messianic messages could. Today, I see clearly that by pursuing these sacred talismans the Nazis were attempting to justify their total disregard for humanity, and their lack of conscience, as if in order to get closer to God they first had to make a pact with the devil—as if God and the devil were one and the same.

"To me it sounds very exciting," said Montse.

"You like the prince, that's all there is to it," I blurted out.

At last Montse descended from her winged horse of happiness.

"And you seem to care that I do," she said.

What could I say other than that she was right? But it was not the moment to make a confession that would put me at a disadvantage.

"I think we should get out of this madness before it's too late. We're not spies. Tomorrow I'll meet with Smith and tell him we've changed our minds," I said, returning to the main topic of our conversation.

"I think it's already too late. I have another date with Junio in a few days," Montse admitted. Then she paused. "And now we must separate before my father suspects that something's going on."

Did she mean that she didn't want her father to think that I was trying to meddle in her relationship with Junio? I wouldn't have minded giving Señor Fábregas that impression, but my distress was so great at that moment that the only thing I wanted to do was strike back. Now, remembering this from such a distance, I think that Montse's resolve set in motion the change in my attitude toward the war raging in Spain and the situation in the rest of Europe. It dawned on me that if I didn't take myself seriously it was precisely because I hadn't committed myself; I began to detest the insipidness of trying to remain on the margins of what was going on in the world, as if all I had to do was close my eyes for the problems to disappear. The worst of it all was that I didn't have a shred of pretense: this was, quite simply, who I was. Perhaps in other circumstances, in times of peace, my behavior would not have mattered as much, but with Spain bleeding to death and Europe on the verge of exploding, the world needed people like Junio, like Smith, even like Secretary Olarra, who were capable of committing themselves to a cause. Halfway measures weren't enough; one had to take sides and commit to them until the ultimate consequences. This was the only way to live with any modicum of dignity under the current conditions. I think it was at that moment that I decided to commit myself seriously to Smith, even if it was only because to join his cause I didn't need to wear a military uniform or act with bravado, or speak out authoritatively at meetings and in front of the masses. The fact was, I had never felt drawn to Fascist pronouncements. Apart from any ideological issues, I rejected them instinctively because of my individualistic spirit, my refusal to form part of a flock; I had always been guilty of intolerance for the masses. What I didn't know was that the decision I had just made would lead me to behave recklessly sooner than I could ever have imagined.

IO.

MONTSE DIDN'T COME DOWN for breakfast. Apparently, she had a cough and a sore throat. I considered the possibility that the prince had poisoned her during their meeting the day before. One of those undetectable poisons that kills slowly. Like love.

"I'm preparing an onion for the cough and slicing a tomato for her throat," Doña Julia said.

"An onion and slices of tomato? Good God, are you trying to turn my daughter into a salad, Doña Julia?" Doña Montserrat, Montse's mother, exclaimed. She was a discreet, diffident woman who lived in the shadow of her husband's overbearing personality.

"I assure you, my dear, there is no better cure for a cough than cutting an onion in half and placing it on the bedside table. The fumes it gives off work miracles. And the same thing with a poultice of tomato slices on the throat: it works like the hands of a saint," Doña Julia insisted.

"Hands of a saint? Don't talk such nonsense, my good lady. Your remedies make a mockery of science. Don't forget, even though it might not seem so, due to the unusual circumstances, this house is still an academy where superstitions have no place," Secretary Olarra said.

"Is there anything more scientific than Mother Nature? I'd wager whatever you want that the girl will be completely cured by dinnertime," Doña Julia added, then grabbed a knife and made a small cut on the tip of one of her fingers.

"May I ask what you are doing now?" Olarra asked disapprovingly.

"I'm going to show you your true science. Cut yourself like I have," Doña Julia ordered.

"Cut my finger! Doña Julia, you have clearly lost your mind."

"Just make a little cut," insisted Doña Julia, "and then I'll rub it with a little alcohol and iodine; I, on the other hand, will pour white sugar on mine. Tomorrow morning your cut will be just starting to heal while mine will have already healed completely. Pass me the sugar, Doña Montserrat."

Montse's mother obeyed, and Doña Julia poured a spoonful of sugar onto her cut as if it were a cup of coffee.

"Now I understand why you are the only one who sees that ghost," Secretary Olarra said.

"Yesterday it came back into my room during my siesta. It was looking at me, leaning on the window frame," Doña Julia said.

"So it has a head after all," Doña Montserrat mused.

"Like you and me. Brown hair, huge brown eyes, eyelids full of blue veins, and almost translucent skin. A beautiful young woman," Doña Julia said.

"That's just what they said about Beatrice Cenci. That's why her father did what he did to her," Doña Montserrat pointed out.

"And that's why she did what she did to her father," Doña Julia responded.

"A father who rapes his daughter deserves to be castrated," Doña Montserrat pronounced.

"Death, he deserves death. I have promised the ghost that this very afternoon I will put a candle in the church of San Pietro in Montorio, and I'm also going to do everything possible to find out where her head is. After all, the poor thing just wants to get it back and be able to rest in peace."

"I heard that a French soldier took her head," Doña Montserrat said.

"His name was Jean Maccuse. But according to what Beatrice herself has told me, he never knew peace again after committing such a horrible crime. Don't you know how Jean Maccuse died?"

"I have no idea, Doña Julia."

"He was decapitated, and his head was mounted on an urn that belonged to an African sultan. You know what they say . . . he who lives by the sword dies by the sword. Those are the words of Beatrice Cenci's ghost," Doña Julia said solemnly.

Doña Montserrat crossed herself twice in quick succession.

"Please, ladies, next you'll start shouting 'Long live death!'" Olarra exclaimed.

"The only thing wrong with the girl is that she has fallen in love with that prince," Señor Fábregas observed, returning to the subject of Montse's illness. "I took her temperature and she has no fever. What she has is a lost look in her eyes, and she doesn't stop sighing."

"Just like me. When I fell in love with my husband, I had to stay in bed for two or three days. I had heart palpitations and dizzy spells every time I thought of him," Doña Montserrat said in a tone of voice that made one think she was talking about somebody other than the man standing next to her.

I was trying to digest Señor Fábregas's comment when I realized that he was staring at me. I needed only a split second to read the message in his eyes: "Tough luck, kid, you'll have to make do with the leftovers."

With the excuse that I was checking on the patient, I went to see Montse. Like all the other rooms in the academy, her room was freezing, and Montse was shivering under a couple of blankets. She had one of her mother's shawls around her shoulders, which gave her a chaste air, and she was propped up against some large goose-down pillows. She was pretending to read, but, just as her father had said, she seemed exhausted; her eyes were focused on some indeterminate spot on the wall opposite her bed.

"How do you feel?" I asked.

"Papa assures me the war will end in a few weeks; Junio says it will last years. Who do you think is right?"

I understood by Montse's question that Señor Fábregas had not been wrong in his diagnosis: love had severely undermined her health. I preferred to keep my own prognosis to myself.

"Who do you hope is right?" I answered evasively.

"I want the war to end soon, tomorrow even, if at all possible, but at the same time I don't want to leave Rome," she admitted.

"The other day you told me that you were longing to return to Barcelona," I reminded her.

"The other day was the other day. Have you forgotten that we are now spies?"

What I suspected Montse wanted to say to me was, "Have you forgotten that I've fallen in love?"

"How could I forget? But I also can't seem to forget that Mata Hari was accused of high treason and executed. I'm frightened for you."

"If the prince likes me, there's nothing to fear. And I'll make sure that he does," Montse said defiantly. "I've spoken to my father, and he agrees to spend a little money upgrading my wardrobe. He trusts me; everything will work out fine."

Montse's words caused me acute pain. In spite of the fact that I didn't want to become her confidant, it seems this was the role she had assigned to me.

"You're sure your father doesn't suspect us?"

Using the plural pronoun was the only way I could feel connected to her.

"Relax! My father thinks I want to catch the prince, and he approves."

"And what do you want?" I asked her.

"If we manage to save humanity, perhaps we can also manage to save the prince," she reasoned.

Montse didn't seem to realize that the plan was not to save the humanity of the prince and others like him but to defeat them. I chose to remain silent on that point so as not to make matters worse.

"Yes," I said, in a deliberately offhand way, "perhaps you can."

"My mother says a woman can do anything, even impossible things.

There are good Fascists and bad Fascists, like in the vineyards of the Lord, and Junio belongs to the first batch. He himself told me that a man does not carry nobility in his name, no matter how much of a prince he is, but rather in his heart."

To think that Montse saw Junio as the Good Samaritan was enough to drive me crazy. But I can't reproach Montse for her behavior or how she felt; she clung to her fantasy of reforming Junio the way I clung to her, as some remote and unreachable ideal. Now I see that we were all victims of our times, of a murderous world gone mad.

II.

I REACHED THE PROTESTANT CEMETERY five minutes before the appointed time after having given my code name to the waiter at the Pollarolo Pizzeria, eaten a pizza margarita with a basil leaf, and feeling utterly idiotic. As I was forbidden from writing down what Montse had told me the day before, I took the streetcar from the Piazza del Popolo al Testaccio reciting the story to myself like a schoolboy memorizing a lesson, even though the message could be summed up quite simply: Junio had sent the book in question to the head of the SS, Heinrich Himmler, who was collecting proof of the supremacy of the Aryan race. As far as German plans to remove the map from the Vatican, Junio had said nothing to Montse, either because there were none or because the prince did not completely trust his princess.

The moment the cemetery gate closed behind me, I felt a chill run up and down my spine. I knew I lacked the skills and shrewdness to be a simple messenger, let alone a spy. But I carried on, for Montse's sake.

After walking through the gateway that separated the newer section from the ancient one, I recognized Smith's awkward figure sitting on a wooden bench—the gift of an English organization of friends of poetry, according to a small plaque—right in front of Keats's grave. I say awkward because his body was leaning to the left, as if he were looking for something on the ground. It is curious how our deeply buried survival instincts alert us when we detect something anomalous while our conscious mind still hesitates to grasp what is going on. Suddenly, that instinct surfaces, our muscles tense, and our response to danger becomes rational. At those moments we are capable of efforts that under normal circumstances would be far beyond our reach.

I know this might sound strange, but I smelled Smith's death from far away, long before the rest of my senses could have possibly perceived anything. I have since learned that death announces itself with a characteristic acrid smell, an odor that prevails above and beyond any other sensory perception. I approached him with extreme caution, as if I were really afraid of waking him from a deep sleep. A stream of blood flowed out of a hole between his eyebrows. I saw that it had moved toward the corners of his eyes, where it blossomed again as tears. I stared for a few seconds to see if a breath of life was left in any part of his body. He seemed to be almost examining me with wide-open eyes, avidly, but it was only the empty, absent stare of death. Once I fully grasped the situation, I realized that Smith's assassin could be waiting for me. Paralyzed with fear, I somehow commanded my legs to walk toward the exit—only to find the gate locked. I felt like a cornered beast and began to shout, hoping the guard would hear me. Then, as if my worst nightmare were materializing in front of me, an army of the living dead began to appear from behind the gravestones. Certain they were from the other world, I watched them surround me, then saw they were members of the feared OVRA, Mussolini's secret police, very much of this world. I knelt down, either to beg for mercy or to pray, knowing my own moment of death had arrived. Someone threw a hood over my head and tied my hands together. I was led to a car and shoved into the trunk.

"Don't shout or make any noise at all. . . . It will be only seven or eight minutes," a man's voice said from inside the car.

This, I thought, was the amount of time I had left to live: seven or eight minutes. In my cooler mind, which still hadn't fully prevailed, I considered that if their intention was to kill me, they didn't need to remove me from the cemetery, unless they wanted to torture me first. In any case, I had no intention of offering any resistance; on the contrary, I planned to tell them anything they wanted to know to save my skin. Then, with growing horror, it occurred to me that Montse might have met the same fate and that we would see each other in the torture chamber. Perversely, I wished with all my strength for that to be the case, not only because I thought that with her beside me it would be much easier to explain to our captors that it had all been a misunderstanding, that we were just a couple of crazy kids, but also because in case we didn't survive, I would have the chance to see her one more time.

When the car stopped and the trunk opened, my sphincter muscles gave way.

"*Porca miseria!* This guy has shit himself," shouted one of the men.

The stench was nauseating.

"Calm down. Nothing will happen to you," said the man who had spoken to me from the car.

I had never had such a humiliating experience, and for a moment I wished I were already dead. With a little luck, I thought, my heart would fail during the interrogation.

"I can't breathe," I managed to stutter.

"Find him some clean pants," ordered the man who seemed to be directing the operation.

Two other pairs of arms dragged me into a room where they untied my hands and took off the hood. There I found a new pair of pants and a washbasin with soap and water. "So you are Trinidad," said a short stocky man with an infinite number of wrinkles, eyes as black as coal, and olive-colored skin: a true southern Italian. "If you had arrived ten minutes earlier, you would be wherever Smith is right now. You were saved by a hair," he said.

"My name is José María Hurtado de Mendoza," I corrected him, having decided not to admit to anything he said.

"But your alias is Trinidad. Relax, you are among friends," he assured me.

"You have a strange way of showing friendship," I snapped back.

"Our goal was to rescue you, and that's what we did."

"Rescue me from whom?"

"From the same people who killed Smith."

"And who might they be?" I asked.

"OVRA? The Nazis? The Vatican? Who knows," he answered.

"You are forgetting Prince Cima Vivarini," I said.

The man smiled before answering.

"No, I assure you I am not forgetting Prince Cima Vivarini."

"If you aren't OVRA, who are you?" I asked him.

"Let's say my name is Smith."

"Smith is dead," I reminded him.

"Here, we are all called Smith . . . John Smith," he asserted as he swept his hand in an arc to include all of his colleagues, even though they had long since quietly disappeared from the room.

"At least John Smith looked like a John Smith. You, on the other hand . . ." I blurted out.

"How I look is of no importance; the important thing is that we are all struggling to rid Europe of Fascism," he replied.

"From your uniforms I would have sworn you belonged to Mussolini's secret police," I said.

"Again you trust appearances. If you dress like your enemy, you free yourself from him. As I said, we are friends."

Whoever they were, I was ready to tell them whatever they wanted to hear.

"What do you want from me?"

"The message you had for the other Signor Smith."

"Then you'll let me go?"

"You can go now."

There was a distinct possibility that as soon as I spoke this new Smith would shoot me right between the eyes, but I did so anyway.

"Prince Cima Vivarini has turned the book over to Heinrich Himmler. He is now awaiting orders. For now there is no plan to steal the Creator's Map."

"Anything else?"

"The Germans are also looking for a manuscript about Atlantis, a text that supposedly describes a superior race of men. That's all."

"You see how easy that was? Oh, yes, lest I forget. For the next meeting we'll change the procedure. Go to the same pizzeria, and Marco will tell you the time and place of the meeting. After today we'll have to tighten up our security measures." He stopped and looked at me with a measure of concern. "Whenever you travel by tram, get on and off several times, and go into shops that are full of people and have several doors. Never use the same one to go in and out."

"You think that after what happened today I'm going to continue to play at being a spy?"

"Don't take it as a game, then, but rather as work that will benefit many people," he suggested.

"Those are only words. You people are killing each other over a stupid map, over a . . . superstition. You are the ones who are playing a game," I said angrily.

"We couldn't care less whether or not Hitler and Himmler believe in the esoteric properties of a 'stupid map,' as you call it; however, we are worried that if they get it, they will use it as an excuse to invade neighboring countries. It's not the map that's dangerous but rather the theory of vital space, the idea that Germany is overpopulated and needs new territories. Now do you understand how much is at stake?"

"What? Like democracy? Don't make me laugh. What has democracy done for poor people other than give them the possibility of voting for what kind of poverty they prefer? Yes, I know, now you'll tell me that democracy is the least evil of all possible systems of government, and I will tell you that I agree with you, but that I prefer to remain on the margins."

The new Smith listened to my tirade without losing his smile. I thought I saw in his eyes the same expression I saw in Montse's when she tried to tell me that I needed ideals to make life less unbearable. Deep down, it was a look of deep compassion, as one might bestow upon a person who is terminally ill.

"So, do it for your friend," he added.

"For her this is just a game. She thinks she's in love with the prince and will do whatever it takes to be able to spend time with him."

"If that's true, and she is in love with him, she won't give up her mission. She will carry through till the end, because people in love never leave their work undone. Even when things go badly, they believe there will be another chance. No, your friend won't give up."

"She will when I tell her that Smith has been murdered, probably under orders from her prince," I said, like somebody turning over the card he hopes will win him the game.

"Are you sure? Can you prove that the order to kill Smith came from Prince Cima Vivarini? If not, you're only going to make your friend think ill of you, that you are acting out of jealousy."

Were my feelings for Montse so obvious that even a stranger could guess them? The new Smith was right. It was best to say nothing to Montse. I didn't have a single shred of evidence to prove that Junio was involved in Smith's murder. I began to feel the same surge of panic as when I had found myself locked in the cemetery.

"What if the prince decides to do away with her?" I asked.

"He won't, because even he is aware of what is going on. He will use your friend to get information or, possibly, transmit false information. It is a common practice among spies."

"The spied-on spy. And what will happen when my friend is no longer useful to the prince?"

"We'll pull her out of active service before she gets hurt, I promise you. We know how to read the signs when things start to go badly. We are the first to want to avoid problems. We don't want to call attention to ourselves."

The new Smith spoke with confidence, sure of himself; for me, his words were meaningless, his mouth a fissure leading into a bottomless pit.

"So why did Smith end up with a bullet through his head under your very noses?" I retorted. "Frankly, your arguments are not very convincing."

"Smith's case is different. Whether or not you like my arguments, you don't have much choice: if you don't continue to collaborate with us, your friend will take on your job and that will put her life in much greater danger."

He was right, of course, and so I reluctantly agreed. "But if things get really ugly, I want you to promise to evacuate us from Rome."

At that time, I still didn't understand the basic rules of espionage: when things go well, nobody thanks you; and when things go wrong, nobody knows you.

"We will get you out of Rome if the situation gets complicated," Smith agreed. "Now, one of my men will put your hood back on and drive you to a safe place. It is better for you not to know where you've been."

I didn't answer. I had begun to get tired of formulating objections that led nowhere. I let them put the hood on and I got back into the trunk of the car. For a moment I again longed for Montse to be there with me so I could tell her that it was all her fault.

When they finally released me, I found myself at the door of the Villa Doria Pamphili on the Gianicolo, a five-minute walk from the academy. When I reached the Fontana dell'Acqua Paola, I saw a view of Rome that was as somber as my mood. Then I thought of Smith and what he might think if a dead person could analyze the reasons for his death. Would he say: "It was worth it"? Which led me to ask myself: *Is all this really worth it?*

12.

THIS NIGHT, UNLIKE OTHERS, Rubiños didn't seem to be dozing but rather sunk deep in thought. He kept shrugging his shoulders, as if in answer to whatever question he was posing to himself, as if resigned to not having solved the problem he was pondering. He looked exactly like what he was: a poor fool stuck on a distant terrace in a foreign land. It's odd, but Rubiños continues to be for me the epitome of the subjugated man, precisely because he was completely unaware of being a pawn, a puppet in the hands of higher powers that considered a mere human being insignificant. Sometimes those powers took on the form of a war provoked by spurious interests; other times they manifested themselves in the form of natural disasters; but the victims were always the same: men like Rubiños. For some unknown reason, when I think, for example, of the bombings of Durango, Guernica, or Madrid, I think of individuals like Rubiños buried under the rubble. I can't manage to picture Olarra, Señor Fábregas, Prince Cima Vivarini, or Smith—only Rubiños, perhaps because he was the kind of man who makes a virtue out of servitude.

"Any news from Spain?" I asked him.

Rubiños crushed his cigarette under his shoe and jumped out of his seat.

"Oh, it's you, *mi pensionado*! You scared me! I thought it was Secretary Olarra! No news more important than what happened this afternoon right here in the academy."

"What happened?"

"A miracle! Doña Julia cured Miss Montse with an onion and three slices of tomato. Secretary Olarra has protested to the heavens, but the refugees have interpreted it as a sign from God. They say that if a poor and defenseless woman is capable of changing the course of an illness with only an onion and a tomato, what can't Franco do with the cannons and aircraft that Mussolini is going to send? The Duce announced it this afternoon in a radio address."

"I see."

"Señor Fábregas has spent the afternoon shouting slogans like 'May history tremble in the face of our Caudillo, our Generalissimo Franco!' or 'For Spain! He who defends her dies in glory, and the traitors who abandon her will find no shelter in holy ground, no cross on their graves, nor the hands of a good son to close their eyes!' Then, to show their gratitude for the Duce's help, they all went to Mass." After taking a breath, he added, "Did you know that sugar heals cuts faster than iodine?"

"Yes, Rubiños, I had the pleasure of having breakfast with Doña Julia this morning."

"Well, if Doña Julia is right, tomorrow I'm going to rub my butt with white sugar because these hemorrhoids are killing me."

"Doña Julia's remedies are completely explicable by the laws of nature. The problem is that few people really understand those laws."

Rubiños returned to his chair and stretched himself out, rolled another cigarette, and said, "There's something that intrigues me about you, *mi pensionado*. May I ask you a question?"

"Go right ahead, Rubiños."

"I'd like to know why you come up to the terrace every night and stand there contemplating the view like a . . . excuse the expression, *mi pensionado* . . . like a fool."

"Rubiños, I come up to this terrace because it has one of the best views of the city, as well as a spectacular view of the Milky Way. Not to mention the quality of the air," I answered, inhaling deeply.

"That's the problem, however. Do you really see the city when you look out there?"

The rings of white smoke rose slowly over Rubiños's head, where they hovered briefly like little halos and then dispersed.

"Of course I see the city, Rubiños, what else could I see?"

"I don't see Rome," the telegraph operator admitted.

"What do you see?"

"Galicia, I see my native Galicia. I see the towers of the Santiago Cathedral, the walls of Lugo, the María Pita Plaza, the Ribadeo Estuary, La Toja Island. When I look out, it's like I'm looking out over the balcony of my house; but of Rome, I see nothing at all."

"Rubiños, you see that because you are looking through homesick eyes. I can assure you that the city at our feet is Rome."

I turned my head toward that same city, sunk as it was in gloomy darkness, and I understood that for Rubiños, who did not know it by heart as I did, who had never gotten to know it by day, its nighttime silhouettes might look strange indeed.

"I even get whiffs of seafood," he added nostalgically.

"How long have you been in Rome?" I asked.

"Ten months last week."

"And how many night shifts have you done?"

"So many that my sleep patterns have changed."

"There you have it, that's why you're seeing things."

"You think so?"

"When you live by night you lose your sense of reality because you no longer have any perspective. The world becomes a dark wall and your only choice is to imagine it. And since you rarely leave the academy, you barely have any memories of this city, and you have only familiar smells and images to turn to. You simply project your own movie on the shadows."

"Yes, that's just it!" Rubiños exclaimed, his mouth hanging open. "'It's as if I'm watching a movie."

. . .

AS A FINAL TOUCH to that night full of ghosts, I dreamed of Smith. He stood in front of me, his back turned, facing Keats's tomb. He repeated like a litany the epitaph on the gravestone: "Here lies one whose name was writ in water." I touched his shoulder so he would know I was there. He turned his face to me, and I saw that he had no mouth, even though I could clearly hear his voice reciting a fragment of a Keats poem: "My spirit is too weak; mortality / Weighs heavily on me like unwilling sleep, / And each imagined pinnacle and steep / Of godlike hardship tells me I must die / Like a sick eagle looking at the sky." "You lied to me. You told me there was no danger and now you are dead," I rebuked him. "We all want to be different than we are, we all harbor a restless soul, that's why living can be so dangerous," he answered. "What do you mean?" I asked. Smith smiled, squinting his eyes and puffing out his cheeks before adding, "The answer to your question is, yes, it was worth it. Don't waste any more time with me; get back to your business."

I awoke, startled and in a sweat, as if I had been running for a long time, running away from those images, from a waking much more fearful than death.

13.

B UT IT WAS MONTSE'S RELATIONSHIP with Prince Cima Vivarini that upset me most of all. Their meetings were becoming more and more frequent. For two weeks, Montse's "spying" consisted of going to the movies, wearing dresses made of the finest fabric, and enjoying candlelit dinners and nighttime promenades in the most romantic city in the world. It is uncanny how much the play of the eyes or the line of the mouth can tell us about a person's state of mind, especially if that person attempts to hide her feelings. So it was with Montse, who assiduously avoided displaying any confusion or upset, any lack of composure. Sometimes, a mere trembling of her chin, a widening of her nostrils, a brighter shimmer in her eyes were the only signs that revealed to me the quiet ferocity of her love for the prince.

My only chance of seeing her was at breakfast (thanks to Junio, she had begun to take a course in cataloging at the Palazzo Corsini library, which took up most of her days), when she would bring her mother and Doña Julia up to date on her relationship. She did so, however, unconsciously, or at least with veiled intent, ostensibly recounting the plot of the movie she had seen with the prince the day before. I can still remember the titles of some of those films because of the melodramatic significance (they were, in fact, mostly melodramas) they took on for me. One was *Under the Southern Cross*, by Guido

Brignone. According to Montse, it showed the importance of experiencing unfamiliar emotions in order to mature. It was obvious that Montse was immersed in a similar process. The conversation would then turn to what Montse should wear that night. Señor Fábregas had fulfilled his promise, and Montse's wardrobe had increased by four or five new outfits, in addition to the dresses the other women of the academy had placed at her disposal. The dining room suddenly filled with words that were incomprehensible to me: accessories, appliqué, bias, binding, blouson, bodice, cap sleeve, cardigan, clasp, darts, double-breasted, all the way to z. It was at those moments that she would lower her guard and I could best read her face. With all this going on, I often sought refuge on the terrace half an hour before sunset, when the light of the *tramónto* was minimal and imbued the city with a golden glow, then a moment later gave way to a rainbow of sepia tones followed by violet hues. It sometimes seemed as if the departing day were clinging to the dying city for all it was worth. I liked to watch the way Rome dissolved in front of my eyes like a beautiful dream and how, once it was reduced to vague and ghostly shapes, my eyes transformed the landscape into a host of threatening oneiric figures. It was as if the shadows set the buildings in motion. The churches seemed to leap over the barbicans; the distances between the towers and the domes filled with darkness, forming one gigantic, darkened mullioned window; the imposing marble mass of the Vittorio Emanuele Monument became the sheet of a terrifying ghost; and the Aventine, Palatine, and Capitoline hills, vantage points of great beauty by day, blended their wealth of temples and ruins into a horizon that appeared sculpted in stone. At that moment I began to think that the Eternal City's true tragedy was precisely that it was condemned to live eternally. Writers such as Quevedo, Stendhal, Zola, and Rubén Darío had sung of its decadence or predicted its dissolution—none of them realizing that Rome was condemned to persist, for better or for worse, in the vast world of memories.

Then something happened that made it clear that the ground Montse was walking on was not as firm as she had thought. In fact, I realized that she had no idea what kind of ground she was walking on at all.

One afternoon I found her on the terrace occupying my habitual spot, accompanied by Rubiños, who was attempting to teach her with rather imprecise instructions how to use a pair of binoculars.

"What are you doing?" I asked them.

"The young lady is looking for some ship anchored on that mountain, mi pensionado," Rubiños explained.

"I'm trying to find the Aventine, but this contraption is useless," Montse said as she handed the glasses back to the telegraph operator.

"Tell him about the ship, Miss, because if there is anyone who can tell you about everything you see in Rome from here, it's him," Rubiños added.

"It's probably nonsense. It's a story Junio told me."

"What story is that?"

"This afternoon he asked me if I wouldn't mind accompanying him to the Priory of the Order of Malta in the Piazza dei Cavalieri di Malta. It seems he has to give them some documents because the Knights of the Order are preparing some kind of trip . . ."

"So?"

"Once we were inside the front doors, he told me to look through the keyhole—"

"And you saw a view of St. Peter's Basilica framed by an avenue of cypresses, like a picture postcard," I interrupted her.

"How do you know?"

"Because everybody in Rome has looked through that buco. The whole thing is the creation of Piranesi. In fact, it is Piranesi's only work as an architect, and if I am not mistaken, his remains lie in the mausoleum in the church of St. Mary's Priory, which is part of the complex."

"It amazed me," Montse said.

"That was Piranesi's intention. His purpose was to triumph over the distance—perhaps it would be more exact to say *space*—between the Aventine and St. Peter's Basilica through an optical illusion, so when you look through the keyhole, you have the impression that the cupola is right at the end of the garden and not several kilometers away," I explained.

Montse tried to digest my explanation for a few moments before asking, "What do you have to say about the ship?"

"What ship?"

"You say that everybody in Rome has looked through that keyhole, but nobody seems to have heard the story of the ship. At the end of our visit, Junio told me that the hill the Priory of the Order of Malta sits on is in fact a gigantic ship ready at any moment to set sail for the Holy Land. And when I told him this wasn't possible, he made me promise that as soon as I got back to the academy, I would come up to the terrace so that I could see how the southern face of the hill has been cut in the shape of a large V for a prow."

"A ship needs something more than a prow to be able to sail," I pointed out to her.

"I know. The door into the villa of the Knights of the Order would be the entrance to the hull, the labyrinthine gardens would be the tangled rigging, the parapets of the park represent the quarter deck, and the obelisks decorating the plaza are the masts."

"And you believed this story?"

"You are obviously much too Cartesian," she accused me.

"And Junio is a peddler of dreams," I retorted.

"I have managed to get the Aventine in focus," Rubiños interrupted.

Montse brusquely grabbed the binoculars out of his hands.

"It's incredible, but it really does look like a ship," she said.

"Let me see," I said.

What I saw through those lenses was nothing more than a couple of buildings hanging on to the side of the Aventine Hill, and a landscape of trees, hedges, and parterres.

"Yes, it does look like a ship, but it doesn't look like it will set sail this evening. You can relax, I don't think the prince will run off in that ship before the tide rises in about ten thousand years," I teased.

"Very funny," she answered mockingly.

Finally, it was Rubiños's turn.

"It reminds me of a church in Galicia. After it's had a good cleaning, that is. It must be all that marble."

It took me a while to explain to Montse that many different cities coexisted in Rome—imperial, medieval, Renaissance, Baroque, Neoclassical, Mussolini's, to which you would have to add a Rome on the surface and another underground, built beneath the houses, a sinning Rome and a redeemed Rome, a rich Rome and a poor Rome, a living Rome and another that had been exhumed like a cadaver—and that the one that took delight in the Baroque love of deceptions and tricks was the Rome of the trompe d'oeil, of Palazzo Spada, of the false dome of the church of St. Ignatius de Loyola, of Mount Testaccio (built upon the detritus of the wine and oil amphorae that arrived in the city's ancient port), of the Cestius Pyramid, of the Egyptian obelisks, of extemporaneous monuments in the capital of Christianity—the Rome, definitely, of Piranesi's keyhole.

I thought I had convinced Montse when Rubiños took a final shot.

"You see, I'm not the only one who sees strange things from this terrace," he said. "It's because there are things out there, even though nobody can see them, mi pensionado. I'll give you an example. One day I was walking barefoot along the beach in Galicia, and I felt a sharp pinch on the bottom of my right foot. I stopped to see if it was a piece of glass, but I couldn't find anything. The pain got worse and worse, so I decided to dig around in the sand. I found a fish, a scorpion fish, which stays buried in the shallows at low tide and has a powerful poison in its fins. It was buried in the sand. Maybe it's the same thing with the young lady's ship."

I recalled the metaphor Secretary Olarra always used to describe the general situation of the academy, of a ship pushing against the current. Maybe, I thought, we were the ones drifting off course. Yes, this just might be the image one would get of the academy, looking through binoculars from the Aventine: that of a vessel plowing through the Roman sky.

14.

THREE WEEKS LATER, Junio invited Montse to visit the Vatican Library. Fearing that he might use the opportunity to steal the Creator's Map, I asked to join them. To my surprise, Junio didn't object at all; on the contrary, he sent a car to the academy to pick us both up.

Gabor, the chauffeur, greeted us with a smile so cocky I was certain he knew what had happened at the Protestant Cemetery. I realized that he was responsible for Smith's murder, as diligent in driving as in killing—and probably when he gave somebody a beating or tortured him as well. Gabor did the dirty work, while the prince read Byron's poetry, which he would then whisper into the ear of a woman sitting across from him in a fashionable café. "This is the patent age of new inventions / for killing bodies, and for saving souls, / All propagated with the best intentions."

We drove from one side of the Giancolo to the other, crossed St. Peter's Square, and continued along the Leonine Wall until we came to the Saint Anne entrance.

"The prince is waiting for you at the door of the Vatican Library," Gabor informed us. "Walk down that alleyway until you get to Via di Belvedere." We found Julio at the entrance of the Cortile del Belvedere, accompanied by a man with a large crucifix hanging from his neck. They were conversing in the relaxed, easy manner of men of long acquaintance who trusted each other. I was certain that as soon as I looked into the prince's eyes I would know of his complicity in Smith's murder, as if committing a crime left a footprint or a stain, something visible. However, I perceived nothing out of the ordinary: Junio was the same as always. It was I who had been deeply affected by Smith's death, and, combined with my brooding jealousy of the prince himself, I was in danger of jumping to unfair conclusions.

"Montserrat, José María, this is Father Giordano Sansovino. Giordano, these are my Spanish friends," Junio said, by way of introduction.

The priest shook our hands politely. "I'm sorry about what is happening in your country," he said. "It is like an open wound in the heart of Catholicism." He crossed himself.

He was a grave man with a shriveled face, sunken eyes, and thick eyebrows. Even though he was not wearing a cassock or a collar, his suit looked equally severe. Junio later told us—as if the revelation of such a secret were of little consequence—that Father Sansovino belonged to the counterespionage unit of the Vatican, created at the beginning of the century by Cardinal Merry del Val under orders from Pius X. In its day, he said, this organization had been involved in the so-called Russicum, a school that trained priests who were then brought clandestinely into the Soviet Union as spies.

At this first meeting, however, Junio merely said, "Giordano and I were fellow students at the School of Paleography and Diplomacy founded by Pope Leo XIII. Presently, he is a librarian, a *scriptor* of the Vatican Library, and today he will be our guide."

"And that's all I'll be. I do not wish to spend the afternoon discussing fantasies," the priest asserted, looking askance at Junio.

"I've spent the last hour trying to get my friend to tell me where they have hidden the Creator's Map, the one mentioned in the book I bought from you," Junio continued, unabashed, "but he refuses to give me even a clue!"

To this day I wonder what the prince was up to, speaking so plainly, showing his cards from the start. At times I think his behavior was a reflection of the euphoria the triumphant Italian Fascists were feeling at that moment. Not in vain, for the Vatican owed its continuing existence to the Fascists. St. Peter's no longer had only one God; now they also had to worship Mussolini. Perhaps that was why Junio and his people strutted around as if they owned the place, like gods in their own temples, with the right to demand tribute from the Holy See. Word had it, however, that by signing the Lateran Pact in 1929, which recognized the Vatican as an independent state, Mussolini had intended to keep "the black cockroaches"—a nickname Fascists used to refer scornfully to the members of the papal Curia—confined and under strict vigilance.

"I've already told you thousands of times that the map doesn't exist, and that even if it did exist and were here, it would not have been cataloged," Father Sansovino said.

"Because of its secret nature?" Junio asked provocatively, ignoring the priest's desire to change the subject.

"Nothing of the sort," Father Sansovino said curtly. "Simply because the library contains more than a million and a half volumes, a hundred fifty thousand manuscripts, as many maps, and sixty thousand codices in about thirty collections. Out of all that, we know the contents of only about five thousand, even though we've been cataloging since 1902. One person cannot catalog more than ten a year. It takes a long time to read, check, systemize their contents, so it will be another century before we can know what is really hiding in the Vatican Library. In fact, every year a discovery is made—recently, Book VI of Cicero's *On the Republic*, for example—but I highly doubt that someday a map will turn up that was created by . . . God. That would be . . . "

Father Sansovino crossed himself again.

"If God gave Moses the tablets of the Ten Commandments, I don't see why he couldn't have drawn a map of the world," Junio observed.

"Because there is no record in any text of the existence of such a map."

"Yes, there is," the prince persisted. "The *princeps* edition of Pierus Valerianus mentions it, as do Joseph Severn and John Keats in their letters."

"I assure you I have read John Keats's letters and not one mentions the existence of a map."

"Keats didn't know what he had in his hands, nor did Severn, which is why when the poet died, and with the excuse of preventing the spread of a contagious disease, the Church requisitioned the map and burned the letters where Keats made reference to the papyrus Severn bought in the Protestant Cemetery. It is probably in the Secret Archives."

For a moment I thought I was listening to Smith rather than Junio.

"Ridiculous! The Secret Archives were created to store official documents, not to hide anything."

"Everybody knows that within the Secret Archives there is a secret archive. One cannot help wondering why you have never declassified a single document down there."

"Perhaps the answer lies in the fact that the Vatican has existed as a state for only eight and a half years. Do you think a child of eight has secrets he cannot confess? No. At most, innocent little venial sins."

Junio laughed before launching a new assault.

"The Vatican City State is newly established, but the Church has existed for more than nineteen hundred years, and its survival has relied to a large extent on its ability to control the information generated by its own activities and that of its enemies. In this respect, the Vatican is the same as any other country, and thus your little State is founded upon a gigantic gloomy vault where you can hide anything that someone considers unadvisable, out of decorum or convenience, to bring to light. If the Vatican resembles anyone, it would most definitely not be an innocent child of eight years old, but rather the devil himself."

By this time, the trust and complicity between the two had soured into muted conflict.

"Sometimes I have the impression that you have become anything but a scholar, and undoubtedly politics has a lot to do with these changes I see in you. You know perfectly well that most of the collections in the Secret Archives cannot be brought into the open. Some books and manuscripts cannot even be handled without running the risk of losing them forever. It is one thing to bring a text to light and another to expose it to the light of the sun. Deliberate secrecy has nothing to do with it."

"That's why it would be the ideal place to hide such a singular document as the Creator's Map. If you don't help me," said Junio, "I'll have to get the collaboration of another *scriptor*."

Junio's insinuation that he was willing to bribe a librarian apparently didn't try the priest's patience. On the contrary, he responded with evident politeness, "I suggest we go inside before your guests die of boredom."

"Seems like a very interesting subject to me," Montse said.

"It's nothing compared to the treasures hidden behind these walls," the priest said. "Follow me."

Most likely at that moment neither Junio, nor Montse, nor Father Sansovino himself was able to appreciate it, but the library's foremost treasure was the building itself, designed by Domenico Fontana, the architect who laid the foundations of modern Rome. We climbed a staircase that separated the Cortile del Belvedere from the Cortile della Pigna and, after passing through several corridors and rooms that brought us to the Cortile del Pappagallo, we reached the ancient palace of Pope Nicholas V, site of the first Vatican Library. It was spread out over four ample rooms of unequal size whose walls were covered with frescoes. From there we continued on to the vestibule and salon of Pope Sixtus V, where we could feast our eyes on the exquisitely inlaid writing desks lined up along the walls, the work of Giovannino de Dolci, the architect of the Sistine Chapel. It was exciting to think that at those desks sat artists such as Raphael and Bramante. Our next destination would be the Sistine Chapel and Gallery itself, which occupied a huge area more than sixty meters long and fifteen wide.

"Manuscripts were originally kept in the wooden cabinets you see lined up against the walls, but during the reign of Pope Paul V, at the beginning of the seventeenth century, it was thought preferable to keep the documents in a different room. It was then that the Secret Archives, as it is known, was founded," Father Sansovino explained. "But right from the start there was never any intention of hiding anything; it was simply that many large collections were acquired during the seventeenth century, such as the Palatine Library of Heidelberg, the manuscripts of the Dukes of Urbino, and those of Queen Christina of Sweden, and this created the need for more space."

We then moved through other rooms with fresco-decorated vaults depicting the transfer of the Egyptian obelisk to St. Peter's Square. Finally, we came to the reading rooms. The first, the Leonine Library, named in honor of Pope Leo XIII, was the largest. From there we made our way to the Cicognara Library, dedicated to books about art and antiquities; passed through the numismatic gallery; and concluded our tour in the Sala dei Manoscritti, or Manuscripts Reading Room, a medium-size room full of tables with lecterns and pure white walls that felt like an artisan's tidy workshop. A dozen scholars wearing gloves and peering through magnifying glasses were working on deciphering documents under the watchful gaze of the librarians. One heard only the rustle of the pages, like gigantic butterfly wings, which released a fine layer of dust when turned. But if the manuscript room distilled a serene beauty, the deeper interest lay in what the library hid in its bowels. Not in vain was this the "Library of Libraries," as the experts often called it, the most important center of historical documentation in the world. Within those walls could be found the famous "Codex B," the Bible Constantine gave to the most important basilicas after his conversion to Catholicism following the Nicene Council of 325; there were manuscripts of Miguel Angel and Petrarch, of Dante and Bocaccio; texts by Cicero; letters from Lucrezia Borgia to her father, Pope Alexander VI; letters from Henry VIII to Anne Boleyn; missives from the Emperor Justinian, from Martin Luther; codices in Arabic, Greek, Hebrew, Latin, Persian.

"The keys that guard these treasures are prudence, temperance, and wisdom," Father Sansovino said. "I now want to show you twelve kilometers of new steel shelves that the Holy Father has recently ordered."

"Twelve kilometers!" Montse exclaimed.

"Add to that the thirteen already here, and you have a total of twenty-five kilometers. Not to mention the shelves in the Secret Archives. In all, between the Vatican Library and the Secret Archives, we are talking about some fifty kilometers of shelving. And I can assure you that we still need more space."

"Pius XI was a librarian before he became a friar," Junio added. "At one point he sent ten priests, all expert librarians, to Washington to learn the classification system of the United States Library of Congress."

"It's forbidden to touch anything," Father Sansovino warned us.

As we took several turns around that labyrinth of books, I had the impression that we were going deeper and deeper into a mysterious and sinister world. Perhaps it was due to the darkness or the lack of fresh air, but I began to have the same sensation that overwhelmed me when I visited the San Calisto catacombs on Via Appia: all the corridors looked the same, all the shelves identical. I thought about how strange it was to be there, walking behind Father Sansovino and Prince Cima Vivarini, who was probably already preparing his heist now that he had concluded his final reconnaissance mission.

"Nothing interesting in this hallway. Only books here!" Junio complained.

"What else would you want there to be in a library?" Father Sansovino replied.

"Secrets, Giordano, we want secrets!" the prince exclaimed.

"I will now show you what we call the 'clinic,' one of the most important sections of the library," the librarian said, ignoring the prince. "Though this may sound strange, the greatest threat to a book—besides dirt, tears, microbes, insects, and previous restoration attempts—is humidity. If it goes above fifty-five percent, it's very bad, and if the temperature falls below eighteen degrees centigrade or rises to more than twenty-one degrees centigrade, bad again. Which means that the worst enemy of a library is the library itself."

We were looking at the different kinds of inks, glues, gold leaf, and the various instruments the specialists used for restoration work when the prince said, "I am ready to offer you two hundred and fifty thousand lire for that map."

At first I interpreted Junio's words as yet another provocation, but I immediately saw by his face that he was serious, that his proposition was a way to test Father Sansovino.

"I think the rarefied air in here has unhinged you," the librarian answered.

"You're right, perhaps I am losing my mind. I raise my offer to half a million."

As it was, the prince's offer bordered on the absurd. "As you see, Junio," the priest said with resignation, "you've won: you have managed to try my patience. Let's go outside."

"Montse and José María are witnesses that I have tried to persuade you by honest means. You will be responsible for whatever happens from now on," Junio warned.

"You think I would be any less responsible if I allowed myself to be 'persuaded,' as you say, by your lire?"

"Believe it or not, I would like for us to work together."

"Working with you would be like working with Mussolini or, even worse, his boss, Hitler. I obey only the Holy Father, the shepherd of the Church of Our Lord Jesus Christ." Again the priest crossed himself.

"I am not asking you to turn your back on Christ; but just as there is a heavenly power, there is also an earthly one. Didn't Pius XI say that Communism is intrinsically perverse because it undermines the basis of the human, divine, rational, and natural concepts of life itself, and because in order to prevail it needs to be rooted in despotism, brutality, the whip, and the prison?"

"True, that is what the pope said, but I assure you his idea of Nazism isn't much different. No, my friend, faith, and therefore the Church, is not in danger, unlike your ideologies. Can anybody really believe that the Third Reich will last a thousand years, as its leaders proclaim? You can rest assured that there is no eternal power in history, other than the power of God. The eternal is not subject to humans, not even to the human soul. And don't think these are only my words. They were written long ago, and history itself has proven them to be true. I am afraid you're being guided by political rapture, which has swept the world like some new kind of fad."

"You might be right, but the Church won't survive another thousand years if the Communist regime manages to extend its tentacles across Europe. My offer stands," Junio said.

And so our visit to the Vatican Library ended abruptly, with Junio and Father Sansovino in a standoff. But one didn't need to be particularly astute to see that the differences between them, though significant, actually complemented each other. Something similar transpired between Junio and Montse; and between Montse and me. We all needed each other; we were all links in the same chain, even though our needs and interests were so different.

15.

ON CHRISTMAS EVE, by mandate of Secretary Olarra, we all gathered in the Santa María de Montserrat Church on Via di Monserrato to attend midnight Mass. Built for Catalán pilgrims by Pope Alexander VI, the church has been the meeting place of the Spanish colony in Rome since the seventeenth century. There was no festivity remotely connected with Spain that did not have its religious expression in that church. The front steps were an informal hangout where those recently arrived recounted the latest news from Spain, and those on their way home collected letters and messages to pass on to friends and relatives. Not surprisingly, it also served as a center for intrigue and gossip.

"How happy I am to see you, Prince!," Señor Fábregas said as he greeted Junio, whose attendance had not been announced. "But what are you doing waiting at the door in this cold? Come in with us, I beg you."

"I'm grateful for your offer, Señor Fábregas, but I'm waiting for the king," Junio replied, to everyone's surprise.

"Of Italy?" Señor Fábregas asked. He seemed both delighted and perplexed that Vittorio Emanuele III would be attending a religious function.

"No, I'm waiting for *your* king, the king of Spain."

Señor Fábregas had not taken into account that for the nobility, kings do not lose their rank even when, like King Alfonso XIII, they had been forced to escape with nothing but the shirts on their backs.

"Then we'll see you afterward. I would love to shake hands with the monarch," Señor Fábregas confided.

Later that evening, Junio would tell Montse that his presence at the church had been directly ordered by the Duce, to whom Don Alfonso XIII had turned for help in reclaiming his throne. Despite his full support for the political activities of the Falange movement, Mussolini wished to maintain good relations with the Spanish royal family as a kind of insurance against any unexpected turns of events. Who better to send on such an errand than a Fascist prince?

Five minutes after the church had filled to capacity, the king arrived, accompanied by his queen, his children, and the journalist César González-Ruano, who followed the exiled king around everywhere and wrote about him in the Spanish press.

During the Mass, the responsory for the fallen took up more time than the sermon itself; so much that we spent almost the entire Mass praying. We prayed for the 16 bishops summarily executed, the 7 who had disappeared, the 5,800 monks who had been murdered, and the 6,500 massacred priests, not to mention the tens of thousands of civilian victims. Nobody remembered the priests Franco had executed in Guipúzcoa and Vizcaya, nor the civilian victims on the other side. The only thing left for us to do was to pray for that ex-king—sitting in the front row with a sad, waxen face that looked like a half-burnt votive candle—to recover the throne the popular vote had taken from him. Word had it that Alfonso XIII was depressed, that the only pastimes left to him were bridge and women. He was not particulary skilled at cards, and those who played with him felt pity when they won; as far as women went, however, nobody doubted his credentials as a ladies' man: he had accumulated a prodigious list of lovers in Spain. His status, however, had changed radically since he arrived in Italy. He now had to invite his mistresses to his hotel room, where the family lived; moreover, his chronic halitosis had worsened as a result of the trauma of exile, and the ladies had begun to lose interest. Considering that a Bourbon without women is only half a Bourbon, as someone once said, the king had become first a ghost, and then a jinx—if an Italian dared utter his name, he simultaneously touched wood. In this regard as well, Junio was different from his compatriots: he had no qualms about sitting on the king's left, shoulder-to-shoulder, and even giving him his hand when Don Alfonso kneeled after receiving Communion.

When Mass was over, I remained at the door of the church with a group of Spaniards, including the Fábregas family and Secretary Olarra, who wanted to wish the king a Merry Christmas. I still remember overhearing Don Alfonso say to César González-Ruano as they left the building:

"I don't understand why anybody complains about hotels. They're far superior to palaces."

That was the first and last time I heard Don Alfonso speak, but based on the quaver in his voice, it seemed true what one newspaper commentator had said about the nomadic life the monarch was leading: "His soul seemed set on distancing itself quickly from a past that always accompanied him . . ." From up close, Don Alfonso's face showed traces of every epithet chroniclers and historians had used to describe him: controversial king, paradoxical king, perjured king, criminal king, rejected king, slandered king, Carlist king, patriotic king. I don't know which of these best suited him and his behavior, but it was clear that although Don Alfonso justified his abandonment of Spain by claiming that he was trying to avoid a bloodbath, the truth was that he left the country because he could not count on the support of the army to carry out the bloodbath that would have allowed him to retain his throne.

Many years later, I understood that when César González-Ruano wrote that "death can consist of losing the habit of living" he had Alfonso XIII in mind; looking back it seemed to me that already, by Christmas of 1937, he had lost the will to live, perhaps knowing that he would die in a hotel room—no matter how comfortable—and that his remains would end up in the church he had just left, which is exactly what happened.

On that Christmas Eve, however, another surprise awaited me. As Rubiños and I ascended the Via Garibaldo on our way back to the academy, he told me he was going back to Spain.

"You've persuaded them to send you home? That's great news! Congratulations!" I exclaimed.

"I'm not going home, *mi pensionado*, I'm going to the front. I volunteered."

"Volunteered? I have a friend in Spain who says that the only thing worth volunteering for is a trip to the whorehouse," I said.

"You were right. I couldn't continue to live in that darkness."

"I've never been right about anything, Rubiños. Anyway, now who's going to tell me I'm a fool when I stand on the terrace and look out at the view like an idiot?"

"I have a cousin who is a priest in Barcelona. They found his body with a cross stabbed into his jaw."

"I'm sorry."

"What I'm sorry about is being stuck in this city full of nuns and dandies. Olarra has censored the news to avoid any diplomatic problems, but a lot of the Italians they sent to Spain have to be led to the front at the point of a bayonet, because as soon as they hear the whistle of a bullet, they shit in their pants. Do you know what happened in Guadalajara? I'll tell you since Olarra won't. After they were routed, the Italian troops ran off, and the military police had to intervene. Finally, they managed to round up about ten thousand Italians in the concentration camp of Puerto de Santa María; there were three thousand deserters, and another two thousand were declared unfit for duty and sent back to Italy. Meanwhile, those of us gladly willing to shed our blood for Spain are sunning ourselves on a terrace in Rome."

Rubiños punctuated his speech by pretending to spit on the ground.

"You'd shit in your pants too if you had to fight in somebody else's country," I retorted. "That's fine, Rubiños, if you want to go and fight, go, but don't tell me I put you up to it, because if something happens to you I'd feel—"

"Don't worry, you're not responsible. I am a man of action, not ideas. In case it's any comfort to you, I'd say you're a bit like one of those perfumed Italians."

Rubiños's contempt for me calmed my spirit.

"Just so you know I'm not complaining for no reason, just look at the haircut the barber gave me this afternoon," he continued. "I told the man to cut it all off and give me a good shave, simple, and instead he started rubbing my scalp and smearing lotions all over my face and pouring on perfume and powders until I felt like vomiting. He made me so nervous, I flinched and got my cheek cut."

"That's what the Romans call *fare bella figura*, which means to cut a fine figure. The Roman barber thinks of himself as an artist, and his job is to make his clients as beautiful as possible."

"If Spanish barbers tried to *fare bella figura*, as you call it, they'd all go straight to jail for deviant behavior."

"And what if once you get to Spain you end up missing Rome?"

"Rome won't miss me and I won't miss her. The relationship I've always had with this city is the same as I had with Marisiña, my first girlfriend: look, but don't touch. No, I never fell in love with Rome, so don't you worry about me," Rubiños replied.

"When do you leave?" I asked.

"The boat sets sail from Ostia tomorrow afternoon. It'll take me to Malaga, where I'll join Queipo's army."

"I see."

We continued the rest of the way in silence, each absorbed in his own thoughts, avoiding the clouds of dust swirling about us like miniature hurricanes. As we reached the top of Monte Aureo, and the academy came into view, an icy gust from the west served as a sudden reminder of the winds of insanity sweeping across the world. When we recovered our breath, Rubiños and I embraced and wished each other good luck.

16.

THE DAY AFTER CHRISTMAS, Cesare Fontana, the academy's butler, came to me with a somewhat convoluted story. It seems that Rubiños had left him a book with instructions to give it to me discreetly (in other words, without Secretary Olarra finding out), and inform me that I should pass it on to Montse after reading the note inside, for the volume belonged to the academy library.

Don Cesare, as he was called, had a cold, impassive face and great physical dexterity; he usually spoke in a rather ornate, flowery language he seemed to have learned from Olarra himself. He was, in fact, the secretary's eyes and ears within the prosaic and perplexing world of domestic affairs, though he had begun to exploit the position for his own benefit, throwing around his weight like a miniature tyrant. He was the domestic administrator, or housekeeper, so whoever needed a lightbulb or a new chair for their study had to come to him to negotiate the deal. Failing to submit would entail punishment through neglect and delays. All dealings with the butler, as a result, had become a business transaction in which each party attempted to obtain the maximum advantage.

"What do you want to guarantee your silence?" I asked him without any preambles.

"It's a banned book, so it will cost ten lire," he told me.

"You're a thief, Don Cesare. There are no banned books in the academy, at least as far as I know," I said.

"You're mistaken. Many of the books in this house are from the Republican era, and in the Spain of Franco, Republican books are banned."

"Franco still hasn't won the war, so not a single book has yet been banned," I pointed out.

"True, but since this institution is on the side of our valiant crusaders, everything that smells of the Republic stinks. I have heard the secretary say that he is planning to build a bonfire any day now to burn the Reds' books."

I didn't want to continue this discussion, so I agreed to his blackmail without further objections.

The supposedly banned book he handed me was none other than *The Revolt of the Masses* by José Ortega y Gasset. I could only smile.

What the devil was a simple man like Rubiños, with no apparent philosophical concerns, doing with that book? I assumed it had something to do with Montse. Then I found the note the butler had mentioned. It was a single page covered with surprisingly even handwriting.

Mi pensionado, I beg you to forgive me for words I blurted out the other night. You are not responsible for anything (I mean, my decisions), and you don't even smell too strongly of cologne (even if I said otherwise). I have spent several months trying to straighten out my thoughts, because sometimes I don't understand why I do the things I do. I have tried to solve the problem by listening to the Vatican Radio and talking to you, but the noise kept ringing inside my head like one of those tapeworms that feed off what others eat. I don't know if I'm making any sense, but in this case the facts are the important things. Miss Fábregas has always seemed like an angel to me, and I have never known anybody in my life so good or who knows so much about books, so I thought that maybe she could help me. After explaining my situation to her, she told me that my problem was existential (and so I wouldn't seem like an idiot I didn't tell her that I didn't even know what that meant, and to tell you the truth, I still don't), and she handed me a book. Yes, it is this one you have in your hands. According to Miss Montse, the author was a very important philosopher who said, "I am I and my circumstances and if I do not save them

I cannot save myself," which seems to mean that we are all influenced by the world around us. I'm not laughing at philosophy because I don't even really understand it, but it seems criminal that a philosopher has to write a book to say such a ridiculous thing. Not because I don't agree with him, but because it is something that any newborn knows the first time he opens his eyes. It's true I didn't manage to read beyond chapter three, but that was enough for me to reach certain conclusions. First: nobody can understand Señor Ortega y Gasset, which often happens with people who are too smart. He writes Spanish so well that it seems like a different language. Second: if I don't like my current life, it is because of the circumstances around me. Third: in order to go back to being really myself, the circumstances have to change. Fourth: only then will I go back to being myself and the circumstances will go back to being themselves. And in order to bring about the fourth thing, I have felt it necessary to go to the front.

Long live Spain!

Soldier Rubiños

P.S. Take care of Miss Fábregas because I have a feeling her circumstances also aren't the best they could be. That ship she sees anchored on the Aventine Hill will one day set sail.

I went to find Montse to carry out Rubiños's second request; I also wanted to show her the note and ask her to explain.

"I recommended that book because Ortega is a humanist in a dehumanized world, and I thought that Rubiños could use some human warmth and understanding," she said.

"Ortega might well be what you say he is, but Rubiños is a bullet in the chamber of a gun pointed at that dehumanized world. Maybe you should have recommended he read the Bible," I said.

"He told me that whenever he talked to you up on the terrace, Rome would look to him like someone's stomach torn open with its intestines hanging out. He said the twisted streets were like tangled guts whose gastric juices were little by little digesting buildings, churches, and monuments. According to him, the city would soon be regurgitated and converted to ruins because everything that is decaying and putrid will finally collapse. Frankly, I should have recommended he go see a head doctor."

"Anybody who looks over the balustrade to contemplate the city at night can see whatever he wants, even if it doesn't exist," I protested.

"Rome for him was worse than a jail," said Montse.

"I hope it never becomes that for you," I said.

"Why would it?"

"Because you believe that the Aventine Hill is a ship ready to set sail. You also begin to see things that don't exist."

"We all see things that only exist for ourselves. These visions contain the root of what we call hope," she observed.

"Well, let's hope that Rubiños has done the right thing."

I knew that Prince Cima Vivarini had left for Venice that same morning to spend a few days with his family. I had lost a lot of ground in the last few weeks, so I wanted to take advantage of the opportunity to invite Montse out to eat.

"For old times' sake," I added when I saw her hesitate.

"I accept under the condition that you then come with me to do something. But don't ask me what. It's a secret."

"Agreed."

I chose Alfredo's, one of the city's most famous restaurants. Perhaps because Montse had already become used to going to such elegant places with Junio, she didn't reproach me for being ostentatious. We ordered *zuppa all'ortolana* for starters, then *fettuccine all'Alfredo*, a dish whose fame had crossed the Atlantic.

I waited until the butter in the *fettuccine* had melted into the slivers of Parmesan to say, "I miss seeing you. We should make a date to eat together every so often."

"Junio might get jealous," she answered.

"Which would only enhance his interest in you, and the greater his devotion, the greater his trust will be. And if you gain his trust—"

"Your view of jealousy is typical of someone who has never experienced it," she interrupted me. "Jealousy leads to suspicion."

"And if I told you that I *was* consumed with jealousy? That now, at this very instant, I feel jealous—"

"I would tell you that what you feel for the person you think you love is not love, since if it were, you'd know that jealousy leads to distrust, not the opposite."

I had to make a great effort not to feel as if I had just been told to go straight to hell.

We concluded our lunch with a couple of *profiteroles*, which we ate in silence.

Montse then asked me to excuse her for a few moments, got up, and disappeared through the service door. When she returned, she had a big smile and was carrying a huge bag.

"What's that?" I asked.

"Leftovers for the cats," she answered proudly.

"What cats?"

"The street cats. I like to feed them once in a while."

Had she accepted my invitation only to get leftovers for the cats of Rome?

"When you go out with Junio do you also collect leftovers?" I asked.

"No, because I'm not as comfortable with him as I am with you. Come on, let's go feed the cats. You promised."

There wasn't a single Roman ruin that didn't have its share of resident cats, a plague the Romans didn't seem to mind. Montse chose the Área Sacra di Largo Torre Argentina, a vast, recently built plaza under which one of the most important archeological sites in the city had been discovered. Hundreds of cats lived there: brindled, white, black, gray, striped, and red, all parading their supreme indolence among fallen columns and broken stones.

When we arrived after walking from one end of Via del Corso to the other, night had already fallen, and the Área Sacra had turned into a ravine overflowing with darkness. It was not too preposterous to think of the cats as ghosts of the ancient Romans who once lived there—praetors, quaestors, orators, or members of the plebe—as the more superstitious Romans claimed, for there was something evanescent about those arrogant animals with their shining eyes that seemed to melt away as we approached.

"Do you know why I like cats?" Montse asked me as she poured out the contents of the bag on the spot where Julius Caesar had fallen, mortally wounded.

"No."

"Because they do not submit to humans, even though their survival depends on us. They've learned that to get what they need from human beings, it is in fact in their interest to turn their backs on us."

"It is a rare virtue," I said.

"It's called freedom," she said.

Neither she nor I could possibly imagine that the day would come when the cats of Rome would be sacrificed for the survival of the city's inhabitants. Whenever Montse and I speak about the subject, her most idealistic side always comes out, and she asserts that the spirits of the cats the Romans ate rather than starve to death had infused the population with the desire for freedom and the strength to fight the enemy.

17.

THE YEAR 1938 BEGAN with several significant events. Montse had her twenty-first birthday on January eleventh; on the thirty-first of the same month Franco's air force bombed Barcelona, killing 153 and wounding 180, a cause for rejoicing among the academy's "refugees"; the Nationalist army retook Teruel, which had been occupied by the Republican troops; and finally, on March 14, my twenty-ninth birthday, Hitler announced that Germany was annexing Austria to the Third Reich, thereby confirming Smith's worst fears. Even more worrisome was the announcement the following month that the Führer would be visiting Rome the first week of May.

I believe it was the second day of that month when Don Cesare told me that I had a visitor. It was Father Sansovino. At first I thought his agitation could be attributed to the strenuous climb up Via Garibaldo, but I soon understood that there was another reason for his state. He did not even pause long enough to greet me.

"Do you know where our friend, the prince, is?" he asked.

"I think he's off making Nazi banners and buying hors d'oeuvres for Hitler to enjoy," I said sarcastically and, as it turned out, somewhat naively.

I told him what Junio had told Montse: that they would not be able to see each other for two or three weeks because he had been selected to be part of the Führer's welcoming committee. As we later learned, he was to play an even bigger role; he had been assigned the much more important task of negotiating a meeting between Hitler and the pope, thereby allowing Hitler to visit the Vatican Museums. Pius XI's response, however, had been uncompromising: "If Hitler wishes to enter the Vatican, he must issue a public apology for the persecution suffered by the Catholic Church in Germany." Hitler did not agree to these terms, so on the day of his arrival, the Holy Father said that he felt sad to see a cross—the swastika—other than Christ's flying over Rome, and he moved to his residence in Castel Gandolfo after giving orders that the Vatican Museums would remain closed and the Vatican's newspaper, *L'Osservatore Romano*, would not publish a single word about the visit of the German chancellor. The enmity between Pius XI and the Führer had already lasted a full year, since the former published the encyclical *"Mit brennender sorge"* ("With Deep Anxiety"), in which he laid out the pagan nature of Nazism and condemned its racism, and Hitler responded by arresting thousands of well-known German Catholics, three hundred of whom ended up in what at the time was still thought to be the "labor camp" of Dachau.

"Damnation!" the priest exclaimed.

"May I know what's going on?"

"I'm afraid Junio has carried out his threat and, even more seriously, that it has cost a man his life."

Instinctively, I thought of the second Smith, but Father Sansovino immediately set me straight.

"Four hours ago we were informed that one of our *scriptores* was killed after leaving Signor Tasso's *antica libreria* on the Via dell'Anima. Someone shot him several times." His face was grim.

I thought of the first Smith.

"What does the prince have to do with the death of a *scriptor*?" I asked.

Deep down I was hoping that Father Sansovino would tell me that Junio had been seen actually pulling the trigger, but his answer surpassed my expectations.

"The *scriptor* had stolen the Creator's Map," he said.

I was speechless. I waited, hoping the priest would say more, but in the end, I spoke first.

"But you said the map doesn't exist!"

This time, it was Father Sansovino who knit his brow, looking decidedly uncomfortable.

"In a way, that's true. The map only partially exists," he said, trying to justify himself.

"What does that mean?"

"It is true that the Church requisitioned an Egyptian papyrus from John Keats's house after his death, and that the experts who analyzed it said it contained a strange map that, among other things, showed the world was spherical. I believe it even contained precise drawings of the continent of Antarctica, which wasn't discovered until the nineteenth century. It was written in cuneiform characters and, given its antiquity and considering that it was a very advanced map for its time, the experts did indeed begin to call it the 'Creator's Map.' It could just as well have been called 'Map of Anonymous.' The point is that just because the map was baptized with that name does not mean its author was God. Unfortunately, the map began to deteriorate so quickly after being handled repeatedly that it would simply perish if it were opened now. In other words, it cannot be looked at without destroying all the information it contains, which is why I say it only partially exists."

"What makes you so sure that the map is not the work of God, as the prince claims?" I asked him.

By now, Father Sansovino had calmed down and seemed prepared to discuss the matter. "There are many reasons," he said. "To begin with, it is not mentioned in any of the sacred texts. But there is another, more practical reason: if God had wanted to draw a map of Creation, let us say, he would never have used a material as fragile as papyrus. Weren't the Ten Commandments carved in stone? The ancient Hittites and Babylonians used clay tablets, which are much more durable than papyrus, so it would be totally absurd to think that God, given his infallibility, would commit such an error."

"There's something in this whole story that doesn't add up. You claim that the map got its name in the nineteenth century, after it was stolen from John Keats; but Pierus Valerianus's book mentions the Creator's Map two and a half centuries earlier," I pointed out.

"So it does, but there is no contradiction. The experts gave it that name precisely because they knew of the existence of Valerianus's book. But in his book Pierus Valerianus is simply referring to an ancient Egyptian legend. He never set eyes on the map, either."

After a brief pause, Father Sansovino continued. "The subject of relics is extremely complex, especially when it comes to establishing the authenticity of each object. For example, the Holy See has recorded the existence of more than sixty fingers belonging to John the Baptist. The foreskins of Our Lord Jesus Christ are worshipped in the cathedrals of Antwerp, Hildesheim, and Santiago de Compostela. There are umbilical cords of the baby Jesus in Santa Maria del Popolo, in San Martino, and in Châlons. Throughout the world there are two hundred coins that Judas supposedly was paid for his betrayal, there are several sites that claim to have Lazarus's skull, and even in the Vatican's Sancta Santorum there are lentils and bread left over from the Last Supper, as well as a bottle containing a sigh of Saint Joseph, which an angel left in a church near the French city of Blois. Considering that Our Lord Jesus Christ could have had only one umbilical cord and one foreskin, that John the Baptist had only two hands with a total of ten fingers, that there were thirty, not two hundred, coins that Judas earned for his betrayal, we must reach the conclusion that we have an abundance of relics, an overabundance, I would say. Thus, to speak about a map created by God is almost a . . . *boutade* . . ."

"I understand. So will they arrest the prince for the murder of the *scriptor*?"

"They would sooner arrest the Holy Father than Prince Cima Vivarini," the priest answered. "I'd wager anything that tomorrow's press calls the murder of our brother an attack perpetrated by atheist anti-Fascist forces in order to destabilize Mussolini's regime."

"But the police can't just stand around and twiddle their thumbs . . ."

"Above the police are the secret police, and it's men like the prince who control them," he interrupted me. "Junio wanted to pay me back for the blow I dealt to his pride a few months ago."

"Pay you back?"

"Didn't he tell you the other day that I was a spy for the Vatican?"

I was surprised that Father Sansovino would have assumed as much.

"Yes, right after we left the library," I said.

"He told you the truth. I was until very recently. I worked in the Sodalitium Pianum, the Vatican counterespionage service of the Holy Alliance. My mission was to uncover moles, and Providence led me to trap the most important one of all. About a year ago we detected a leak inside the Holy See. After a discreet investigation, we found that the traitor was Archbishop Enrico Pucci, who had been recruited by the Fascist police around 1927. We then circulated a false document stating that we had discovered that one Roberto Gianille was a British agent who had been passing on sensitive information from the Kingdom of Italy and the Vatican City State. As soon as this document reached Bishop Pucci, he informed the chief of police, who immediately issued an order for the search and capture of Signor Gianille. The catch was that Gianille didn't exist; he was my invention, and as a result, all the members of the Pucci network were unmasked. Needless to say, my position became compromised, so I turned to other duties. But I left the Fascists without an informer in the Vatican, and now they are paying me back by stealing the Creator's Map from right under my nose. By bribing a *scriptor*, they are telling me that they don't need a spy network to get what they want, and by murdering him they are proving that they hold earthly powers in their hands."

"That sounds quite alarming," I said.

"It is. Above all because behind this vendetta of Junio's is a message Mussolini is sending to the Holy Father to get him to submit to the secular state Mussolini represents. The Duce has confessed to his most intimate associates that he is ready to "scratch off the scabs" of the Italians and turn them against the clergy if the pope doesn't change his attitude toward Hitler and himself. He claims that the Vatican is full of foolish, dessicated old men and that religious faith is practically worthless, for nobody can really believe in a God who cares about our sorrows. Yes, times have changed; to commit a crime now against the Church gains you applause from the State."

"So the *scriptor*'s murder will go unpunished?" I said, appalled.

"At the most, when the diplomatic arm of the Vatican demands a full investigation, they will arrest an innocent man and charge him with the crime." The priest got up to go. "Will you keep me informed about the prince's whereabouts?" he asked as I showed him out. "I think Junio should be watched, just in case."

I didn't entirely trust Father Sansovino's motives for asking me to spy on Junio—and my suspicions only increased the following day when neither the Vatican Radio nor the official Vatican newspaper, *L'Osservatore Romano*, mentioned the murder.

18.

HITLER'S VISIT *in pompa magna* to Rome could be summed up by the
comment I heard from a young Italian girl. Seeing swastikas everywhere, she exclaimed, "Rome is full of black spiders!" She was expressing
what so many of us, children and adults, felt: we were being pursued by a
plague of uniformed arthropods that was disrupting our daily lives. For a
whole week the city was transformed into a gigantic stage decorated with
banners, fasces, eagles, and ancient Roman insignias; public buildings
were equipped with portable grandstands Mussolini used to address the
nation. Demonstrations, parades, and military maneuvers were organized,
as were receptions and tours in honor of the German chancellor. They
even washed the façades of old palaces so the Führer and his entourage
might get the impression that they were visiting the capital of a super-
power. As the Roman poet Trilussa wrote in an epigram that was doing
the rounds: "*Roma de travertino / rifatta di cartone / saluta l'imbianchino / suo
prossimo padrone.*" ("Travertine Rome / remade in cardboard / greet your
new patron / the housepainter.")

I'll never forget the incredulous look on Montse's face when I told her
about my conversation with Father Sansovino and about Junio making
good on his threat to bribe a librarian, whom he then ordered to be executed once he had the Creator's Map in his hands. I suspected the news
might affect her deeply—that she might even refuse to continue her mis-

sion of seducing the prince. I was right, but when I saw her determination flagging, it was I who buoyed her up, reminding her that our lives were now part of a higher destiny, one that required us to place our personal desires second.

Montse and Junio met two weeks later at the Dreher Beer Hall, a popular watering hole for the German community in Rome. The prince had just returned from Wewelsburg Castle in Westphalia, the training center for leaders of the SS. He had gone there with the Reichsführer-SS, Heinrich Himmler, after traveling back to Germany in Hitler's train. During the trip, Junio was taken to the Führer's carriage so that he could personally hand him the Creator's Map. According to Montse, he'd said that the initial joy of the Nazi High Command had turned into disappointment when they discovered that they could not open the map without essentially destroying it. While waiting for German scientists to find a solution, however, Himmler reminded those present that the object itself had immense value. "The importance of an object of power is to possess it. It is like having a key that opens the doors of the world," he said. Hitler agreed and ordered the map to be brought to the castle.

Himmler's plan was for Wewelsburg to become for the Third Reich what Marienbad had been for the Teutonic Knights or Camelot for King Arthur. Guests were personally selected by Himmler, and there were never more than twelve, for there had been twelve members of the Round Table, twelve Apostles, and twelve Peers of Charlemagne, the founder of the First Reich. In the enormous dining room was a massive oak table and twelve high-backed chairs upholstered in pigskin, each one with a silver plaque engraved with the name of the SS knight it belonged to and his coat of arms. Under the central hall was a crypt with twelve niches called "The Sphere of Death"; in its center was a crater containing a stone chalice to be used as a funeral pyre. Most extraordinary was the black sun carved into the floor of the Marble Hall, a symbol of the supposed existence of a tiny heavenly body in the center of the earth—which was hollow, according to some esoteric theories—that shed light on the superior civilizations residing therein. Himmler was convinced that as soon as the Creator's Map was opened, they would discover the roads that led to these remote places. Once there, the Third Reich's control of the world would be absolute.

That Himmler could believe in such hoaxes and that Junio would agree to encourage them puzzled as much as frightened me, and it was not difficult to imagine how far a person could go who blindly believed that the earth was hollow. Unfortunately, my worst imaginings came to pass when Himmler became the supreme advocate of what was to be called the "Final Solution," which ended the lives of millions of European Jews. Such an insane plan could be concocted only by someone as demented as he, someone convinced he was the reincarnation of Henry I the Fowler, founder of the royal Saxon lineage in the tenth century, someone who rejected Catholicism and worshipped the pagan god Wotan.

Finally Montse had asked Junio why Gabor wasn't around. Junio proudly explained that his chauffeur had been recruited by Himmler to assist in the so-called procreation of a superior race. Specifically, he explained that Gabor was staying in a home belonging to the Lebensborn, an institution created by Himmler to "manufacture" the *Herrenrasse*, the master race, using the techniques of selective reproduction. He was, it seems, copulating with previously selected Aryan women to engender a new race of genetically perfect beings.

I interrupted Montse and asked her if they had talked about the *scriptor*'s murder.

"Things will no longer be as they were," Montse answered, clearly in reference to their relationship.

"He assured me he had had nothing to do with that disgraceful affair," she continued. "He said that Rome is full of anti-Fascist groups hoping to destabilize the regime at the slightest opportunity, that a priest with his pockets full of money was an easy target, and that he was only responsible for the bribe. I told him that that was exactly what Father Sansovino had said he would say."

"How did he respond to that?"

"He told me that Father Sansovino could not be trusted. So, naturally, I asked him to be more explicit."

"And?"

Montse took a few moments before reciting Junio's response from memory.

"'Once someone has been involved in a spy network, he never again tells the truth, the whole truth, and nothing but the truth. Do you know why? Because truth and lies are the head and tail of the same coin, and anybody who has spied knows this is so.' That's what he said."

"He also cannot be trusted," I said.

"He's even gotten rid of the ring with his family's crest and is wearing a horrible silver skull ring that Himmler gave him as a gift," Montse continued, without hiding her disappointment.

Years later, when the Third Reich collapsed, we found out that the ring in question was the talisman carried by those initiated into the SS, into whose ranks Junio had been admitted in gratitude for services rendered.

"The fact that Junio has changed rings doesn't mean that his behavior has changed," I pointed out to her.

"Are you trying to justify him?" she asked.

"Absolutely not. I'm just trying to tell you that Junio is the same as he's always been even though the ring has changed. He is not a different man than he was a few weeks ago."

"Yes, he is. No person who changes his family ring for a skull ring can be the same."

Montse didn't realize it, but it was she who had changed. Because of a simple ring, she had lost her regard for the person she had thought she was in love with. It was enough to see the expression on her face to understand that her large green eyes had seen the light and that, having shaken off the stupor of love and recovered her senses, her heart had closed like a fist.

"I don't plan on ever falling in love," she said, as if she had truly lost her ability to feel.

It was clear that Montse's pride had been hurt and that she was seriously angry with herself. She didn't realize, however, that the real victim of her emotional withdrawal was me rather than Junio. My only crime was to have fallen in love with her; in the code that governs the laws of love, such a crime is too often punished by indifference. Several months still had to pass before Montse showed any interest in me. And when she did, we had to struggle to find common ground, for the passion I showed her turned out to be as uncomfortable for her as her lack of commitment was for me. In fact, her behavior most of the time was more like a zombie than a woman in love. I have finally understood that the long, feverish years of the war worked on her like a chronic illness, undermining her emotional well-being and diminishing her life spirit.

"But it is now that you need to pretend to be more in love," I told her.

"Lovers break up when one party ceases to feel attracted to the other," she replied.

There was both sadness and disillusionment in her obstinacy.

"What do I tell Smith?" I persisted. "That you don't like the prince anymore?"

"Tell him the truth. Tell him we're dealing with a ruthless killer."

"Smith already knows that."

What Montse didn't know was that the Smith she was talking about was another of Junio's victims (that is, at least, what I believed). My animosity toward the prince had transcended the purely personal realm, but I was now the one who saw the necessity for us to remain firm in our positions.

"I know you have always disapproved of my lack of commitment, but if you decide to not see the prince again, you will be the one betraying your ideals. If you put feelings before reason, many people could get hurt," I said, trying to persuade her.

I didn't know who exactly I was talking about, but I had already begun to experience all the symptoms of the disease of idealism. We couldn't allow Junio to have his way. It was no longer a question of jealousy but rather one of principles.

"I have lost faith in love," Montse said, trying to justify herself.

"So act without faith. Do you think Junio has faith in love? He's too busy ordering people killed, committing robberies, and pleasing the Nazis."

"Okay, I'll hide my feelings and simply make the best of it," she finally agreed.

I hoped that Montse's naturally optimistic temperament would help her overcome her low spirits, and that she would soon be able to master the situation.

19.

A T MY SUGGESTION, Smith and I arranged to meet in E42, the new
city Mussolini was building south of Rome to host the Esposizione
Universale di Roma, the world's fair planned for 1942. The leading Italian
architects of the time were involved in this colossal project, and all of
them understood that in order to astonish the world it was not enough to
design and build a collection of spectacular buildings. The Duce had asked
them to construct a metaphor for the superiority of Fascist ideology. I
speak now with the benefit of hindsight, for the Universal Exposition of
Rome never took place, and the EUR buildings were never occupied and
never served any purpose during the Fascist dictatorship. The buildings
that were completed faithfully reflected the paradigm of Italian Fascism:
monumental exterior and empty interior, with no purpose other than to
serve as an efficient propaganda tool of political power. Today, when the
authorities again speak about giving a new and final impetus to the project now known as EUR, it has become a clear example of "authoritarian"
or "ephemeral" architecture.

But that morning toward the end of May 1938, E42 was still in its in-
fancy; under the State's watchful eyes, it was taking its first steps, devouring
bags of cement, having tons of earth removed with heavy machinery, and
being fed tons more of travertine marble. Hundreds of workers pretended
to incarnate the requisite "vitalism" and order demanded by the regime,
while curious onlookers ventured there each morning to applaud the prog-

ress being made or simply to ask if in this "third Rome" (the one Mussolini was building for the people), so long after the first (that of the Caesars), and so different from the second (that of the popes), there would be affordable apartments. The charlatans responsible for disseminating the regime's propaganda did not hesitate to respond: "There will be apartments with views of the sea." And in case anybody dared to point out that the sea was more than ten kilometers away, Mussolini ordered the following sentence to be carved into the façade of the Palazzo degli Uffici: *La terza Roma si dilaterá sopra altri colli lungo le rive del Fiume sacro sino alle spiagge del Tirreno.* ("The third Rome will spread over the hills and along the banks of the sacred Fiume River to the beaches of the Tyrrhenian Sea.")

In the midst of that construction site, surrounded by workers and the prying eyes of curious bystanders, his figure silhouetted against the cerulean sky, the second Smith looked like a building contractor. He was wearing a camel hair coat, and he looked around as if truly interested in everything he was seeing. As he approached, he seemed to be expecting me to offer him a bribe.

"What's happening?" I asked him.

"Lots of things. What specifically are you referring to?" he answered, lifting the collar of his coat to protect himself from the nonexistent cold.

The din of jackhammers and cement mixers brought to mind the war raging in Spain, but I knew these sounds had little in common with the whistle of bullets and the blast of cannons. I shook my head to dispel that association.

"Prince Cima Vivarini has given the Creator's Map to the Germans," I said, going straight to the point. "He bribed a librarian in the Vatican Library, then arranged for him to be killed. It happened on the second of May, although nothing was mentioned in the news the following day."

"What did you expect, with Hitler's visit to Italy scheduled to begin the following day?"

"Well, it doesn't say much about either the Italian or the Vatican news sources."

"Mussolini wouldn't have allowed the pope to create another scandal during Hitler's visit. One could say that Pius XI's departure from Rome to avoid meeting Hitler was the last straw. If Pius XI now has a complaint to make to the Duce, he will have to do it sotto voce and through diplomatic channels."

The second Smith's explanation, though not wholly convincing, made sense; I decided to continue.

"It seems the Germans have been unable to open the map because it is so fragile. Hitler has ordered Himmler to take it to Wewelsburg Castle to be studied. Apparently, Himmler believes that when they do manage to open it, they'll find the instructions for reaching the center of the earth, and from there, they will rule the world."

Smith's face reflected his astonishment.

"The center of the earth? What the devil do the Germans plan to do in the center of the earth?"

"Why are you surprised? You were the ones who told me about the Reichsführer's outlandish beliefs. Himmler is convinced that our planet is hollow, and that inside lives a civilization of superior men. The Creator's Map would be the means to reach them. And I suspect this is not all they believe," I continued. "They have also set up a network of so-called 'reproduction farms', where young Aryan men and women copulate in order to procreate a superior race. Himmler has recruited the prince's chauffeur, a Hungarian named Gabor, to participate."

This didn't surprise the second Smith. "The Lebensborn is part of Professor Haushofer's lebensraum doctrine," he explained. "In order to occupy that so-called vital space you need to create a race that matches the magnitude of the project, so it is of the utmost importance to have a fertile population capable of engendering a large number of healthy children. By educating these children at special indoctrination centers, the Nazis are not only attempting to create a superior race but also trying to guarantee that it remains true to itself. For Hitler, people who refuse to maintain the purity of their race are also renouncing the unity of their souls. He wrote in Mein Kampf that the State that devotes itself to its best racial elements will one day rule the world."

"In Germany, then, love is also under the jurisdiction of totalitarianism," I said.

"They are even studying ways to reduce gestation by half in order to increase the number of children a woman can bear."

I laughed. "That sounds like a hen farm!"

But Smith was deadly serious. "They also encourage members of the SS to have sexual relations in old cemeteries in order to procreate reincarnations of ancient German heroes. The SS newspaper *Das Schwarze Korps* has even published a list of the ideal locations," he added.

At that time, neither of us could have imagined that once the German invasion of Europe had begun, the principal activities of the Lebensborn project would include the kidnapping of children who looked Aryan—handsome, healthy, well built, with blond or light-brown hair, blue eyes, and free of any Jewish blood—from occupied nations, or that these children, after extensive medical and psychological examinations, would be sent to special indoctrination centers or offered for adoption by families of the Aryan race. In Poland alone two hundred thousand children were kidnapped or taken from their families; only forty thousand of them were returned to their homes after the war. In the Ukraine the number of children reached several thousand, and more or less the same number in the Baltic states. But there were also Lebensborn children in countries such as Czechoslovakia, Norway, and France, all part of an ambitious plan to incorporate into the Third Reich all those who should, by reason of race, be part of it.

"There's something else I wanted to tell you. Have you ever heard of Father Sansovino?"

Smith shook his head.

"He is a *scriptor* at the Vatican Library and a friend of Prince Cima Vivarini. It seems he used to be a member of the Vatican's counterespionage services. He wants me to keep him informed about the prince's activities."

"And do you plan to?"

"No, I don't plan to tell him anything."

"Perhaps it would not be such a bad idea to maintain an open channel to the Vatican," Smith suggested.

"What do you mean?"

"It's simple. You tell him about the prince's activities, just as you do us, then you tell us what the priest tells you: quid pro quo."

"What if Father Sansovino is a Russian agent?" I asked. "He was a member of the Russicum, the department of the Holy Alliance that specialized in sending spies into Russia. Maybe he's playing both sides."

"There's only one way to find out," said Smith. "You maintain contact with him, and we'll keep an eye on him. If we find anything out, we'll let you know."

20.

THE BATTLE OF THE EBRO kept us all on tenterhooks from the end of July until the middle of November 1938. The terrace became the Academy's meeting place, in spite of Secretary Olarra's opposition. Given the fact that nothing less than the future of Spain depended on the outcome of that battle, he had no choice but to relent and allow the Academy's refugees to maintain a permanent siege of the radiotelegraph. On July 25, when the Republican army began its offensive by crossing the Ebro River and directly threatening Franco's army, Doña Julia suffered a fainting spell, as if the battle-hardened soldiers of the Popular Front had just crossed the Tiber and were poised to attack the Academy. In total, eighty thousand soldiers took part in the operation, supported by eighty artillery batteries and Russian fighter aircraft. They advanced so quickly and unexpectedly that a Nationalist general in La Fatarella was taken prisoner while he slept peacefully in his underwear with his wife; in Gandesa a Moroccan soldier drowned in a barrel of wine he had hid in to avoid being captured by the Republican troops; and in Terra Alta, the imminent arrival of the Reds' army forced a parish priest to interrupt Mass and flee on foot. The following day, Doña Montserrat became indisposed after hearing on the radio the Nationalist announcer's description of Lister, the Republican general, whom he characterized as a demonic beast with skin flushed from heavy drinking, sharp incisors due to eating red meat daily for breakfast, and a devil's tail, given his penchant for promiscuous and dissolute living. After the Republicans' initial success, however, the Nationalist army managed to reduce by half the strength of the Republican offensive by opening the sluices on some nearby dams. The refugees' morale rose as quickly as the waters of the Ebro, especially when the infantry regiment of Our Lady of Montserrat, to whom they attributed invincible strength, entered the fray. When Lister lost control of Sierra Magdalena on August 14, Franco's army began to gain the upper hand, and Doña Julia, Doña Montserrat, and the other women turned their attention back to the sufferings of Beatrice Cenci's ghost, the infernal heat of the Roman summer, and other light-hearted subjects that lent balance to the warlike fever transmitted over the airwaves.

On August 16 the prince joined the evening "salon" to listen to the summary of the bulletins from the front. Apparently, he was personally interested because he had a cousin fighting with the Littorio Division in the Terra Alta. He repeated his visit seven or eight afternoons in a row, and as the heat and the humidity were unbearable even at night, he brought ice cream for the ladies and *limoncello* and a chunk of ice for the gentlemen. Gabor was in charge of breaking it up with a pick, which he did with unusual violence and speed while the ice's reflection shone in his already frozen and defiant blue eyes. Having brutally assaulted the ice, he discreetly retreated and awaited orders from his master.

In that context, Montse's beauty stood out in particularly sharp contrast to the subjects being discussed. She seemed to have decided to make the prince suffer as much as possible. Her strategy was to emphasize her most appealing attributes—she let down her hair, applied her makeup perfectly, got a manicure, wore high heels and sheer summer dresses that exposed her shoulders, and a perfume that successfully competed with the fragrance of summer evenings—while at the same time showing interest in everybody and everything except him. Whereas Montse used to listen to him in raptures, as if at the mercy of her lover's will, she now began yawning whenever he addressed her, as if his conversation bored her no end. If the prince offered to bring her an ice cream or a lemonade, she declined, but a moment later she would get up and serve herself. The more Montse's indifference grew, the more solicitous the prince became, as if he felt guilty without even knowing what crime he had committed.

I have never again seen Junio so defenseless, so disconcerted and insecure, perhaps because he was aware that Montse's apparently capricious behavior was utterly justified.

On one of those nights, Señor Fábregas took me aside and asked with some embarrassment, "Do you have any idea what game my daughter is playing at? She is going to ruin everything! Life isn't made to be throwing princes off like this."

"She's putting the strength and quality of his love to the test," I assured him. "To be perfectly frank, Señor Fábregas, Montse thinks her relationship with the prince has stagnated, and that it's about time for him to take the next step."

Few things gave me as much pleasure as misleading Señor Fábregas, knowing as I did that he had little regard for me because of the close friendship I had with his daughter.

"Women don't want to take chances if they don't see a future in a sentimental relationship; in this way they are like businessmen in skirts," Señor Fábregas said philosophically, ever true to his commercial spirit.

On November 7 the Nationalist troops occupied Mora de Ebro; on November 13 the Republican army retreated, bringing the Battle of the Ebro to an end. In the end, 116 days of fighting caused more than seventy thousand deaths. According to the statistics, which in many cases offer a good indication of a battle's ferocity, the Nationalist army managed to shoot 13,600 cannons in one day; in response, General Rojo, the top general of the Republican army, declared, "In the Battle of the Ebro, there was no art, only the most distilled application of brute force."

"There will be no winter this year, José María. In three or four weeks spring will be upon us," Secretary Olarra again predicted, just as he had the previous year.

The following day we received word of Rubiños's death in Ribarroja the week before. An antiaircraft battery hit a Republican airplane, which crashed behind Nationalist lines, killing four soldiers. I realized that I didn't even know his first name.

That night when I looked out over the balcony, I saw only a dense stain of darkness. I understood then that my view of Rome from that terrace really had been nothing more than the projection of a dream.

21.

WHILE THE FUTURE OF THE WAR in Spain was being decided on the front in Catalonia, Hitler was carrying out his plans elsewhere. In September 1938, at an international conference held in Munich, France as well as England accepted Germany's annexation of the Sudetenland, hoping this would be the Third Reich's last territorial claim.

At the beginning of October, Junio was urgently summoned to Wewelsburg. Upon his return, he told us that the two scientists responsible for opening the Creator's Map without damaging it had died handling the papyrus in a dark room. The autopsies revealed that they had inhaled a large quantity of anthrax. At first Himmler and his men thought that the ancient Egyptians, who used naturally occurring poisons to kill their enemies and to commit suicide, might have doused the document to keep it from falling into unworthy hands, but as neither Keats nor Severn were reported to have suffered any ill effects when they had come into contact with the map, they discounted this hypothesis. Suspicion then fell on Prince Cima Vivarini himself, who was arrested in Wewelsburg and accused of having tried to use the map to make an attempt on the life of the Führer and half a dozen high functionaries of the Third Reich while they had all been in the train traveling back to Germany from Italy. Junio, who reported this with a cool head, said he had easily refuted the accusation. "I was the one who warned of the danger of opening the map in front of the Führer," he told us he had pointed out to his interrogators. "If my intention had been to kill him, all I would have had to do was allow someone to open it and all those present would have inhaled the anthrax." In spite of this logic, he was forced to submit to a quarantine (as he called it) of two weeks while his life was meticulously examined. He was confined to a room in Wewelsburg and expressly prohibited from communicating with the outside world while the investigation was being carried out. Once the prince was exonerated, Himmler concluded that the anthrax had been the work of the Holy Alliance, the Vatican's secret service. By dousing the Creator's Map with a toxic substance they could achieve two objectives: first, to render the map useless, at least temporarily; second, to put an end to Hitler, or Himmler, or perhaps both at the same time. Thus it seemed that the *scriptor* who had sold the map to Junio had not been bribed but was instead probably following orders from the Holy Alliance.

This setback did not change the Nazis' plans, and a few days later an armored train guarded by the SS left Vienna on its way to Nuremberg, the Nazis' spiritual home, carrying the Hapsburg treasures, the objects of power both Hitler and Himmler longed to possess, and foremost among them, the Holy Lance of Longinus.

The Holy Lance was a piece of rusty metal thirty centimeters long; its blade was split down the middle and had a nail encrusted in it—supposedly one that was used to crucify Jesus Christ—which in turn was held in place with a gold thread. In addition, two gold crosses were embedded in its base, near the handle. Although it hardly resembled a lance, according to the tradition of the Teutonic Knights this was the object the Roman soldier Gaius Cassius Longinus had used to pierce Christ's side. Naturally, such an object would become highly valued and endowed with enormous legendary powers. It was also said that the Holy Lance of Longinus was a talisman of Charlemagne, who carried it with him on the forty-seven victorious campaigns he waged. According to tradition, he died after accidentally dropping it. Henry the Fowler, the monarch of whom Himm-ler believed himself the reincarnation, was also said to have once possessed the relic. Federick Barbarossa as well used the Lance of Longinus to his advantage, conquering Italy and forcing the pope into exile. Like Charlemagne, Barbarossa committed the folly of dropping the lance while fording a river in Sicily and died shortly thereafter. Given its history, it was understandable that Hitler wanted to possess the Hapsburg lance. The Führer's blind faith in that object led him to ignore one crucial detail: the Hapsburg lance was not unique. Three other Holy Lances of Longinus existed—in the Vatican, in Paris, and in Krakow, each one of a different provenance.

The prince's gregariousness, combined with his strangely solicitous attitude, made Montse think that he had had a truly difficult time in Wewelsburg. It was as if he had finally understood that affection made life more bearable, and he was now anxious to pursue the goal of nurturing that element in his life. According to Montse, he was struggling to express something besides words, something that did not come easily to Junio, who was essentially a cold, unsentimental man. I have always contended that Junio's sudden change of behavior had nothing to do with his trips to Germany, nor with the fact that—it seemed—his life had been in danger, but was rather a simple change of strategy designed to win back Montse's trust. Though loquacious, often too much so, he was never truly open with others; on the contrary, he seemed to continue to trust only his own dogmatism, in which he took refuge the way others do in silence.

In the end, I believe that Junio's effusive demonstrations of affection hid nothing more than his interest in maintaining his relationship with Montse, because he knew of our activities and wished to use us for his purposes. Fortunately for Montse, the danger posed by love had already passed, and she now acted with greater impunity.

In any case, the events immediately following Junio's return from Germany fully bore out our worst fears about the Nazis' will to power. On November 9, 1938, there was Kristallnacht, the Night of Broken Glass, a pogrom that included the sacking of the homes and businesses of thousands of Jews, the burning of books and synagogues, the murder of two hundred people, and the internment in work camps of thousands more. But Kristallnacht was just the tip of the iceberg. In the following days Hermann Göring promulgated three decrees that made absolutely clear the National Socialists' intentions regarding the "Jewish question." The first decree forced the Jewish community to pay a billion marks in indemnity, whereby the victims of the attack became the responsible party, the instigators. The second decree marginalized the Jews from the economic life of Germany, and the third forced insurance companies to pay the State the claims resulting from the incident, thereby making it impossible for Jews to receive any compensation.

At lunch on November 10 Secretary Olarra told us about what had happened in Germany the night before.

"But what have the Jews done to make the Germans dislike them so much?" Doña Julia asked.

"They are responsible for Germany's defeat in the War of 1914; they created Wall Street's unbridled capitalism and its subsequent collapse; they are also the instigators of Bolshevik Communism," Secretary Olarra replied.

"Don't forget that it was the Jews who handed Our Lord Jesus Christ over to the Romans," Señor Fábregas added.

"You see, they are even responsible for Our Lord's crucifixion." Olarra smiled.

Doña Julia crossed herself before speaking.

"The way you explain it, they really do seem awful."

"That's all foolishness!" Montse exclaimed. "You're just trying to find some moral justification for those crimes, and that makes you all accomplices."

His daughter's outburst left Señor Fábregas speechless. He flinched under Secretary Olarra's reproachful stare.

"What are you talking about, child? What do you know about the Jews? Go to your room this instant," Señor Fábregas said.

"I am an adult and I have no intention of going anywhere," Montse replied calmly.

Provoked beyond reason, Señor Fábregas lurched forward with his hand out, as if to slap her. Instinctively, I dived toward him and grabbed his arm before his palm could reach her face.

"Let go of me, you brute!" Señor Fábregas hissed.

"Not before you know that if you hit her, you will have to deal with me," I responded.

"Did you hear? Did you hear, Secretary Olarra? He threatened to hit me," Señor Fábregas shouted, red with rage.

"Everybody, calm down," Secretary Olarra intervened. "You, José María, let go of Señor Fábregas; and you, good man, don't raise your hand against your daughter. Let's all calm down."

Once Señor Fábregas had shaken me off, he turned to me, his face contorted.

"This is all your fault for filling the girl's head with all your Bolshevik ideas. And all because you can't tolerate her going out with the prince! You think I haven't noticed how you drool when you look at her? I'm going to denounce you to the embassy as a Communist. I'll have them deport you to Spain and shoot you."

"You are the only one to blame for the situation we're in, Papa," Montse said in my defense.

"Me? You think it's my fault we're here? Bolsheviks like your friend here are the ones you should blame."

"It's Franco's fault we had to leave Barcelona. He was the one who took up arms against the Republic. And if now, when I'm twenty-one years old, you suddenly want to slap me, it is also Franco's fault. If you are going to denounce José María as a Red, you'll have to denounce me as well!"

Montse's tirade left everyone momentarily speechless. But I had little doubt that Señor Fábregas would quickly recover and go on the counterattack, spewing even more venom than before.

"We'd better leave," I said to Montse.

"Yes, please do, and seriously reflect on what has just happened here. When you return, José María, I would like to see you in my office," Secretary Olarra said, obviously relieved at having averted a fistfight.

Thanks to another fainting spell feigned by Doña Fábregas, we managed to get away before Señor Fábregas could come after us. When we reached the esplanade of San Pietro in Montorio, Montse turned to me.

"You behaved like a knight in shining armor," she said somewhat melodramatically.

Despite the compliment and the appreciation it expressed, I understood that Montse would never allow anybody to prevent her from standing up for her own principles.

"I think my days at the academy have come to an end," I said.

"I'm sorry for involving you in this whole family mess."

I shrugged. "It was only a matter of time."

"What are you going to do?"

"I still have a bit of money left from an apartment I inherited from my parents, so I guess I'll rent a room somewhere and look for a job."

"I know—let's ask Junio for help."

Although I was initially horrified at the idea of turning to Junio, of all people, for help, the neutral and unenthusiastic tone of her voice made me realize that her only motivation was to help me.

"Do I really want help from someone with blood on his hands?"

"I'm beginning to think that by now we all have blood on our hands. Didn't you hear what my parents and Olarra said about the Jews? And I fear they are not the only ones. Anyway, if the civil war ends soon, as it seems it will, I'll return to Barcelona, and it would be good for somebody to maintain contact with Junio to tell Smith what he says."

Montse was right. Though I had tried to avoid thinking about it, I knew that one day she would return to Barcelona.

Suddenly, I wished the war would never end. As we began to descend to Trastevere, the academy vanished around a bend in the road and I imagined for a moment that it might never appear again, that it had never existed—and that neither of us would ever have to go back there. As if Montse had read my thoughts, she took my hand.

"The academy often feels to me like a prison," she said softly. "But then I think that if I had never been there, I never would have met you."

22.

M Y LAST CONVERSATION with Secretary Olarra turned out to be the most honest one I'd ever had. I found him sitting in his armchair in his office with the light on behind him, listening to a military march playing at full volume on the gramophone, as if the vibrations of that infernal music infused him with vitality and nourished his soul. Even if I listened very carefully, I could hear nothing more than a clamor of grandiloquent and incomprehensible voices under a blanket of trumpets and drums. Olarra waited until the last note had sounded before he spoke.

"Are you calmer now, José María?"

"I suppose so."

"Please, have a seat."

I did as I was told and waited.

"Today's little outburst has the potential of turning into a very ugly affair. Señor Fábregas is determined to carry out his threat of denouncing you," Olarra began. "Of course I have told him that there is another solution . . ."

I began to feel like a prisoner mercifully granted the choice to end his own life or undergo a dishonorable execution, so I anticipated Secretary Olarra's conclusion.

"You needn't worry; I'm leaving this afternoon."

"That would be for the best," he said. "But before you go, I would like to talk with you about something that has been bothering me for a long time. I want to be frank with you, José María: I have never liked you. Do you know why? Because you have always acted like someone who is . . . lukewarm. And these days, there is nothing more indecent than being lukewarm, indecisive, indifferent, a proponent of partial measures. I have been so concerned about this that at one point I took the trouble of speaking with your colleagues, yes, Hervada, Muñoz Molleda, Pérez Comendador, and a few others, about what they think of you. You know what they said? That you are a cold, detached person, without strong likes or dislikes, without passion, and, even worse, without any apparent worries or concerns. Is there room in this world for a man with no worries when a country is bleeding to death in a civil war? No, I told myself, and that's when you sank further in my esteem. I then asked them to find out what political ideas you had, who you voted for in the last elections. They were also unanimous about this. 'He didn't vote,' they said, and then all the red flags went up. For weeks, even months, I've listened carefully to you, I've watched the expressions on your face, followed your steps, and finally I've reached the same conclusion: you are a bystander. What then intrigued me, and continues to intrigue me, is whether you are an active bystander, that is, a rebel, or if, on the contrary, you are motivated by incompetence, passivity. You must know, whether you belong to one side or the other, the bystander is an empty vessel, without loyalty and, consequently, without virtue."

"That may have been true, but I have changed," I said.

"Are you talking about what you did this morning?"

"I'm talking about people like you who turn cowards like me into heroes."

Olarra shook his head to show his disagreement. "You, a hero? Don't make me laugh," he said mockingly. "You really believe that taking on a man like Señor Fábregas makes you a hero? Perhaps in Montse's eyes, but not in mine."

"I've always wondered why it's so difficult for you to admit that some people are simply unwilling to accept the rules society imposes on them."

Immediately after speaking, I realized it would have been better for me to remain silent rather than give Olarra the opportunity to lash out at me again.

"Precisely because we do live in society, we have created norms that regulate our coexistence, and those who do not abide by them are excluded," he answered. "Social instinct is inherent in man's very nature, and it's impossible to conceive of an individual living apart from the infinite chain of beings that make up humanity as a whole. Nietzsche said it and the Duce never tires of repeating it: the world of 'do what you like' doesn't exist; the only world possible is 'do what you must.' No, you cannot explain society by placing yourself outside of it. But not even this is the case with you. I know you come from a well-off family, that you have never wanted for anything; I also know you completed your architectural studies brilliantly. I don't believe you are the sort of person who wants to live on the margins of society. You are not even a particularly unusual person. No, your problem is one of conscience. Your life suffers from a lack of action, a lack of vigor and enthusiasm. The disease that afflicts you is fatalism, and the means you have to fight against it is your own willpower. Only by uniting all our power will we build the foundation on which to forge the future."

Oddly enough, rather than being irritated by Olarra's words, I found myself intrigued by the ease with which he found a reasonable explanation for everything. I saw that this flowed freely from his deep commitment to a Fascist political ideology, his bulwark against ambiguity or contradictions. "Have you finished?"

"One more thing before you go: leave the Fábregas girl alone. Her parents think that stuck-up prince is pining away for her. I wasn't born yesterday and I know that a conceited Italian prince would never set his sights on a bourgeois girl from Barcelona, no matter how many factories her father owns in Sabadell, unless it's to enjoy the poor girl's virginity and then, at the hour of truth, claim never to have touched her. In either case, you'll get nowhere with her. Forget about Miss Fábregas, and I'll make sure the denunciation against you goes nowhere."

"I presume you won't mind if I don't offer you my hand to seal the agreement."

Olarra lifted his right arm, then quickly transformed it into a Roman salute.

"I wish you luck, José María. You'll need it," he said after I had already stood up to leave.

I found Montse waiting for me on the balustrade next to a small fountain in the courtyard. She looked like one of the many figures painted by Il Pomarancio on the tiles adorning the walls: simple, inexperienced characters, almost naive.

"What happened?" she asked me.

"I have to leave."

"I talked to Junio. He told me the job problem is solved."

"I'm going to pack."

"Let me help you. It's the least I can do."

"It's better if they don't see you with me," I said, looking around. "Olarra has made me promise I won't bother you anymore; otherwise he'll denounce me to the embassy."

"As soon as you get settled in your new house, I'll come visit you. We'll meet every afternoon, secretly. We'll carry on."

I had no plans for the future beyond leaving the academy as soon as possible. Nor did I want to pay much heed to Montse's words or count on her promises. Only time would tell if we would continue to see each other. I felt no nostalgia; on the contrary, I swore to myself I would never set foot in the academy again.

23.

I HAD JUST BEGUN the long walk down Via Garibaldo when I heard the soft purr of a car approaching me from behind.

"Was it that serious?" asked a familiar voice.

It was Junio. He was sitting in the backseat of his Italia with the window rolled down, in spite of the cold.

"So it seems," I responded laconically.

"The Duce always says, 'molti nemici, molto onore,' which means that now that you have more enemies, you must have more honor."

"My only enemies are Secretary Olarra and Señor Fábregas."

"Would you like me to talk to Olarra?" he asked.

"No, thank you. Let's just say that our differences are irreconcilable. I should have left quite some time ago."

"You should offer more resistance to the enemy," he suggested.

I was starting to tire of everybody giving me advice, so I responded with irritation. "Leave me alone. I'm in no mood for more sermons."

"Get in. I'll take you."

"Where?"

"I suppose, given that you are carrying those suitcases, the first thing is to find you a place to sleep. And I know just the place. A room next to the river, on Via Giulia. Come on, get in."

Gabor drove past me, braked, then got out and opened the trunk. The strong smell of cologne inside the vehicle reminded me of Rubiños's "perfumed Italians."

"If the smell bothers you, open the window," the prince said when I got in the car, as if he could read my mind. "I usually put on too much, sometimes so much I almost suffocate myself. I have a friend who says I do that because I have a guilty conscience. And it's true. Even somebody like me has things to confess."

I felt like confessing to him that I was aware of his illicit activities, and that he would need more than a few liters of cologne to cleanse his conscience, but I held my tongue.

"So we're competing for the same woman, and, paradoxically, in order to maintain her esteem, I must help you. It doesn't seem quite fair, does it?" he asked.

"Tell your driver to stop!" I said.

"Come on, don't take it like that. It was a joke!" he said, as if to cover his tracks. He threaded his arm through mine and whispered in my ear, "*Montse prova grande affetto per te*. She's always talking about you."

For a few seconds, Junio's words acted as a palliative, but I quickly recovered my senses.

"Foolishness," I replied.

"Believe me. The problem is she's always had you too close. Living together for so long . . . almost like siblings."

I was afraid he was going to tell me that he was giving up Montse, that he did not want to come between her and me. Since I couldn't bear to hear such condescension, I made an attempt to seem disinterested.

"Well, when she's with me she talks about you," I told him.

My words seemed to please the prince, as if they dispelled some doubts he had been harboring.

"So she speaks about both of us," he said.

"So it seems."

"She speaks about both of us, but does she act the same with both of us?" he asked out loud, his eyes glued to the floor of the car.

"What do you mean?"

"No woman treats two men equally, unless she is not interested in either."

"That's also a possibility," I admitted.

"Women are a great mystery, don't you agree? They do not think the same way we do. And even if it seems we share the same world, it's not true. They despise what we appreciate, and love what we are incapable of having any feelings for. For us, instinct is primordial; for them, they think about the consequences before taking the first step," Junio continued in solemn tones.

"I suppose you're right," I said.

"You know what I like best about Montse?"

"No."

"That in spite of living through the war and exile firsthand, she has learned everything she knows about life through books. She still trusts her reading more than her own experience, and this makes her vulnerable. She believes that only what's written in books is useful to society. For example, she believes that justice should be dispensed exactly as it is written in the books, as if that could ever be possible. Montse is the kind of person who doesn't understand how people can commit crimes when the law prohibits them. And all because she doesn't know human nature. She is so deeply enchanting that she deserves to be transformed into a princess in a fairy tale, though I don't think that would be possible given the times we live in."

Junio's words about Montse sank me into a reflective silence. It was clear he understood Montse better than I had thought he did. Or so it seemed by the fondness and longing reflected in his eyes as he spoke. Why, then, I wondered, had he tried to throw her into my arms just a few minutes earlier?

"Now, tell me," he said, changing the subject abruptly, "until we find you work as an architect, would you be willing to do something else?"

"As long as it's respectable, yes."

"Of course, I'm thinking of something quite respectable. And easy. I'll tell you all about it."

As we got onto the road that led from the Lungotevere dei Tebaldi to Via Giulia, I turned my head to the left and found myself facing the silhouette of the academy, whose towers seemed to levitate above Trastevere.

We had just passed under the bridge that linked Palazzo Farnese to the shores of the Tiber when Gabor spoke. "What number on Via Giulia, Prince?"

"Eighty-five," Junio answered. Then he turned to me and added, "This is the house where Raphael de Sanzio once lived, at least according to tradition. The owner is a Roman aristocrat who has come down in the world. She is an old family friend. She rents rooms out to people she can trust."

I must admit that I was pleasantly surprised. If I could have had my choice of a street and a building, I would have chosen that modest Renaissance house on Via Giulia. Often, when I took a walk, I would end up strolling down that lovely street from one end to the other. I would begin at the Fontana del Mascherone, one of the most beautiful fountains in Rome, where I would dip my hands into the granite basin until the cold water numbed my fingers; from there I would walk to the iron gate at the back of the Palazzo Farnese, where I could contemplate the garden and the impressive loggia; later, I'd walk under the same ivy-covered bridge we had just crossed in the car. I'd sit down for a quick rest on the so-called sofas of Via Giulia, a row of stone pedestals belonging to the Palace of Justice, designed by Bramante for Pope Julius II, but remaining unfinished at the death of the pontiff. Finally, I'd continue in a straight line to the monumental Palazzo Sacchetti and conclude my walk at the Church of San Giovanni dei Fiorentini.

My new landlady turned out to be a singular woman, tall and thin, with deep, inscrutable black eyes and a shrill voice that whistled like a poorly sealed valve. She introduced herself as Signora Giovanna, and told me that the only rule in the house was that boarders should make as little noise as possible, not only to safeguard the privacy of others but also because she suffered from serious migraines and at times, as she put it, "the mere sound of a pin dropping on the ground is enough to kill me."

"José María is as quiet as the dead, right?" Junio said, turning to me with a smile.

I nodded. At that moment I wished I were dead, far from that house, from Rome, from the world.

The woman continued. "I like to live alone, but I can no longer afford to. I suppose the prince already told you about my situation. Nor do I like to live with men; they tend to be untidy and unkempt, so I expect you, for as long as you live here, to strive to maintain high standards of cleanliness as faithfully as a saint seeks spiritual ecstasy."

Her analogy left me speechless. I looked at Junio, as if to say, What the hell am I doing here?

"Signora Giovanna is an orderly, serious woman," Junio explained, as if to dispel my fears, "and she does not meddle in the lives of her lodgers. She will give you a key and you can come and go as you please."

The woman conscientiously filled out a long questionnaire. "The police require this," she explained, as she peppered me with questions.

As for the room, it was as unusual as its owner: the door was of frosted glass; the floor was covered with a thin layer of sawdust, which a servant swept up and replaced every morning; at noon the same servant perfumed the room with lavender, leaving it aromatic for the rest of the day; the sheets and towels smelled of camphor; and the walls were covered with old wallpaper of an iridescent sulfur color. The bed frame was made of iron and creaked like the brakes of a train. On the mattress lay a brazier and under the bed was a chamber pot and a bag of coal. Each lodger was responsible for emptying his own pot and for changing the coal in the brazier. In addition, there was a porcelain water jug and washbasin. Out of the room's only window, which faced a lighted patio, one could glimpse a piece of the sky pierced by the last lights of the day.

"What do you think?" Junio asked me as we surveyed it.

"A bit seedy, but I'll manage," I said with a wink.

The prince smiled. "Now," he said, "let's talk about your job. Tomorrow you will go to the pharmacy on Corso del Rinascimento and ask for the pharmacist, Signor Oreste. Tell him you are picking up Prince Cima Vivarini's order, and take what he gives you to the second floor of number 23 Via dei Coronari. Do not speak to the person who opens the door. Just hand over the package. That's all, for now."

"That's not a job!" I exclaimed.

"Yes, it is, because I'm going to pay you to do it."

"You're going to pay me to be a messenger boy?"

"No. I'm going to pay you because I need somebody I trust to deliver that package."

Knowing what had happened to those who had handled the Creator's Map, I didn't want to take any chances.

"What's in the package?" I asked.

"That's not important."

"What if it's a dangerous substance and I drop it?" I asked.

"You have nothing to fear. If you drop the package, you are in no danger," Junio said. "Enough questions for now."

After he left, I wondered if working for Smith, for Father Sansovino, and for the prince at the same time was too risky. Especially because collaborating with Junio was the same as collaborating with the Nazis, even as far as the danger involved. I consoled myself, however, by convincing myself that this was an excellent opportunity to learn about Junio's plans firsthand.

I unpacked my bags and hung up my clothes in the wardrobe. Finding an old Bible in the drawer of the bedside table, I opened it at random. In Exodus, I read: "Thou shalt not raise a false report: put not thine hand with the wicked to be an unrighteous witness. Thou shalt not follow a multitude to do evil; neither shalt thou speak in a cause to decline after many to wrest judgment." I felt a twinge in my stomach and realized I hadn't eaten anything since breakfast.

24.

I WOKE THE NEXT MORNING feeling exactly as I had when I went to bed: full of apprehension. I had the uncomfortable sensation that I was in an unknown city rather than Rome. During the night I used the chamber pot so as not to have to go to the bathroom, a common enough practice, but now I had to empty it. I didn't like the idea of a stranger seeing me in my pajamas, so I waited until after I'd washed and dressed before leaving the room an hour later.

Following the recommendations of the second Smith, I went to visit Father Sansovino at the Vatican Library. I was intrigued by the question of the poison, and I was worried about Junio taking revenge. But Father Sansovino wouldn't receive me. He sent a note to me through a *scriptor*. It said, "Meet me at four in the afternoon in the crypt of the Basilica di Santa Cecilia. If not possible, inform the carrier of this note."

As I was free for the rest of the morning, I decided to carry out the prince's errand. I started toward Borgo, crossed the Tiber at Castel Sant'Angelo, turned left onto Via dei Coronari, and walked to number 23, where I was supposed to deliver the package they would give me at the pharmacy. It was an ordinary building, one of many similar ones in the neighborhood. I then continued walking to Corso del Rinascimento.

The pharmacy was across the street from a bookshop, where I stopped to look in the window; I didn't dare enter the pharmacy until all the customers had left.

"*Che cosa desìdera?*" the clerk asked me, eager to wait on me in the pharmacist's temporary absence.

"I am looking for Signor Oreste."

"*Un àttimo*," he said with disappointment, indicating I should wait there while he went to the back room.

A minute later a middle-aged man with a robust complexion appeared; he looked more like an athlete than a pharmacist, in spite of the impeccably white coat he was wearing. "May I help you?"

"I've come to pick up the order for Prince Cima Vivarini," I said.

"I've been waiting for you," he replied, as he took out of one of his pockets a small package wrapped in brown paper. It measured no more than five centimeters long and two and a half centimeters wide. "Here you are."

"Is this all?"

"Put it in your jacket pocket," he said.

Once outside, I felt tempted to open the package, but I refrained, afraid of being found out. I returned to Via dei Coronari, where I briefly stood in front of the building and looked things over. I wanted to make absolutely certain that I was not walking into a trap. When I grew tired of waiting in vain for something to happen, I entered and climbed the stairs cautiously to the second floor. As there was no bell, I knocked on the door. Nobody answered, so I knocked harder. A moment later the peephole opened and a woman's glassy eye, her lashes coated with mascara, peeked through. The peephole closed and the door edged open, only enough for the woman to reach out her arm and extend her hand. When I placed the package in her palm, her arm withdrew into its lair like a snake, and the door closed. Then I heard the voice of a man inside the room repeating one phrase in a foreign language, perhaps German. I thought I recognized the expression *Mein Gott*. That was it.

For a while I wandered aimlessly through the Piazza Navona and Via del Governo Vecchio until I decided to take refuge in a café. By now my initial nerve had given way to a kind of bewilderment that had me sitting for a long time in front of a *cappuccino* I paid absolutely no attention to. I understood nothing about what might be going on, much less what that package might contain. Did a German, who for some unknown reason needed to hide, live in that house? Was he ill? What was the prince's role in all this? I decided that at the first opportunity I would share this experience and my doubts with Montse as well as with the second Smith.

I had a bite to eat and began walking toward Trastevere along the banks of the river, which looked like a brown rope poised to strangle the city.

Before descending into the crypt of the Basilica di Santa Cecilia, I paused to contemplate the statue by Stefano Maderno. According to tradition, this exquisite masterpiece depicted the saint in the identical position she was in when Cardinal Sfondati found her in her tomb during Clement VIII's reign. Her head was facing backward and wrapped in a scarf—at the last minute the martyr had been decapitated—and her body was lying on its side facing forward; most striking were her hands, three fingers spread out, an allusion to the mystery of the Holy Trinity. I couldn't help thinking that thanks to the war in Spain and to Hitler, the time for martyrs had returned in Europe.

When I finally descended the stairs into the crypt, I had the sensation of delving into one of Piranesi's prints I had seen in Signor Tasso's back room. I advanced along a long corridor dimly lit by small skylights that opened into the church and lined with half a dozen dark rooms that exuded an unpleasant, rancid odor. In one of these I saw seven basins of rough stone for dyeing cloth, and a niche with a bas-relief of Minerva, the goddess and protector of the home; in another I counted five superbly carved Roman sarcophagi; in a third were some stored columns and remnants of the original paving stones. Further to the right, sunk in shadows, I saw the boiling hot springs where the saint had been tortured for three days before being decapitated.

Father Sansovino arrived late, and, just as on the day he visited the academy to inquire about Junio's whereabouts, he approached silently.

"Please forgive me for being late, José María, but for several days now I have thought I was being followed, so I was forced to take the Circolare Rossa."

The priest was referring to the tram that went around the outskirts of Rome. I assumed it was Smith's men that were tailing Sansovino, and so I attached no further importance to the matter.

"So, have you had any news of our friend?" he asked me once he had caught his breath.

"Something terrible has happened," I blurted out. "The German scientists responsible for opening the Creator's Map have died. It seems the papyrus was infected with anthrax."

Father Sansovino's face became indescribably sad. "When will we men learn that the answers to our problems cannot be found in darkness?" he said with deep feeling. "When will we understand that causing death never allays our fears, but rather the contrary? When will we realize that we carry the enemy around inside us, and that it is with ourselves we must wage the fiercest battle? May God have pity on us all!" the priest implored from the depths of his distressed soul.

"Junio believes you are responsible for the poisoning," I said.

"The prince is mistaken, although by now it doesn't matter," he added. "Remember the *scriptor* who sold the Creator's Map to Junio? We found a piece of paper in one of his pockets; on it was drawn an octagon with the name of Jesus on each side, and the following inscription: 'Willing to suffer torments in God's name.' That is the slogan of the ancient Catholic group called the Octagonus Circle. Its members, always working in groups of multiples of eight, were fanatics who were willing to defend the Catholic Church at all cost, even through the use of violence. The sect was founded in the times of the religious wars in France at the end of the sixteenth and the beginning of the seventeenth centuries. Have you ever heard of a monk named Ravaillac?"

"No," I said.

"He assassinated Henry IV of France, stabbed him with a knife, on

May 14, 1610. It has always been believed that Ravaillac was a member of this sinister organization, which has appeared and disappeared throughout history at its own convenience, without anybody being able to reliably prove its existence or find out who its members are. The last time the 'eight' showed signs of life was during the Napoleonic Era. Of course, the enemies of the Church have always claimed that the Octagonus Circle was intimately connected to the Holy Alliance. But I assure you that the murdered *scriptor* had no ties to the Vatican's espionage services."

"Are you suggesting that this man voluntarily sacrificed himself, that he knew that after giving over the map he was going to be assassinated?"

"Yes, he knew the risk he was taking."

"That must be the reason the Vatican didn't publicly report his death. It would have been equivalent to admitting to the existence of a sect of assassins in the heart of the Church," I mused out loud.

"We wanted to cut the evil out at the root. Nothing would be more prejudicial to the Church than for its name to serve as an excuse for a group of murderers, no matter how Catholic they are. His Holiness's position toward Hitler is well known throughout the world, but this doesn't mean that the Holy Father wishes—and much less instigates or encourages—the committing of violent acts that could endanger the German chancellor's life."

I didn't say so to Father Sansovino, but his story made me think that understanding those who speak in the name of God was every bit as difficult as understanding the Nazis. "So now what is going to happen?" I asked.

"We suspect that a criminal plot was behind the sale of the Creator's Map, and we will redouble our efforts to find out if we are dealing with members of the Octagonus Circle."

"The problem is that Junio seems to know nothing about this sect of fanatics and, as I said, he believes that you committed this crime. He might try to take revenge."

"I am willing to suffer torment in God's name," the priest answered, his arms outstretched.

"Isn't that the Octagonus slogan you just quoted?" I asked, genuinely perplexed.

"At a certain point, it can also be applied to anybody willing to become a martyr. A priest must always be ready to sacrifice himself, following the example of Our Lord Jesus Christ," he said.

That was when I understood that his choice of the crypt of the Basilica di Santa Cecilia was not random. Between these very walls the saint had lived and suffered martyrdom. By meeting me there, he wished to show me the kind of weapons the Church could count on in its struggle against its enemies: faith and resistance; shrewdness and determination. And the conviction that the blood of martyrs is not shed in vain.

I FOUND MONTSE WAITING for me at my new lodgings. She was pacing back and forth in front of the door, and though stiff with cold, she exuded the tranquillity I lacked. I had the sensation that she was moving across a stage and that the fractured shadows of the building were its edges. At her feet, a puddle reflected the last light of the day. I wondered when it had rained and what I had been doing so that I hadn't even noticed.

"Why didn't you go on up and wait for me inside?" I asked her in a slightly reproachful tone.

"I tried, but your landlady told me that female visitors were forbidden, then she shut the door in my face."

"That witch is worse than Secretary Olarra," I said.

"That's impossible!" Montse laughed. "Olarra doesn't trust me anymore, either. I can see it in those steely eyes of his. I had to make a date with Junio so he wouldn't follow me. We drank coffee, then Gabor brought me here in the car. In an hour he will pick me up and take me back to the academy. I fear that in order for us to see each other, I am going to have to take up again with the prince."

I remembered my conversation with Junio the day before, how I had wondered if she behaved the same way with both of us. "I see nothing has changed at the academy," I said wryly.

"Doña Julia has predicted that the war will be over in April, and when Olarra asked her if she was secretly working for the Nationalist government of Burgos, the good woman answered that her source was Beatrice Cenci's ghost, who had developed an interest in the affairs of our nation after wandering for so many centuries through the Spanish Academy. Olarra, playing along, asked her if Cenci's ghost had given her any other news of interest. Doña Julia's answer was definitive: 'The Holy Father will die on February 10 of next year.' You can imagine the uproar that followed. Some have even placed bets. What do you think?"

"How should I know? I've got enough problems in this world."

"Junio told me you're working for him, at least until you get a job as an architect."

"He's using me as a delivery boy. This morning I picked up a package at a pharmacy and took it to an apartment on Via dei Coronari. I wasn't allowed to ask any questions, but I think a German lived in the house; he started shouting with relief when he had the package in his hands. Several times he exclaimed, '*Mein Gott!*'"

"Perhaps he is ill, and he was thanking God for his medicine."

"I thought the same thing, but the fact that the man is ill does not explain why the clerk at the pharmacy couldn't deliver the order himself, and even less so why the whole thing had to be transacted so secretly. Junio assured me he needed somebody he could trust, and that's precisely what doesn't sit right; if there is anybody he mistrusts, it's me."

"Maybe he's changed his mind," Montse suggested.

"No, at least not while he keeps thinking that you talk about me too much."

"Is that what he told you?"

"Don't worry, I told him that you never stop talking to me about him."

Montse smiled complacently before saying, "A couple of spoiled brats. Will you take me to get something hot to drink?"

"I thought you already had coffee with the prince."

"So I have, but the half hour I spent waiting for you in this weather has left me frozen stiff."

"Do you want me to go up and get you a coat?"

"I'd prefer that you hug me," she said.

When I had her in my arms, I felt how her body, so fragile and weary, trembled, a chill, perhaps, but also an onrush of emotions. She leaned her cheek against mine, and I felt her cold skin as intensely as her body's docility. It was evident that Montse had decided that I should take the initiative. I led her to a nearby doorway already sunk in shadows and pressed her lips against mine. It was a kiss without reserve; we abandoned ourselves until we were breathless, a mutual release, which, I think, frightened her. I, on the other hand, felt as if I had just won a great battle.

"Now we can go have a coffee," I said, my voice trembling, only in part from the cold.

As the increasing darkness spread its dense veil over the city's every nook and cranny, I hoped that Prince Cima Vivarini were watching us, just so he would know that although Montse spoke about both of us, she kissed only me.

25.

THANKS TO THE REPORTS I got from Montse during her afternoon visits, I knew that the joy of the academy's refugees at the events in Spain was somewhat tempered by news of Pius XI's precarious health, which worsened in November. After surviving the start of the new year, he suffered a heart attack on February 4, and complications from kidney failure developed five days later. He died at dawn on February 10, thereby fulfilling Doña Julia's prophecy. That same day, Catalonia surrendered.

Rome was living in a state of consternation and uncertainty, not only because of the death of the Holy Father but also because the imminent election of a new pope made it crystal clear that the principal European powers were vying for influence over who would next sit on Saint Peter's throne. Even Prince Cima Vivarini's activities took a backseat. I met again with the second Smith in the building site at E42, but he didn't seem very interested in the details of my new job. Like everyone else in Rome, he was concerned about the prospects for the election of the new Supreme Pontiff; he had heard that the Germans were ready to put in play an enormous sum of money in order to guarantee that their candidate won, and he asked me to try to draw out Father Sansovino. By the time I was able to arrange another meeting with the priest, Eugenio Pacelli, papal nuncio to Germany for twelve years and ex–Secretary of State to Pius XI, had already been elected pope.

It seems, according to what Father Sansovino told me subsequently, that the process of electing the Supreme Pontiff had been plagued by irregularities that raised doubts about the integrity of the voting cardinals as well as the efficiency of both the secret services and the embassies of those countries with the greatest interest in having a pope on their side. The ideal candidate for the North Americans, the English, and the French was Pacelli, although some members of the French curia preferred Cardinal Maglione, an ancient nuncio in Paris with markedly anti-Fascist ideas. The candidates favored by Italy and Germany were the cardinals Mauricio Fossati of Turin and Elia Dalla Costa of Florence. In order to make sure that one of the two would be victorious, the Nazis sent three million marks in gold ingots to a man by the name of Taras Borodajkewycz, a Viennese of Ukrainian parentage and an agent of the Sicherheitsdienst, or SD, the SS intelligence agency. Borodajkewycz, who had contacts in the highest spheres of the Roman curia, told them that this would be enough to buy the necessary number of votes. Nevertheless, when the sixty-two members of the College of Cardinals met in conclave, they elected Cardinal Eugenio Pacelli on the third round on March 2, 1939.

Immediately thereafter, the Nazi leaders demanded that Borodajkewycz return the gold to the Reich. But by then the spy had vanished.

Some said that Taras Borodajkewycz had been an agent of the SS, though a different version also held a certain sway, that Borodajkewycz had been executed by an agent of the pope named Nicolás Estorzi, a tall, good-looking man with dark skin and black hair, about thirty years old and a native of Venice. According to the Italian secret service, Taras Borodajkewycz had spent the day of February 26 visiting various foundries on the outskirts of Rome in the company of a man matching Estorzi's description, and it was thought that both men were looking for a way to melt down the German gold to remove the markings of the Reichsbank. Borodajkewycz was next seen hanging from a crossbeam and Estorzi was spotted at a foundry on the island of Murano, in Venice, where he might have had the German gold recast and stamped with the Vatican seal. The treasure might then have ended up in an armored vault of a Swiss bank. At this point in the story Father Sansovino posed an extremely disconcerting possibility.

"One does not need to be particularly lynx-eyed to recognize the numerous similarities between Nicolás Estorzi and Prince Cima Vivarini," he whispered.

"What do you mean?"

"Estorzi is about thirty years old, like our prince, both are Venetian, and both are good-looking, dark-skinned, and have dark hair."

"Are you suggesting that Estorzi and Prince Cima Vivarini are one and the same person?"

"I am only pointing out a series of coincidences."

"If it were so, the prince would be an agent of the Holy Alliance, in which case you would know about it," I reasoned.

"Perhaps he's unscrupulous, posing as an agent of the Holy Alliance and taking advantage of the trust of the Nazi leadership to rob them of three million marks," the priest suggested.

"The prince is a wealthy man," I added.

"No wealthy man believes he is wealthy enough."

To this day, nobody knows what happened to those three million marks in gold the Nazis invested in the election of the new pope. What is known is that the election of Cardinal Pacelli—who four days after being seated on Saint Peter's throne wrote a somewhat conciliatory letter to Hitler—ended up smoothing out the enmity between the Vatican City State and the Third Reich in Germany.

That same month, Hitler occupied Czechoslovakia by invading Bohemia and Moravia, took over Memel, in Lithuania, and restored German sovereignty over the so-called Polish Corridor and the free city of Danzig—territories it had lost after the First World War—making manifest its policy to reunite the entire Germanic population of Central Europe.

Whenever I met with Junio, I tried to imagine him as Nicolás Estorzi, an agent of the Holy Alliance, who had stolen three million marks in gold ingots from the Nazis, but his demeanor did nothing to support this supposition, and he continued to behave as usual, sporting his black shirt with its Fascist slogan. I finally convinced myself that Junio was not and could never be Nicolás Estorzi.

Montse fulfilled her promise to visit me whenever possible. For twenty days, from Pius XI's death until the election of his successor, she wore deep mourning. This did not deter me from stealing a kiss from her when my desire was stronger than my will. Each time I hoped to reproduce the intensity of our first physical encounter, but no kiss was as intense as that first one, no embrace as voluptuous. Montse did not reject me, but her thoughts seemed far away. Perhaps she was getting herself prepared psychologically to return to Barcelona.

"I told you I didn't plan to fall in love again," she said as if to justify herself when she perceived my despair.

But behind that façade of indifference, I sensed her sorrow. I believe that she admired my decision not to return to Spain; by her doing so, she felt she was betraying herself now that Rome had become the city of her adulthood. Montse knew that she had changed forever, as had Barcelona. Both, so deeply affected by the war, now ran the risk of not recognizing each other.

After the capitulation of Catalonia, the end of the war awaited only the surrender of Madrid. This happened on March 28 and was made official on April 1 by Franco's final military assault. By then the refugees had packed their belongings, awaiting the right moment to set out from the port of Civitavecchia for their journey back home to Spain.

For Montse and me, these were days filled with anguish, uncertainty about our immediate future dogging us at every step, like shadows of lost opportunities glued to our heels. Neither of us dared bring up the subject of our parting. We preferred to deceive ourselves, clinging to the idea that the best thing would be for the good-byes to catch us both off guard, giving us no time to react.

One morning in April my landlady told me that Montse was waiting for me in front of the house. When I went down to her, Montse said simply, "I'm leaving. I'm returning to Barcelona."

"When?" I asked, still thinking we had time.

"This afternoon, at five."

I was so stunned, all I could do was ask her if she would write to me.

"We would suffer if I did."

"I'll suffer if you don't."

"I know, but it will be a passing pain that time will soften. You will forget me; we will forget each other."

"But I love you!" I exclaimed. I held firmly onto her wrists in a vain attempt to keep her with me.

"Let go of me, you're hurting me!" she said.

"Stay with me, please!" I said.

"That's not possible. At least not at the moment. So many things have happened, and I have to sort out my thoughts and my feelings, and this is something I can do only in Barcelona."

"Why only in Barcelona?" I asked her.

"Because that is my home. Because we all have a past and the war has deprived me of mine."

"Doesn't the future mean anything to you?"

"No, it means nothing. Nobody can ever know the future."

All of a sudden, I sensed that the distance between us was growing, as if Montse were already sailing away and I was remaining in the shadow of the door watching her depart. After giving me a kiss on the cheek, a moist, cold kiss like the brush of a marine breeze, she spoke again.

"I'd rather we say good-bye here. Take care of yourself, José María. Farewell."

I lowered my eyes, trying to absorb her words. By the time I lifted them again, she was already walking away down Via Giulia.

As I watched her, I felt physically ill, dizzy, as if I were the one boarding that ship. Everything began to move under my feet. I felt utterly powerless: our separation was irrevocable. Montse and I had broken loose from each other and were drifting in opposite directions. Everything was lost.

At two in the afternoon, still distraught, I stationed myself at one end of the Ponte Sisto, where there was an incomparable view of the academy. It was impossible from that distance to see anybody coming or going, but I didn't care. I wished only to recover for a moment the memories I had left between the academy's walls before time converted them to ghosts. I harbored a pathetic little hope that Montse had changed her mind and would suddenly appear on the other end of the bridge. I stood there, immobilized, until the setting sun made way for the darkness that fell over Rome like a heavy curtain.

PART · TWO

I.

MONTSE'S DEPARTURE proved something I had thought about on many occasions: that a city is, above all, a state of mind. For example, it wasn't until I lost her—until her absence had left me naked and vulnerable—that I noticed the nakedness of certain urban landscapes and discovered that Via Giulia had no trees. I know this might seem trivial, but I had failed to notice it when she was there. Cities do, indeed, throb, but they do so in sympathy with the hearts of their residents. I was embarking on a discovery of a different Rome, in the same way as I was exploring an entirely new part of myself.

In May, coinciding with the new alliance between Germany and Italy, I had a conversation with Junio that shook me out of my lethargy for a few days. After telling me that, for the moment, my work as a messenger had come to an end, he confessed that the situation in Germany had become more complicated because of a Vatican spy the Nazi secret service could not find and whom they believed to be involved in the poisoning of the Creator's Map.

"The Nazis think his real name is Nicolás Estorzi," he confided to me. "They believe he is a member of an ancient Catholic sect called the Assassini, a branch of that other sect of Arabic origin that committed murder for the promise of achieving paradise."

I replied politely, giving no indication that I had already heard of Estorzi's existence. But I was surprised that Junio should wish to discuss this with me.

After meeting again with the second Smith to recount verbatim my conversations with Prince Cima Vivarini, and arranging another meeting with Father Sansovino in the crypt of Santa Cecilia, I lost interest in everything. For several weeks, while Junio was trying to find me work in an architectural firm, I spent my time reading biographies of great men who, for one reason or another, had killed themselves. The tumultuous and frustrated life of the popular adventure-story writer Emilio Salgari became a mirror in which I saw my reflection. I was struck by his troubled existence; his son Nadir wrote that though his father had triumphed in the jungles and at sea, he had succumbed to the prosaic pressure of civilized life, with poverty as his most loyal companion, despite the fact that his books sold thousands of copies. But above all I was impressed by his tragic end: he committed hara-kiri using a Malayan kris with a corrugated blade in a remote region of the Valle San Martino in the spur of the Turin Alps six days after losing his wife, the actress Aida Peruzzi. In the end I decided not to follow Salgari's example, at least as long as Montse was still alive.

At the beginning of July the prince paid me a visit. He said he found me "much altered," and "very thin and with sunken eyes," as Signora Giovanna, the landlady, had warned him; he assured me he was worried about my health—it was true, my sustenance consisted principally of *mozzarella di bufala* with *pomodori pachino*, a little pasta, a piece of pecorino, and bits of sausage—and he suggested I accompany him to Bellagio, a charming little town on the shores of Lake Como, between Milan and the Swiss border.

The idea of spending part of the summer with Junio did not appeal to me in the least, but after the departure of the academy's refugees and *pensionados*, he was the only person I maintained somewhat consistent contact with in Rome. I cannot judge if my relationship with Junio was an authentic friendship (a friendship, after all, can be founded on resentment, in the same way as a smile can express disdain), for it was always subject to ups and down; paradoxically, my awareness that he was not to be trusted made me feel oddly tranquil, and safe. In addition, I was convinced that Junio knew about my activities, and since all these factors contributed to our relationship from my perspective, I finally accepted his invitation. Maybe, having proved myself incapable of committing hara-kiri with a Malayan kris, I harbored some kind of perverse hope of coming to a heroic, if possibly ignominious, end in his company. Perhaps he would send me to kill somebody; perhaps we would be vanquished together at the hands of one of the many enemies I suspected he had.

2.

WE MADE THE TRIP FROM ROME to Como in a comfortable train
headed for Lugano, and we settled into the Grand Hotel Villa
Serbelloni, a private villa built by the Frizzoni family in 1852. Junio and
Gabor occupied adjoining apartments (I think it was at this point that I
began to suspect the prince's sexual inclinations); I settled into a large,
well-lit suite with exquisite French furnishings and fine views of the lake.
Heavy velvet curtains framed the windows, antique Persian carpets lined
the floors, chandeliers made of Murano glass hung from the ceilings, frescoes decorated the walls. Never before or since have I been surrounded
by so much luxury.

Time lost the scaffolding of the days and seemed to grow deep like the
waters of the lake; pure air enveloped everything; the roads were lined
with brightly colored flowers suspended on fragile stems. Life, in short,
grew torpid, like muscles at rest after strenuous exercise—the enormous
effort I had exerted in continuing my life in Rome after Montse's departure. At certain moments, I even came to believe there could be paradise
on earth, a conclusion particularly outlandish given the madness already
gripping the world.

Most mornings we organized outings to the "countryside," as Junio
called it even though we were living so close to nature already. The hotel's
restaurant would prepare a basket of food and a bottle of Prosecco, and
Gabor would drive us to Punta Spartivento, where we could enjoy a mag-

nificent view of the three branches of the lake and of the surrounding mountains, as described by Alessandro Manzoni in his novel *I Promessi Sposi*, with their threatening peaks covered in perpetual snow. On other occasions, we'd visit famous local villas, whose owners warmly welcomed Junio. I still remember the ancient family names of some of our hosts: Aldobrandini, Sforza, Gonzaga, Ruspoli, Borghese.

Most of the time, however, we drove aimlessly along windswept roads with Gabor behind the wheel. One morning, for a change, we took the *traghetto* from Bellagio, then boated through the waters of the lake to Villa d'Este, a magnificent and legendary hotel where the likes of Byron, Rossini, Puccini, Verdi, and Mark Twain had stayed. Not to mention the list of kings, princes, and business magnates who, with all the arrogance of those who know themselves to be the chosen among the chosen, had converted Villa d'Este into a showcase where one could see and be seen. I came to see the extent of Junio's contradictions during those days we shared in Como. He was, in a way, a Jekyll-and-Hyde character: a cold-blooded killer who could be brought to tears reading Lord Byron.

But this was not the only discovery I made. One morning, while we ate lunch on one of the terraces of the Serbelloni with a view of the lake, Junio spoke to me about his childhood, which he described as itinerant, for his family was always traveling and changing residences. They had become too dispersed because their vast wealth allowed each one to do as he pleased. He even referred to the path he had taken to become the man he was today, describing his affinity with the Fascist cause, as well as his devotion to the National Socialist doctrine of Hitler, as "a family obligation," which I understood to mean that there were family ties that united him to both movements. He defined himself as a moderately religious person, opposed to extremism of any kind, for he was, he claimed, a practical man above all else. Junio believed that in the same way the secular State had allowed itself to be infused with Catholic values, the Church should do its part and naturally take on some postulates of secularism, such as tolerance for divorce.

If he had such a strong sense of his heritage, I asked him, why had he chosen to go to Bellagio for his holiday rather than to Venice.

He smiled. "First of all, because the strength of my mother's personality drowns everything else in Venice. She is like a second lagoon, if you can imagine that. And second, because as a young man I gained a certain reputation, and any gentleman with any self-respect has the obligation to keep his bad reputation intact. If my compatriots saw what I have become, they would instantly stop talking about me and even stop talking to me. And they would be absolutely right."

He paused and then continued speaking. "Venice is the only city in the world one need not constantly return to, because there is no difference between visiting it and dreaming about it. You don't even have to be asleep to dream about Venice. Don't misunderstand me; anyone who speaks of dreams must also take nightmares into account."

"I've never been to Venice," I said.

"Really? I thought everybody had by now." He continued, somewhat wistfully, "I suppose you've heard it said a thousand times that Venice is the city of lovers; I am of the opposite opinion: it is an ideal place for couples who are, in fact, not in love. Do you want to know why?"

"Please."

"Because Venice is a stage set, just like false love. In the end, Venice is a collection of old palaces only their residents have access to, palaces surrounded by abandoned hovels and rows of identical mullioned windows that make all the canals look the same, everything infused with a humidity that blends with melancholy, and legions of mosquitoes that constantly remind us that the city's foundations are sinking into the putrid water. There are two ways of seeing a gondola: as a black swan or a floating coffin. I am partial to the second. As for the constant floods, the fog, and the winter cold"—he shrugged—"I'll describe them to you some other time."

One warm, star-studded night, after we had shared a bottle of Tuscan wine, possessing the scent of old leather and the smoothness of velvet, and later two *amaros* mixed with aged rum and pear juice, he asked me, "Has she written to you?"

It was the first time Montse had been mentioned by either of us since she left.

"No."

"Nor to me, but I think that's a good sign," he said.

"What do you mean?" I asked.

"She'd write only if she weren't planning to return," he said.

"You think so?"

"Yes, I do. Montse belongs to us."

But I knew that capturing Montse, reducing her to a possession, even if only in the intoxicated dreams of a couple of drunks, was the same as pretending to snatch one of those stars from the brilliant night sky, and then simply pocket it.

3.

A T THE BEGINNING OF AUGUST I began my job at the firm of an
architect named Biagio Ramadori. He was a man with scant architectural talent but great skill at establishing relationships with the
right people and garnering favors. Thanks to this ability, Ramadori had
been promised a project in E42. A mere month later, however, Hitler
invaded Poland, and France and England declared war on Germany.
What had previously been an advantage for obtaining sinecures now
worked against Ramadori, and on the pretext of Italy's possible entrance into the armed conflict, he was assigned the task of designing a
bunker for the Palazzo degli Uffici that would be built under the supervision of the architect Gaetano Minnucci. Ramadori called this assignment "crumbs, considering my talent and the services I have rendered
to this regime." In order to give Minnucci—the director of architectural services of E42—a slap in the face, he assigned the job to me,
thereby passing both myself and the project off to Minnucci. I never
found out the reasons behind the dispute between Ramadori and
Minnucci (I imagine they're the usual ones: jealously, envy, and arrogance), but as a result, my professional fortunes took an about-face.
From one day to the next, I found myself working for one of the finest
architects of the time. At first my work was limited to that bunker,

but the positive outcome of that project—and the fact that the drums of war were beating more and more insistently—led to many such projects coming to Minnucci's firm. Since most of their efforts were spent on the monumental project of E42, I was left to design and build the bunkers.

There was no great professional or aesthetic merit in this work. I studied the defensive structures used by armies since the First World War—from the famous but ultimately ineffectual Maginot Line (the largest defensive barrier ever built, which included 108 main forts fifteen kilometers apart, a large number of smaller forts, and more than one hundred kilometers of underground barracks and galleries extending along the entire French-German border) to the Belgian fortifications—and I reached the conclusion that the design of Czech bunkers was the most revolutionary and innovative. Traditionally, bunkers had been built facing the line of the advancing enemy. This meant that the adversary's artillery would be aimed directly at the installation of the defensive weaponry. However, the Czech engineers built their fortifications with their backs to the enemy, whereby the least vulnerable part of the structure received the enemy fire, and the bunker could be defended by attacking the enemy's flanks, often the rear guard of the attacking forces, and not head-on. Each bunker was also able to defend the one next to it, and vice versa. In addition, it was possible to maintain communication between them through deeply buried telephone lines and a network of subterranean corridors, which could be used to move troops and supplies. All I had to do was follow the Czech designs, and improve on a few technical aspects.

Junio took advantage of my sudden "renown" to recommend me to a contact of his at Hochtief, the largest construction company in Germany. One of the directors interviewed me at the Grand Hotel in Rome, and though we didn't finalize an agreement then, we parted with the promise of working together in the near future, which finally happened in 1943, four years later.

My new assignment greatly pleased the second Smith, whom I now supplied with the fruits of my labor as an architect—designs, drawings, plans—as well as the information I obtained from the prince. This qualitative leap in my career as a spy filled me with pride. It even made me consider that lying and deception might be considered honorable under such circumstances. Smith, who had always been honest about the risks I was taking, warned me that my life was now in very real and constant danger. But by then I had decided not to turn my back on this new war; this was no longer about the fate of one small country—Spain—but of the entire world.

Looking back, the contradictions I was living may have been a backhanded way of seeking mortification, even the death I was too cowardly to afford myself. On one hand, I felt the emptiness around me growing, as if every day another part of my world were vanishing. It was not the world that was disappearing, however, but rather my interest in it. On the other hand, I now regretted not having participated actively in the war in Spain, a remorse that made me commit myself with greater fervor to this new war that had just begun.

Once I had a steady income, I began to look for an apartment where I could live alone, far from Signora Giovanna and her phobias. Thinking about Montse's absence had become such a constant that it began to isolate me from the outside world. In some sense, I was not really alive when I made the decision to move. I was functioning out of some kind of autism, a total disconnection from reality. The purpose of my work—to build bunker after bunker—became the purpose of my life. Thirteen hours of work and eight of sleep left me only three hours a day, and I could use these to find myself a new place to live.

I decided to rent a top-floor apartment with a terrace on Via dei Riari, a quiet street that ran from Via della Lungara to the Gianicolo. From the terrace I enjoyed a beautiful view of Trastevere and Palazzo Farnese across the river. Soon, as I had done during my residence at the academy, I began to count domes and towers within my field of vision: Il Gesù, San Carlo ai Catinari, Sant'Andrea della Valle, and Chiesa Nuova.

This is the same home I now share with Montse, and I believe the time has come for me to recount how and under what circumstances she returned to me.

4.

THE WAR DEVOURED 1940 as avidly as Germany was gobbling up nation after nation. In the first few months of the year, at the recommendation of the Italian ruling class and the king, Mussolini hesitated to join Germany and enter the war. His reluctance was mainly due to his awareness of the limitations of the Italian army, despite what the propaganda said about its being one of the world's most experienced and well-prepared fighting forces. Finally, when the Duce was certain of France's imminent defeat, he declared war on that country and Great Britain, more out of fear that Italy would be invaded by the Germans if he didn't than out of any hope of scoring a victory on the battlefield. This happened on June 10, 1940, by which time no Italian in his right mind was in any doubt that Germany would win the war.

The Italians' inability to subdue the south of France, whose army had been demolished by the Germans, established a pattern the Fascist troops would repeat throughout the armed conflict. Led by Prince Saboya, who insisted on an entourage of counts, dukes, marquises, and Fascist high officials, the Italian army suffered six hundred dead and two thousand wounded. Only the armistice between the two nations managed to bring an end to the hostilities. And in spite of this being, in theory, Italy's victory, the peace treaty followed all of Germany's recommendations, for the Germans had been the ones to break the back of the Gallic army. Mussolini demanded Corsica, Avignon, Valenza, Lyon, Tunis, Casablanca, and other places of minor importance. Hitler, however, arguing that he did not want to humiliate France, particularly because he wanted to use its territory to launch his assault on England, conceded to Italy only a demilitarized zone of fifty kilometers on the Italian-French border, and another between Libya and Tunisia.

The subsequent defeats of the Italian Fascist army, first in British Egypt, then in Greece, forced the Germans to repeatedly come to its aid, blow after final blow to any confidence the Italians once had in their military and their Duce.

Junio never dared to openly confess his disappointment, but it appears he intensified his contacts with the SS at the beginning of October 1940. On the fifteenth of that month he set off again for Wewelsburg, where he was scheduled to meet with Himmler. He was going to travel with Hitler's party to Hendaya, where the Führer was planning to meet with Franco, and from there continue on to Madrid and Barcelona in the Reichsführer's entourage. Junio told me of these plans in the same conversation that he told me one of those stories the second Smith so much enjoyed hearing. It concerned a Cathar legend, according to which the Holy Grail had been kept somewhere in the recesses of Montségur Castle in the south of France since shortly before the fort had fallen in 1244. Montségur, however, was built on a huge block of stone, which led some scholars to wonder if perhaps it was instead hidden in one of the caves of the Montserrat Monastery, on the other side of the French-Spanish border. Himmler therefore had decided to travel to Montserrat to look through its secret grottoes.

Besides Junio, there were twenty-five people on Himmler's expedition, including a strange character named Otto Rahn. I call him strange because he was an expert in medieval and Cathar literature, author of a book titled *Crusade Against the Grail*, and another, singular title, *Lucifer's Court*, one of Himmler's favorite texts, which was bound in calfskin and distributed to all top SS officials. But Rahn, who had been appointed to Himmler's staff, had a problem: his grandmother was named Clara Hamburger and his great-grandfather Leo Cucer, both typical Central European Jewish surnames. It was therefore decided that he must be "eliminated" so that he could continue to render services to the SS under a different identity. In this way, Otto Rahn became Rudolph Rahn. This same man would be appointed German ambassador to Rome during the final days of the occupation.

I remember asking Junio if he planned to look up Montse.

"No, I am going to search for the Holy Grail. But if I see her, I'll tell her how much you miss her."

"You would really do that?"

"I promise." Then, after reflecting for a few moments, he added, "I think that everything would be a lot simpler if instead of looking for the Grail or some other relic, people tried to find love. Don't you agree?"

"What do you mean?"

"Nothing of much importance. I'm just saying that sometimes we struggle to find something that doesn't exist, and we reject what we have within reach. But I suppose it has always been like that, otherwise there wouldn't be so many gods and myths. Hitler thinks he has found the solution to that problem by resurrecting the concept of the Man-God, or Superman, a superior being that incorporates all the questions and provides all the answers."

ONE WINDY AND DISAGREEABLE November afternoon when I was feeling crushed by a particularly deep sense of melancholy, Junio knocked on my door. He had just returned from his trip to Barcelona and was bringing me some unexpected news.

"The Grail is definitely not buried in Montserrat, but I did see our friend," he said, and I knew immediately he was referring to Montse.

"You saw her? Where?" I asked.

"First, give me a drink."

"I can offer you an *amaro*."

"Averna *amaro*?"

"Yes."

"Fine. I met her at the Ritz, by chance; that's where the Reichsführer and his entourage were staying."

"Maybe it wasn't by chance," I suggested. "Himmler's arrival in Barcelona must have been well publicized, and Montse knows what a close relationship you have with him, so it's perfectly possible she went to the Ritz in hopes of meeting you there."

"Perhaps. In any case, I couldn't see her afterward because somebody stole Himmler's briefcase from his room, and then total chaos ensued. You should have seen the scandal!"

"Montse asked about you," Junio went on, "and I told her you were working as an architect in Minnucci's firm; I also told her about your new home. She was very happy to know things were going so well for you. She asked me for your address so she could write to you."

"And she—how is she? What is she doing?" I asked eagerly.

"She's broken off contact with her father, and no longer lives in her family home. Once a month she meets her mother at the Ritz Hotel, they have tea together, and Doña Montserrat gives her a little money that allows her to survive in a dignified fashion until she can find a decently paying job. She lives in a small room and works as a translator in a publishing house. I tried to persuade her to return to Rome, telling her she'd be better off here and safer than in Barcelona, despite the war. When we parted, I gave her an envelope with money and a safe-conduct pass to get into Italy. She said she would think about it."

Junio's news both upset me and filled me with renewed hope; for some time I had been convincing myself I would never hear from Montse again. I no longer knew if I was in love with her or her memory. I'd assumed that Montse had picked up her life in Barcelona where she'd left it, but Junio's words told a different story. My first impulse was to go to her and help her, but my work commitments, my duties as a spy, and my loathing of Spain held me back. Unbeknownst to me, at that precise moment, Montse was waiting at the port in Barcelona.

5.

I DIDN'T UNDERSTAND why Montse had wanted my address—after all, she was the one who had insisted it was better not to correspond—until one cold, rainy morning in December when she appeared at my door. My first impression when I saw her through the peephole was that she had just emerged from the sea: her hair was wet, and drops of rain were dripping down her face. She wore no makeup and had on an old wool coat that spoke volumes about her financial hardships. In spite of all that, she had not lost a bit of her beauty. Her large green eyes sparkled, and her face was calm, reflecting her solid, pragmatic approach to life. Looking into those eyes made me feel like a sailor who sees the beam of the lighthouse on the horizon and knows it will lead him safely into port after a long and exhausting journey.

"Montse!" I exclaimed.

Instead of kissing me, she touched my lips with her fingers, as if wanting to silence any possible objection I might have.

"I'd better not kiss you; I'm soaked," she said by way of excuse.

For a year and a half I had been imagining a quite different meeting. She seemed for a brief moment like a total stranger, but then I saw the beseeching look in her eyes: she was chilled to the bone if not the soul.

"Come in and take off your coat. I'll get you a towel."

"May I stay at your house until I find a room?" she asked as she followed me inside.

Now she seemed to be sizing me up, trying to determine if I was still as I had been.

"Of course," I said. "This is your home."

After looking around while she dried her hair and face, she went straight out to the terrace.

"So, this is your new place! I like it," she said.

"There's still so much to do. I haven't even had a chance to furnish it."

It was true; within the strict divisions I had made of my time, I had few moments left for decorating or for any other idle pursuit; I had feared that any idle time would sink me back into my depression.

"Junio told me you're working as an architect, designing bunkers for the Italian Ministry of Defense."

"He told me you work at a publishing house as a translator."

"I quit. The work was poorly paid and the books I was translating were completely uninteresting. I've decided to go into exile."

Montse spoke in such a matter-of-fact way that I was convinced she didn't really know what she was saying.

"Exile?"

"I've broken all connection with my family, forever," she said.

"Your father is not an easy man."

"It's more than that. Do you remember I once told you about my Uncle Jaime?"

"Yes, I remember your mentioning him," I said.

"When I returned to Barcelona I decided to find out what had happened to him. For more than a year I had thought he was dead, then about four months ago I found a letter addressed to my father and signed by Colonel Antonio Vallejo Nájera, head of the Military Psychiatric Services of Franco's army. The letter, full of allusions to the psychophysical roots of Marxism, made reference to 'the patient of interest to you,' who had showed no signs of improvement due to the 'democratic-Communist-political fanaticism of the subject in question.' Intrigued by this letter, I began to try to find out more about this colonel. A few days later, in a bookstore window on Paseo de Gracia I saw a book called *The Madness of War: The Psychopathology of the Spanish Civil War*, published in Valladolid in 1939, written by Dr. Antonio Vallejo Nájera. To make a long story short, the book argued in favor of an intimate connection between Marxism and mental inferiority and for the necessity of isolating Marxists as sociopaths in order to liberate society from this terrible plague. It was then that I began to figure out who this patient 'of interest' to my father could be. After pressing my mother, I got her to tell me the truth: my Uncle Jaime was alive. He had been arrested after the war ended, and with the express purpose of saving him from himself, my father had offered him up to Dr. Vallejo Nájera to experiment on, to try to extract the 'Red gene' that had corrupted his soul. It seems the experiment was being carried out at the Miranda de Ebro concentration camp under the supervision of the Gestapo, also interested in learning the results of the experiments Dr. Vallejo Nájera carried out on his patients. As far as I know, my uncle is still there." She paused, then added, "That's why I decided to take revenge."

"Revenge?"

"As soon as I knew about Himmler's trip to Barcelona and his plans to stay at the Ritz, I devised a plan. Twenty years ago, when my Uncle Jaime left home, he did so in the company of a maidservant my grandmother had arranged for him. This woman, named Ana María, loved my uncle like a son, though some said their relationship didn't stop there. When my uncle became estranged from his brothers because of ideological differences and things began to go badly for him economically, Ana María got a job as a housekeeper at the Ritz Hotel, and she has worked there ever since. So I went to talk to her and told her what I had just discovered, that my uncle was alive and being used by that doctor as a guinea pig. I then suggested she give me a copy of the key to the room where Himmler was going to stay and get me a maid's uniform, figuring that among the papers the Reichsführer kept in his suitcase was probably something about the experiments Vallejo Nájera was carrying out in Miranda de Ebro and other concentration camps. My plan, I told her, was to steal the documents. I would then make them public through the international press so that the neutrality Franco so strongly desired would be in danger if he didn't put an end to such medical practices. Ana María agreed and told me what time of day would be best. Getting in and out of Himmler's room was the easiest thing in the world."

"But you had no idea what kind of documents were in his briefcase!" I said.

"That's true. And since I don't read German I still don't know; all I understood were a few drawings of the cellars of the Montserrat Monastery. But I'm sure they're important. That's why I thought they should reach Smith."

Montse went over to one of her suitcases and took out a black leather briefcase.

"You've traveled from Barcelona to Rome with Himmler's briefcase?" I asked her incredulously.

Montse's audacity perplexed me, as it always had and always would: that she could devise such a plan, carry it out, and then have the courage and sangfroid to travel halfway across the Mediterranean Sea with the loot mixed in with her underwear made her worthy of deep admiration.

My silence must have indicated to her that she needed to explain, at least a little.

"What happened to my Uncle Jaime has opened my eyes. I have decided to struggle against Fascism with all my strength," she said.

"From Barcelona?" I asked her. "Or are you here to stay?"

She answered obliquely. "Franco has things all tied up in Spain. But if Hitler and Mussolini lose the war in Europe, Franco won't have any allies and will remain isolated. . . . Do you still meet Smith?"

"Yes, every three or four weeks."

"Will you do me the favor of giving him the briefcase?"

I picked up the briefcase and put it away in a wardrobe without even glancing at its contents.

"Tomorrow I'll set up a meeting with him," I said.

"Thank God," she said with enormous relief. "The whole trip, I never stopped considering the possibility that you had . . . changed."

"I haven't," I said. "I pass on my designs for the bunkers to Smith. I could be charged with high treason."

This was the first time I had spoken about my activities and their consequences out loud. I heard myself as if I were talking about a third person. I certainly didn't feel like a traitor; on the contrary, because my conscience alone dictated my actions, my spirit was totally at ease.

"If they catch you, you'll be executed," Montse said.

Not even Smith himself had dared put it in such crude terms.

"What do you think they'd do to you if they found out about Himmler's briefcase?"

"Maybe they'd execute us together. That would be an interesting twist of fate."

I was further alarmed by how flippantly she spoke.

"The problem is whether or not we would die with dignity, with a sense of having accomplished something," I said, attempting a bit more gravity. "I guess that would be our only comfort. I don't mind thinking about death, but I am incapable of imagining how and when I am going to die. I also don't care about the details, nor do I have any idea how I would behave in front of a firing squad. Right now I think my courage functions only in the abstract, and I don't particularly want to put it to the test!"

"The opposite is true for me," declared Montse. "I can imagine myself facing the firing squad, looking at my executioners, my head held high, but I don't like thinking about death or, rather, what it really means. There have been times I've wanted to die, like when I found out about my uncle, but I think that is part of the empathy we all feel for people who are suffering. It is that desire to die that gives us the strength to keep on living, to fight injustice."

I have never thanked Montse enough for how she dealt with the discomfort that stole upon us as night encroached, when she realized my house had only one bedroom and only one bed. Without any fuss she told

me to get into bed and turn off the light, and after going into the bathroom to change, she lay down by my side, as naturally as if we had been
sharing a bed for years. I don't think I have ever been so frightened. My
lungs contracted and my muscles froze; I became as rigid as a corpse. She,
on the other hand, initiated our intimacy the way she lived her life, prag-
matically and, as cold as that sounds, correctly. Everything, absolutely
everything, that happened that night was Montse's doing, and I always
believed that it set the pattern of our future relationship. I may have been
tempted, at certain moments over the years, to complain about her lack
of passion, but I also know that my own state of tension, my personal fears,
did not allow me to express my own. I have never talked to her about this
directly, but whenever we make love I have the strange and uncomfortable sensation that some part of her is elsewhere. Nevertheless, I have
made my peace with the part of Montse that belongs to me as well as the
part that doesn't, and I have never asked her to prove her faithfulness. I
know that any lover she might have would also have to settle for whatever
part of herself she made available. Whatever happened that night, however unextraordinary, however disappointing, our union was thereby
sealed forever. In exchange for a lack of passion, Montse gave me the
privilege of her intimacy, the chance to sleep with her, to eat breakfast by
her side, the two of us sitting on the terrace of our house looking toward
the leafiness of the Gianicolo, then to eat lunch and dinner with her
while the world was bleeding all around us. When I look back, I think the
most outstanding aspect of our relationship during those years was that in
spite of the differences in our personalities we both knew how to infuse
each other with a sufficient dose of optimism, a commodity as scarce at
that time as meat or imported goods. And so we got married precipitously
a few weeks later, as if by so doing we were taking a stand against the war,
proving to ourselves that it was we who controlled our destinies, not
the war.

6.

THE JOY I FELT at my good fortune in marrying Montse made me more able to accept the fact that we could never have children. The day we talked about getting married, she told me that before I made a final decision there was something she had to tell me, which she referred to as "the saddest episode of my life." she added. Then, calmly and simply, she told me the story of how, years before, when she was very young and very inexperienced, she had met and fallen madly in love with a young man a few years older than she, a man of the world who belonged to a universe of experience that dazzled her. She gave herself body and soul to this man for a few weeks, before her lover's stay in her country came to an end. When, after he had left, she found out she was pregnant, she knew that to carry the pregnancy to term would have meant dishonor for herself and her family. Not to mention the young man, whose work of great importance to a certain political cause would be compromised. With little hope of following the young man to his own country, she decided not to tell him about the pregnancy, and to go ahead with an abortion. She went to her uncle, a person of liberal ideas and great determination, who knew the right people to solve such a problem. Thanks to the fact that she lived in a country where a republic had just been established, she had no problem carrying out her decision without having to give many explanations. But, as a result of the procedure, she was rendered incapable of having children. It took her three years to get over it, and even then, she still experienced spasms of regret, distress that became, she thought, like a chronic illness. "Now you know why I am so grateful to my Uncle Jaime and why I can never have children," Montse concluded.

Once I recovered from my initial shock I tried to reassure her, still not knowing the extent of her resolve. "I don't care. The war will leave a world full of orphans, so if we want to be parents, we can always adopt a child."

"You don't understand, do you?" she said with calm finality. "I could never adopt a child. Every time I'd look at that child's face I would remember that other child I'd had cut out of my womb. No, I'll never be a mother."

On many occasions I have been tempted to ask her to tell me about the lover who had consumed all her passion, but I never quite dare. I prefer to think of him as a dream upon which Montse built her entire subsequent personality, and I tell myself that without him, I wouldn't have found a place in her life. And if ever I have felt jealousy or hostility, it has been an undefined kind of jealousy and a cordial kind of hostility. Somewhere I read that in all marriages there is the need to deceive the other person about some weak point in one's own character, because it is intolerable to live with a human being who is aware of all our wretchedness. That's why there are so many couples who end up miserable, because the accumulation of wretchedness finally outweighs any positive aspect of sharing a life.

The wedding was performed by Father Sansovino, and Junio and a few of my colleagues at work were witnesses. We decided to get married through the Church because having a civil marriage would have been an avowal of the triumph of the Fascist state. Italy's entrance into the war had increased the tensions between the Church and the State. Despite the new pope's attempts to maintain a balancing act (after a few months Pius XII went from being a tightrope walker to being a Nazi puppet) between the powers engaged in the conflict, one faction within the Church had taken off its blindfold and accused Mussolini of being an accomplice to the atrocities the Germans were committing in the nations they were conquering. I took advantage of the premarital talks with Father Sansovino to tell him what Junio had told me about Himmler's visit to Montserrat in search of the Holy Grail.

"I am aware of the Reichsführer's trip to Barcelona. But the Chalice of the Last Supper is in Valencia; this is public knowledge," he said.

"Is there anything to all those legends they attribute to the Cathars?"

"They're nothing more than that, legends. The Grail recognized by the Church appeared in Huesca before the Arab invasion of the Iberian Peninsula. In the year 713, the bishop of Huesca, one Audaberto, hid it in a cave in Monte Pano. The monastery of San Juan de la Peña would be founded later on the same site. Under the reign of Alfonso V, the Magnanimous, the Grail was moved to the cathedral in Valencia. Since 1437 it has been there. That is the official story, and as you can see, the Cathars make no appearance at all."

"So, what was Himmler looking for in Montserrat?"

"I have no idea, but I know that he didn't even want to visit the basilica, so the abbots of Montserrat refused to receive him. Father Ripoll was put in charge of doing the honors because he spoke German. According to him, Himmler was more interested in the surrounding countryside than in the monastery, and he even asserted that the Albigensians, with whom the Nazis believe they have so much in common, found refuge there.

"I don't recall what that heresy was about," I admitted.

"The Cathars, also known as 'good men,' didn't believe Jesus died at the hands of the Roman army, so they rejected the cross. They recognized as sacred only the Gospel of St. John, and wore long black tunics, wandering around the Languedoc region in pairs, helping anybody who needed it. They were completely uninterested in material wealth, and before long they were accepted by individuals from all strata of society who felt the need for a liberating philosophy. But when this small local movement crossed the borders of France and made incursions into Germany, Italy, and Spain, Rome decided to take action. Keeping in mind that these 'good men' believed that Lucifer, whom they called Lucibel, was also a benefactor of humanity, Pope Innocent III found it very easy to launch a crusade against them. So began an implacable persecution that destroyed the lives of thousands of people and was the source of the legend that the Cathars, before being exterminated, managed to stash away immense treasures, among them the Grail. I have no idea what threads Himmler might find in common with the Cathars, except that the Grail the Church recognizes and the one the Reichsführer recognizes are not the same."

"What do you mean?"

"Some ancient pagan legends say that the Holy Grail is not the Chalice of the Last Supper, but rather a sacred stone that can channel celestial energy. The poet Wolfram von Eschenbach said in *Parzifal*, an Arthurian romance, that the Grail is a stone 'of the purest sort.' Others have described it as a 'stone with spirit' or an 'electric stone.' According to some theories it contains a neutral energy and is protected by a group of angels known as the 'Doubtful' for having remained on the margins of the conflict between God and the devil. Von Eschenbach, whose work tells of events that happened during the crusade against the Cathars, wrote about these angels: 'The noble and worthy angels who took neither side when Lucifer warred with the Trinity were sent down to earth as custodians of this stone, which is forever pure. I know not whether God forgave them or destroyed them . . .'"

"So it wasn't Christ's chalice but rather a source of energy that Himmler was looking for in Montserrat."

"That's possible. A neutral energy that can be used for good as well as evil. It seems that between those two worlds, Heinrich Himmler's role is like the evil sorcerer Klingsor, the ancient knight, rejected by the Grail."

"I suppose the Reichsführer now hopes to find out the exact location of this stone through the Creator's Map."

"Maybe. But frankly, I see many contradictions in this story."

"Explain."

"The Cathars rejected the possession of material goods; initiates were even obliged to renounce them. They also opposed idolatry. So to think they possessed a treasure and did everything possible to keep it safe is

absurd; it would go against their most basic principles. I fear Himmler is
a 'Cathar ignoramus.'"

SMITH WAS ABLE TO SHED a little light on all this after he had translated
the documents from the Reichsführer's briefcase. The drawings Montse had
seen were of the dungeons of Montserrat, but there were also others of the
bunkers Franco was building in Linea de la Concepción, a total of 498
concrete fortifications, which, according to the footnotes, the German army
was going to use to invade Gibraltar in an operation baptized as "Felix" and
subsequently scratched after Franco and Hitler met in Hendaya. In addition
to those plans, Himmler's briefcase contained documents that made evident
the collaboration between Franco's secret police and the SS. Finally, the
Reichsführer had in his possession a strange report about the existence of
thirteen underground cities in the Andes Mountains—thirteen cities of
stone artificially illuminated and connected to one another through tunnels, whose capital was named Akakor, and which extended beyond the
Purus River and a high valley on the border between Brazil and Peru. This
underground kingdom, built by the "Grand Masters" thousands of years
before, contained a plant that was capable of softening stone, a treasure the
Nazis wished to possess at all costs.

To me, all these stories seemed as hollow as Himmler believed the
center of the earth to be, despite the Reichsführer's conviction that the
results of his efforts would end up shaking the foundations of the world.

I knew that the second Smith took all this information quite seriously,
but to me it seemed like a waste of time. While we were worrying about
the name of some legendary city in the Amazon, the German military
machine was proving to be increasingly implacable. Pursuing the Creator's Map, the Holy Lance of Longinus, or the Holy Grail made no sense
to me; I would have preferred a different line of action, something more
expeditious, something that might hold back the advancing panzers of
the Third Reich. I wouldn't have hesitated to bomb my own bunkers,
and on more than a few occasions I got angry with Smith for what I

considered passivity on his part, but he always tried to reassure me that the Allied army would know when and how to use the information I was supplying.

Meanwhile, something quite different was happening to Junio. If I reproach him now for anything besides his criminal behavior, it is that he allowed himself to be led by his superstitions. At first I thought this was part of his character, but as time passed I reached the conclusion that his taste for the esoteric was nothing more than a whim, one of those ridiculous pleasures wealthy people indulge in. Aside from his dabbling in paleography and politics, Junio had never done any work. He didn't even interest himself in the family business, which was run by a legion of lawyers, stockbrokers, and accountants. But I suppose this was to be expected of a prince who enjoyed the privilege of friendship with the king of Italy.

As happened to all of us, the war brought out the best and the worst in Junio. And when the Italian army's ineptitude finally destroyed his unbreakable faith in the Fascist movement, he sought refuge in the esoteric with the vehemence of an alcoholic whose drunken state distorts reality. He was always talking about the outlandish missions Himmler sent him on: to find Wotan's Hammer, to encounter the residence of the King of the World, to acquire the Staff of Command, et cetera. Of all of them, I remember most vividly the account he gave one evening at the Nino Restaurant on Via Borgognona. According to Junio, the Reichsführer had assigned him the important task of organizing an expedition to Central America in search of what he called "The Skull of Destiny." Apparently, in January 1924 an explorer named Frederick A. Mitchell-Hedges discovered a death's-head carved in quartz crystal in the ruins of a Mayan temple complex, which he called "Lubaantun" (which means "City of Stones" or "City of the Fallen Pillars"), in the area of the Yucatán that belongs to Belize. The skull, weighing about five kilograms, was perfectly carved out of a single piece; and the precision of its details (the jaw could move) as well as its mineral hardness—seven on the Mohs scale—made it both remarkable and unique. The experts confirmed that it could have been cut and polished only by tools made of corundum or diamond, and if carved by hand, as was considered most plausible, it would have taken the artisan or artisans three hundred years. But there was more: the Kekchis, the indigenous people in the region, claimed there were thirteen identical skulls that belonged to the local priests and that were traditionally used in esoteric rituals, as they were sources of power that could cure or kill. Mitchell-Hedges was convinced that both the ruins and the skull belonged to the lost continent of Atlantis.

At one point, Junio even quoted Rilke, something about our world being a stage curtain behind which the most profound secrets hide.

Although Junio took these missions seriously, I saw his interest as an effort to avoid reality. Not in vain, for the waning of the Italian Fascist movement was becoming more evident by the day, as was the dejection of the population, weary of making sacrifices in exchange for nothing. Everybody could see that the cord was being stretched too tight. The Italians were beginning to discover en masse that behind the Duce's arrogant and hardened expression—once a living symbol of the firmness and security that would lead the country to its greatest glory—there was nothing but obstinacy.

7.

THE YEARS 1941 AND 1942 were ones of shortages and scarcity. The economic assistance Hitler promised never came, and the living conditions of the Italian people deteriorated to an almost unbearable degree. The amount of money in circulation tripled, industrial production decreased by 35 percent, and the dreams of grandeur Mussolini had spoken of so often during the months prior to the war had become an ongoing, waking nightmare.

Rome alone seemed insulated from the war. A city of such unique and vital importance to Western civilization, it had been spared bombardments by the Allied forces. Because of this—and because of the severe shortages elsewhere—the city had attracted from the rest of Italy hundreds of thousands of refugees, who huddled in houses, on stairways, and in doorways.

During these years I continued seeding the north and the south of the country with bunkers under orders of the Italian Ministry of Defense. Montse was hired as a librarian in the Palazzo Corsini library near our house. She was paid only a few hundred lire, but the job allowed her to continue working as a librarian.

In the middle of 1942, I took a trip with Junio, but this time for strictly professional reasons. It seemed the Axis feared an Allied invasion from the south, through Sicily, and they wanted to check (and, if necessary, reinforce) the defenses on Pantelleria, a tiny *isola* located barely seventy kilometers from Cape Mustapha on the Tunisian coast and one hundred kilometers from the Sicilian cape of Granitola. Pantelleria was the port of entry to Sicily, just as Sicily was to the rest of the Italian peninsula. The island had been strongly fortified before the war, and based on what I found there, I could conclude only that nothing more could be done to protect it.

Since there are no hotels on the island, we stayed at a *dammuso*, a typical construction of that region, which showed Arabic influences and surprised me as much for its simplicity as for its efficiency at counteracting the intense heat of summer. Every afternoon, after work, we drove in an Italian army four-wheel-drive vehicle to Cala Tramontana to watch the sunset, with the most beautiful beach on the island in the background and the sirocco winds from Africa forming little whirlwinds at our feet. I have never seen a sea look more like a sky, nor a sky so like a sea.

Our time there was, in a sense, a continuation of our stay at Lake Como, at least as far as Junio's openness with me. I remember one night as we dined by candlelight (electric lights were prohibited in Pantelleria in order to make it more difficult for the Allied bombs to find their targets), he sounded particularly dejected as he told me that the SS had slaughtered more than three hundred Czechs in reprisal for the assassination of Reinhard Heydrich (the ex-chief of the Gestapo, whom Hitler had named the Deputy Reich Protector of Bohemia and Moravia). It hadn't mattered that those responsible had already been caught in Prague and had killed themselves when they saw themselves surrounded by German soldiers; Himmler nonetheless ordered the summary obliteration of the entire population of a village called Lidice. I asked Junio why the Reichsführer had chosen that village and not another.

"Because the inhabitants of Lidice were accused of giving shelter to members of the resistance responsible for Heydrich's assassination. Himmler gave the order to shoot all men over the age of sixteen, deport all the women to the Ravensbrück concentration camp, and send all the children to Berlin for selection and eventual Germanization. Then a squadron of

Jewish prisoners dug the graves to bury the dead. The town was burned, and plowed over, making Lidice literally disappear from the map."

Not long ago I read an Italian newspaper account of the aftermath of the Lidice tragedy; only 143 women returned after the war, and of the 98 children taken to Germany, only 11 had been deemed worthy of Germanization and given to relatives of SS officers. Sixteen others reappeared after the war. The rest perished in the gas chambers of the Chelmno concentration camp.

Junio got up and went outside, as if he needed to stand under a star-studded sky in order to continue speaking about the Reichsführer.

"In the Hague Conventions of 1907, the laws of a land war state that punishment can only be meted out to those who perpetrate acts against the forces of occupation. That man is completely insane. Anyway, Germany will never win the war by slaughtering innocent civilians."

It was the first and last time I heard Junio openly complain about the Germans' conduct in the war. I took advantage of this moment to ask him about rumors circulating in Rome that Jews from all over occupied Europe were being taken to concentration camps to be exterminated. Junio's response, though brief, spoke volumes about his feelings.

"Shortly, Europe will be one big concentration camp and one gigantic cemetery."

That trip brought us closer. The fact that I would lend my skills as an architect to the Italian army made me a part of that army, in his eyes. I don't know if by then he suspected my espionage activities; he never showed any sign that he did. As I have already said, Junio was a pragmatic person, and by the middle of 1942, he seemed to have no doubt that the war would end with Italy's defeat and, therefore, the demise of Fascism. In fact, that trip to Sicily showed us firsthand that Italy had been defeated before a single battle had been waged on its territory, for in addition to the poverty that had spread virulently through the entire south of the country like a malignant tumor, the Italian people had lost faith in their leaders.

Mussolini's downfall was only a matter of time, and by February 1943 his situation had become seriously compromised. His own undersecretary of foreign affairs, Bastianini, was pushing to break off relations with Hitler and make peace with the Allies. One month later, demonstrations broke out at the Fiat factory in Milan when the workers went on strike, claiming long-overdue payments for damages caused by the Allied bombardments. The strike spread to other industries in the north of the country, and the sociopolitical situation became unsustainable. But the worst was yet to come.

JULY 18, 1943, was one of the hottest days of the summer, and Junio appeared at the house to invite Montse and me to the beach at Santa Severa. He had a basket of food and wine, hammocks and folding chairs, towels for everybody, and, of course, a car with a chauffeur. We couldn't refuse.

The day was extremely pleasant. We swam, sunned ourselves, and ate under the ample branches of a pine tree whose shade sheltered half a dozen families who, like us, had used the heat as an excuse to escape from the city and grab a few hours of leisure. Seeing us there, lying in the hammocks or sitting astride the folding chairs, carefree, allowing summer's lethargy to glide slowly over our bodies like drops of sweat, it seemed as if Rome was as yet untouched by the war raging in the other capitals of Europe. After lunch, Montse wrapped herself in a silk blouse and strolled along the beach, looking like a sun-drenched goddess as she collected various types of seashells. Even Gabor couldn't resist the urge to remove his shirt and do a few exercises, impressing the children with his Herculean muscles. Neither Junio nor I left the giant umbrella of shade offered by the pine tree; from there we could contemplate the shore bathed in the emerald sea as we breathed in the sultry breeze strongly seasoned with salt.

The next day, at eleven-fifteen in the morning, the sirens wailed as they often did to warn of the arrival of enemy airplanes. But that day the bombers of the United States Air Force did not simply pass overhead, as they had until then. A cloud of bombs darkened the sky over the city, and the ground began to shake, tremble, and burn. That first bombing left fifteen hundred dead, six thousand wounded, ten thousand homes destroyed, and forty thousand people homeless. There was no water, gas, or electricity for weeks afterward. Rome went from being the *città aperta*, the open city, to being the *città colpita*, the stricken city.

That same day, hundreds of kilometers from Rome, Mussolini met with Hitler in Feltre and received the news of the bombing of Rome; even so, he failed to summon the courage to pull Italy out of its alliance with Germany. Instead, he became sick, and silent.

The next morning the following message was scrawled on one of the buildings struck by a bomb: "*Meio l'americani su la capoccia che Mussolini tra li coioni.*" ("Better the Americans over our heads than Mussolini squeezing our balls.")

King Vittorio Emanuele III, supported by the Fascist Grand Council, decided to disregard Mussolini, break the treaty with Germany, and negotiate peace with the Allies.

Within a few short hours, Rome ceased to be the capital of Italian Fascism and became the anti-Fascist capital of the world. And when, that night, the news of the Duce's removal from office was announced on the radio, the city suddenly lit up and people poured into the streets shouting: "*Abbasso Mussolini! Evviva Garibaldo!*" Bonfires were built to burn every possible object or symbol that had anything to do with Fascism, and the mob even set fire to the editorial offices of *Il Tevere*, one of the newspapers that had supported the regime. A crowd gathered in Piazza Venezia, and another in St. Peter's Square, to thank God and call for peace.

Montse and I also went out to the streets to celebrate Mussolini's fall.

But with the Allied army in Sicily about to cross the Strait of Messina, the Germans couldn't allow the Italians to surrender, so Hitler ordered a show of resistance, establishing a series of defensive lines around Rome and a military occupation of the capital.

On September 10 and 11, battles raged between an Italian contingent (the majority, civilians or soldiers of the dissolved army), which defended Rome, and the German troops, which slowly but surely occupied the city until they were in full control.

On the afternoon of September 11, the Germans plastered the city with the following edict.

THE GERMAN COMMANDER IN CHIEF OF THE SOUTH HEREBY PRO-CLAIMS:

ITALIAN TERRITORY UNDER MY CONTROL IS HEREBY DECLARED A WAR ZONE AND IS SUBJECT TO THE GERMAN LAWS OF WAR.

CRIMES COMMITTED AGAINST THE GERMAN ARMED FORCES WILL BE JUDGED ACCORDING TO THE GERMAN LAWS OF WAR.

STRIKES ARE FORBIDDEN AND WILL BE PUNISHED BY A WAR TRIBUNAL.

ORGANIZERS OF STRIKES, SABOTEURS, AND SNIPERS WILL BE SUMMARILY JUDGED AND EXECUTED.

I WILL MAINTAIN LAW AND ORDER AND ASSIST THE COMPETENT ITALIAN AUTHORITIES BY ALL MEANS NECESSARY TO ASSURE THE WELL-BEING OF THE POPULATION.

ITALIAN WORKERS WHO VOLUNTEER FOR FORCED GERMAN LABOR WILL BE TREATED ACCORDING TO GERMAN STANDARDS AND GIVEN GER-MAN SALARIES.

ITALIAN MINISTERS AND JUDICIAL AUTHORITIES WILL REMAIN IN THEIR POSITIONS.

TRAIN TRANSPORTATION, COMMUNICATIONS, AND MAIL SERVICES WILL BEGIN TO FUNCTION IMMEDIATELY.

UNTIL NEW ORDERS ARE GIVEN, ALL PRIVATE CORRESPONDENCE IS PRO-HIBITED. TELEPHONE CONVERSATIONS SHOULD BE REDUCED TO THE MINIMUM AND WILL BE MONITORED WITH STRICT VIGILANCE.

ALL CIVILIAN AUTHORITY AND ORGANIZATIONS MUST REPORT TO ME FOR THE MAINTENANCE OF PUBLIC ORDER. THEY WILL BE ALLOWED TO CARRY OUT THEIR DUTIES ONLY IF THEY COOPERATE IN AN EXEM-PLARY FASHION WITH THE GERMAN AUTHORITIES EMPLOYING GER-

MAN METHODS FOR THE PREVENTION OF SABOTAGE AND PASSIVE
RESISTANCE.

ROME, SEPTEMBER 11, 1943
FIELD MARSHAL KESSELRING

That night Hitler spoke to the Italians in a radio address from his
wartime headquarters in Rastenburg, in East Prussia. He congratulated
himself on having captured Rome and assured Italy that it would pay
dearly for its betrayal and the downfall of "his most beloved son," referring
to the Duce.

The next day, Mussolini was rescued from his imprisonment in the ski
resort of Gran Sasso by a daring paratroop commander named Otto
Skorzeny and forced to preside over the Italian Social Republic with its
capital in Salò, a small town on the shores of Lake Garda, which was
actually a Nazi bastion.

AMONG THOSE WHO MOST BENEFITED from these changes was Major
Herbert Kappler, who had discovered Mussolini's whereabouts (for which
he was awarded an Iron Cross and promoted to lieutenant colonel), and
his lieutenant, Erich Priebke, who was promoted to captain. Kappler became the SS commander and Himmler's man in Rome. That same day
the Reichsführer called Junio on the phone to ask him to help Kappler in
his difficult new position.

The first order Kappler received from Himmler was to arrest all Jews
in the capital and deport them. Kappler, however, with his firsthand
knowledge of the Italian situation on the ground, knew that such a measure could cause more inconveniences than advantages to the occupying
troops, not to mention the fact that he did not have sufficient manpower
at his disposal to carry it out. His hope, then, was to get Junio and perhaps
the German ambassador to the Holy See, Baron Ernst von Weizsäcker, to
warn the Jewish community. Given how apparently calm the situation

had been and the length of time they had coexisted with the German troops, Rome's Jewish leaders considered Prince Cima Vivarini's and von Weizsäcker's warnings to be exaggerated. They didn't even listen to one of their own rabbis, Israel Zolli, who was convinced that the Nazis' insane plans were for real; he proposed closing the synagogues, withdrawing money from the banks, and dispersing members of the Jewish community among private homes and in Christian monasteries and convents. In the meantime, while Kappler advocated using the Roman Jews to obtain information about the international Jewish "conspiracy," Himmler continued to insist on the necessity of his "Final Solution." Kappler, after meeting with Field Marshal Kesselring in the Wehrmacht commander-in-chief headquarters in Frascati, changed strategies and demanded the sum of fifty kilos of gold within twenty-four hours from the Jewish community in Rome if it wished to avoid the deportation of an unspecified number of its members. Kappler and Kesselring hoped thereby to save the Jews of Rome in exchange for using them as cheap labor, as had happened in Tunisia. Kappler put the gold in a box and sent it to Berlin, to the office of General Kaltenbrunner, hoping that the money would help alleviate the scarcity of funds in the intelligence services of the SS. Himmler responded by dispatching to Rome Captain Theodor Dannecker, who had been in charge of successfully rounding up the Jews of Paris. His message was clear: Kappler and other high-level members of the Nazi command in Rome had been exhibiting erratic and disturbing behavior, having even questioned orders from the high command, and this was unacceptable. Dannecker showed up in Rome with a detachment of the Waffen SS Death's Head Corps, comprised of forty-five men—officers, NCOs, and soldiers. After meeting with Kappler, he asked for reinforcements and a list of all the Jews in Rome. The roundup was planned for the morning of October 16. Though the weather had been unseasonably hot for the autumn, a heavy downpour accompanied the operation. In the ghetto alone more than a thousand Jews were arrested and taken in trucks from the Portico d'Ottavia to the Military College on the banks of the Tiber, barely half a kilometer from Vatican City. The next stop for the prisoners was

Auschwitz concentration camp, from which only one woman and fifteen men survived. When Pius XII found out, he had no choice but to lift canonical restrictions on the city's cloistered convents, thereby providing refuge to the Jews who had not yet been arrested.

Within hours, indignation spread throughout the city. As Kappler had feared, the attack on the Jewish community in Rome spurred on the spirit of resistance in the rest of the population, and acts of sabotage against the forces of occupation multiplied.

That morning after the roundup, I remember Montse got hold of a copy of the clandestine publication *Italia Libera*; one of its headlines read: GERMANS ARE ROUNDING UP ROMANS FOR THEIR CREMATORIUMS IN THE NORTH.

Because of Junio's friendship with Colonel Eugen Dollmann—the nexus of the relationship between the SS and the Italian Fascists—I was sent to work with the Germans on the construction of the defensive lines they hoped would stop the advancing Allied forces.

I was officially proposed for the job over lunch with Junio and Dollmann himself. During the meal, Dollmann spoke extensively about the beauty of Italian women, the hundred ways to cook lobster, how much he liked *tartufo nero*—he was eating blinis with sour cream and caviar—and other banalities related to his refined, sybaritic tastes. His only political comment was a boast about the influence he had over Field Marshal Kesselring, the supreme German military commander in Italy. According to Dollmann, Kesselring had asked him for his opinion about how the Roman population would react to their city being in the hands of the German military.

"I told him that throughout their history, Romans have shown themselves to be averse to uprisings of any kind, whether it's facing the enemy or simply getting out of bed, and that this time it wouldn't be any different. I assured him that they would do nothing more than bide their time, waiting to see whose hands they fell into, the British and Americans or the Germans. And my prognosis was right: that is precisely what they did."

Dollmann was forgetting the more than six hundred Romans who had sacrificed their lives attempting to keep the city from falling into German hands.

He turned to me.

"The prince claims that you are a brilliant young architect. If you agree to work with us, I will grant you the privilege of maintaining contact with your wife, in spite of regulations," he said.

I assumed that Junio was behind that concession. I always wondered why he was so generous with us, assuming he was aware of our secret activities. Even now, the only explanation I can come up with was his love for Montse.

"I don't suppose I have the option to refuse?" I asked, testing Dollmann.

"Of course you do, but then I would have to recommend you for forced labor," he answered without bothering to hide his cynicism.

After downing another glass of wine and forcing out a half-smile, he spoke again in a sarcastic tone.

"Did you know that they call Kesselring 'Smiling Albert'? His smile has frozen on his face, and his patience has run out. He needed 66,000 workers to build the defensive fortifications along the southern front; 16,400 of them were supposed to come from Rome. When only 315 volunteers showed up, Albert got so angry he increased the number of volunteers from Rome to 25,000, and now that they still haven't shown up, he's ordered them to be hunted down in their homes, on the streetcars, and in the buses."

"I was caught in one of those roundups this morning. My driver was getting my car repaired, and so I boarded a streetcar at the Colosseum, and five minutes later the SS surrounded it and ordered everybody off. After examining every man's papers, they took four," Junio said.

"Have you heard the joke General Stahel invented about these roundups? It goes: 'Half of Rome's population is hiding in the houses of the other half.' It's as if the earth had swallowed up all Roman men. But they should realize that if they stay away much longer, we Germans will take their places, and that includes in their beds. I trust you understand me. . . ."

Dollmann let out a loud and grotesque laugh. A few moments later his Italian chauffeur appeared with Cuno, his German shepherd, who trotted over to our table and enthusiastically received the leftovers from his master's meal.

A biography of Dollmann, written in the summer of 1945, was recently published. The author claims that Dollmann was a man of extraordinary intelligence as well as unusual vivacity, for a German, that is. He also suggests that in spite of being vain and lacking any principles, his hedonism probably saved him from committing any acts of abject cruelty.

Clearly Dollmann gave the impression that he was less interested in National Socialism as an ideology than as a means of obtaining his ends, which, in essence, could be summed up as securing for himself the opportunity to live a life surrounded by luxury and dissipation in his comfortable apartment on Via Condotti. From a strictly political point of view, I never met a German official so far removed from the Nazi ethic; by the time lunch was over, I already had my orders, and I hadn't answered a single question. I now think that meeting was just an excuse for Dollmann to eat a sumptuous meal with his friend Prince Cima Vivarini. Junio's recommendation alone would have sufficed; Dollmann couldn't have cared less about me.

I DON'T REMEMBER ever having worked so much and so hard in my life. In addition to the great urgency to complete the project, there were huge distances that had to be covered and a wide range of topographies—from the steep cliffs of La Mainarde to the gentle slopes of the Aurunci Mountains. Also, by this time the Allies had already come ashore on the Salerno beaches and pushed the German Tenth Army to the north, beyond the Volturno River, just forty kilometers from our position. Churchill's intention was to convert the boot of Italy into the Achilles' heel of the German army, opening up a wound that would force Hitler to neglect the Eastern and Western fronts. But Kesselring was a difficult commander to wear down, and he was determined to offer more resistance than expected.

The Gustav Line, the main German defensive structure, began in the mountainous region of Abruzzo, had one of its axes in Monte Cassino, then continued along the Garigliano and Rapido rivers to the sea. We had only a few days, with torrential rains and mercilessly cold temperatures, to clear undergrowth, plant mines, and build defenses that included underground tank turrets, bunkers, casemates with rocket launchers, and sites for eighty-eight millimeter cannons.

When I wasn't rushing from one place to another to oversee the construction, I worked in the cloister designed by Bramante in the Abbey of Monte Cassino. Built in 1595, it reminded me of the Spanish Academy. From the balcony, looking west, there was a splendid panoramic view of the Liri Valley. Even today, when I close my eyes, I can see the Abbey of Monte Cassino, intact, before the bombs of the Allied air forces reduced it to rubble and the Liri Valley became a cemetery for Polish soldiers.

I not only kept constantly busy with work but I found time to write to Montse. Once the second Smith found out about the duties Dollmann had assigned me, he instructed me to get the information from the front to them through her (Montse passed my letters to Marco, the waiter at the Pollarolo Pizzeria). The code we used was very simple: I wrote a series of supposedly innocent sentences that relayed important military information. For example, if I wrote, "The view from the abbey is splendid," this meant that there were no German troops in the vicinity. If I wrote, "I miss holding you," it meant that the German troops were taking up positions in the neighboring towns. One of the advantages of this way of enciphering messages was that we didn't need a book of codes, thus didn't run the risks such a possession would entail.

Even though all letters went through German military censorship, not one of my messages was ever intercepted.

When I finished my work in Monte Cassino, I was taken to the Reinhard Line, situated a few kilometers from the Gustav Line, and then to the Senger-Riegel Line, also known as the Hitler Line, which connected Pontecorvo, Aquino, and Piedimonte San Germano. There was yet another line of defense before reaching the capital, but I did not participate in its construction because I was called away to Berlin.

The shock of such a summons took my breath away. Considering that throughout Italy deportations had multiplied by a factor of a thousand, as had the reasons for which one could be executed or sent to a concentration camp, I feared the worst.

Five hours later I found myself at 155 Via Tasso, the headquarters of the Gestapo in Rome, with Junio, Colonel Eugen Dollmann, and an SS captain named Ernst, who would accompany me to Germany. It seemed the time had come for me to work for the Hochtief Construction Company.

Almost a head taller than Gabor, and a little blonder, Ernst looked like he had come out of one of Himmler's laboratories. He had been trained to receive orders and carry them out, and I swear I have never known anyone who took his work so seriously. If I told Ernst I had to go to the bathroom, he would accompany me to the door and remain there until I came out. During our flight in a modern Junker-52, which could carry fifteen passengers, he confessed to me that he had belonged to the Einsatzgruppen, the mobile killing units that had attacked Jews and Gypsies in Eastern Europe. He had, however, been unable to withstand the psychological effects of shooting defenseless people, often women and children, and had been sent to Rome, where the climate was considered propitious for the recovery of the spirit. Now, after a year, he felt strong enough to return home and continue to fight against the enemy, even if from behind a desk. I asked him what he had done before the war.

"I sold sausages. I owned a butcher shop in Dresden."

I was allowed to go home to pick up some clothes before the trip, and so was able to say good-bye to Montse.

I couldn't find a way to soften the blow, so I simply blurted out, "They're sending me to Germany." Seeing her astonishment, I continued. "There's a German officer waiting for me downstairs, so I don't have much time for explanations. If you want to get in touch with me, talk to Junio. He'll know where to find me."

We fell into a long embrace, which might, I thought, be our last. When we finally let go of each other, she told me the news.

"Father Sansovino is dead; he committed suicide."

My stomach turned. I knew something was wrong. "But priests are forbidden to commit suicide."

"They say that Sansovino discovered that Father Robert Liebert, the pope's personal assistant, was being spied on by the Germans. So Kappler ordered Sansovino's arrest as soon as he stepped outside the Vatican on Roman soil. Junio told me that when the priest saw himself surrounded by the Gestapo, he bit into a cyanide capsule he always carried with him."

"He'll go to hell. We'll all go to hell," I muttered, unable to hide the fury that overwhelmed me.

Hurriedly, I grabbed a paper and pencil and sketched out the Gustav, Reinhard, and Senger-Riegel lines, detailing the spots where the German defenses were placed and making a few notes that would help locate them.

"Make sure Smith gets these plans," I said to her, adding, "The safest place for you to meet him is in the Santa Cecilia crypt. But make sure nobody is following you. If you get arrested, we're both finished."

"Don't worry, I'll be careful."

"One more thing. The Smith you'll be meeting isn't the same Smith you met at the Protestant Cemetery. That first Smith died a long time ago. I don't know why, but I never found the right moment to tell you."

Montse shrugged. "It doesn't matter now."

As I descended the stairs, I felt as if I were descending into hell.

8.

I NOTICED SEVERAL THINGS when I first landed at the airport at Tempelhof. The first was that the installations were in an excellent state of repair. The second was how easy it was to go through customs, because everybody who traveled to Germany had already been investigated and classified. In my case, not only had I been recruited by the largest construction company in Germany but I could count on a report signed by Dollmann that spoke of my contribution to the defenses in the south of Italy. The third was the overall peaceful atmosphere, almost as if the war were something of no consequence. After a brief questioning at Gestapo offices, I was given food coupons for an entire week, and a chauffeur drove Ernst and me downtown.

Berlin was beginning to reflect Hitler's goal of leaving his legacy written in "documents of stone." To this end, he had employed Albert Speer, one of Germany's most distinguished architects, to transform provincial Berlin into cosmopolitan "Germania," the new capital of Germany, which would surpass cities such as Paris or Vienna in both beauty and magnificence. The project, planned for completion in 1950, included an avenue wider than the Champs-Elysées, an enormous arch 80 meters in height, and a kind of conference hall crowned with a dome 250 meters in diameter. It was to be built of stone, for the buildings were supposed to last a thousand years, along with the Third Reich itself. In the meantime, Speer was in charge of the construction of the provisional New Reich's Chancellery, a monumental building of colossal dimensions that he managed to complete in one year.

The magnitude of the buildings was overwhelming, effectively shrinking the individual through sheer size and intimidation. This was an architecture ruled by horizontality and symmetry; it was also pompous and reiterative. But, just like Italian Fascist architecture, behind those inexpressive, fortress-like buildings stood nothing more than an immense vacuum.

I also noticed that flower gardens had been replaced by cultivated fields planted with potatoes and vegetables. In the fall of 1943, Berlin was already the capital of a defeated nation, despite the propaganda claiming otherwise. This was, in fact, corroborated by my very presence. Hochtief had requested my services to assist them in converting the city into a gigantic antiaircraft refuge, something in direct contradiction with the Germania of Albert Speer.

In spite of numerous measures taken to snuff out dissident movements within the country, it was evident that a portion of the population did not share the Nazis' ideology. Germany was carrying on a double life, and that next to the Germany of the swastika-bearing flags, the uniforms, and the columns of soldiers—portrayed exhaustively on the radio and in the movies—there existed another, secret Germany, very different, omnipresent in a vague yet palpable way. One might even assert that Germany resembled a palimpsest or a retouched painting: if you patiently and carefully removed the surface façade, there appeared underneath a completely different text or picture—one possibly damaged in the process of revelation—that formed an integral part of a coherent and harmonious whole.

Nine years have passed since then, and the sounds of the sirens and the incessant noise of the bombs whistling through the sky still echo in my head. After the middle of November, the bombing of Berlin intensified. First it was the British Royal Air Force, the RAF, whose incursions always occurred at night. Later the skies of Berlin began to be furrowed by the Flying Fortresses of the United States Air Force, which preferred to dump their deadly cargo during the day. Thus the city was transformed into an immense crater, and many of its streets became jagged scars. Two-thirds of the buildings collapsed or suffered some kind of damage, and all who could, fled from the city.

But those of us who had no possibility of leaving Berlin were forced to spend a good part of every day and night in one of the subway stations—foreigners were not allowed in the antiaircraft bunkers reserved exclusively for people of the Aryan race.

One night, while waiting in one of the tunnels of the Niederschöne-weide station for an RAF bombardment to come to an end, a Spanish member of the SS approached me. His name was Miguel Ezquerra, an ex-officer of Spain's Blue Division, who had chosen to remain in Germany after the division's dissolution. He was now a member of the German intelligence services, and the Nazis had sent him on a mission to recruit all the Spaniards he could find to form a Spanish unit of the SS. He claimed he had already recruited more than a hundred men, most of whom were workers sent by Franco to the weapons factories; they had lost their jobs when the factories were destroyed by bombs.

"What do you say? Will you join?" he asked.

"I'm working as an architect for Hochtief," I answered evasively.

"I don't mean now, at this moment, but later, when things get worse."

At that moment a bomb exploded a few meters away, and a fine shower of dust fell over our heads.

"That damn butcher Harris! That was close," Ezquerra said.

Sir Arthur T. Harris, air marshal of the RAF, had earned this nickname from the residents of Berlin after giving the order to replace explosive bombs with incendiary ones, which were much more effective in undermining the morale of the civilian population.

"I live in Rome. My family is waiting for me there," I said when calm had returned to the shelter.

I used the word *family* in order to give legitimacy to my desire to return home.

"The way things are going now, you might not be able to leave Berlin."

If there was anything that made me despair, besides the fear of getting wounded or killed in a bombardment, it was considering the possibility of having to remain in Berlin until the end of the war, far from Montse.

"If I can't return to Rome, it will mean that Germany has lost the war," I pointed out.

I must say I was surprised that subway stations such as Niederschöne-weide, Friedrichstrasse, or Anhalter were full of men like Miguel Ezquerra: Latvians, Estonians, French, Georgians, Turks, Hindus, even a few English Fascists, willing to give their lives for the Third Reich.

I met Ezquerra again during the intensive bombing raids that took place between November 22 and November 26. This time he was accompanied by one of his subordinates, a man named Liborio. He had a lost look in his eyes and a nervous tic in his eyelids, and his only concern was to appease his constant hunger. When the news spread that the Allied firebombing had destroyed the Berlin Zoo, he said, "If we hurry, maybe we can find a dead crocodile or bear! Maybe they're even barbecued already! That's the only good thing about these damn firebombs: they leave the meat cooked and ready to eat."

"Do you like bear meat?" Ezquerra asked me.

"I've already eaten, thank you."

"Oh, yes, of course, you people who live in places like Unter den Linden and Alexanderplatz, you eat every day, don't you?"

"Regulation food, like everybody. Cabbage, potatoes . . ."

"Wrong there. In Berlin *everybody* has stopped eating. If things go on like this, I predict we'll start eating each other," Ezquerra said.

Clearly, I had no choice but to invite them to eat at the Stoeckler Restaurant on Kurfürstendamm. I took twenty-five grams of meat, a few more of potatoes, and thirty grams of bread from my rations, and we got three powdered flans for free. The powdered flans were invented by IG Farben, who also produced eggs, butter, and other nutritious foods using a chemical process. Later I learned that IG Farben was the largest chemical factory in the world, and that it produced the Zyklon B gas used to kill millions of Jews, Gypsies, and homosexuals in the concentration camps.

Ezquerra, feeling generous now that he had a full stomach, invited me to the Humboldt Club on the Sunday before Christmas. There the German authorities would be giving a reception in honor of foreigners living in Berlin.

"There'll be food and dancing, in spite of the restrictions," he confided to me. "At least last year they let us sing and dance," he added.

I made my excuses, claiming to have already been invited to dinner that night with the directors of Hochtief.

We went on to talk about the probability that the Russians would reach Berlin, and how scared the population was at this prospect.

"Ivan"—for this is how the people of Berlin referred to the Russians—"will never step foot in the streets of Berlin," Liborio declared, "because the Führer is holding an ace up his sleeve: secret weapons, deadly weapons that will change the course of the war."

Then Ezquerra, exercising his authority, pulled on Liborio's sleeve and pointed to a poster on the wall of the restaurant, the same one that was in all public buildings and vehicles: CAREFUL: THE ENEMY IS LISTENING.

By the time we left the restaurant, the city had fallen under a dense and murky darkness you could almost touch; as usual, as soon as night came, the residents of Berlin covered their windows with black paper.

On another occasion, the bombs began to whistle through the air while I was walking down the street. Not knowing the city well, I couldn't find an entrance to an underground station fast enough, so I took refuge in a doorway. There I bumped into a small Asian woman who had thrown herself to the ground and was covering her head with her arms. At her side lay her *Luftschutzkoffer*, the small antiaircraft bag everyone was required to carry at all times with personal documents, ration coupons, a change of clothes, and some food. Perhaps she was a servant who, like I, was forbidden from entering the antiaircraft shelters. Two minutes later a bomb hit the roof of the building where we stood, and a shower of glass and rubble fell through the stairwell. That shower was followed by another of water and sand, possibly from a bathtub or the buckets of water and sand every house was supposed to keep behind the door. Then a second bomb fell in the middle of the street, about sixty or seventy meters from where we were standing, forming a gigantic crater. When a third bomb tore off the façade of the building across the street, I realized we had better get out of there as soon as possible. The problem was figuring out where to go. I motioned to the woman to follow me, but she was paralyzed by fear. I picked her up in my arms and carried her to the crater just as another bomb hit the building and destroyed it. We had just barely escaped. The roar of the antiaircraft bombs and artillery became unbearable, and the woman curled up in my arms like a flower closing up at night. We remained there for about half an hour, our bodies pressed tightly together, leaving no chink through which death could squeeze. Although we did not exchange a word, each knew what the other was thinking at every instant, after each explosion. When the bombing stopped, I peered out over the edge of the crater to see what was going on. I found myself face-to-face with hundreds of German soldiers running back and forth through the rubble, like a column of ants though more chaotic, building fortifications with bags of earth and placing pieces of heavy weaponry here and there. Another group was working on extinguishing the incendiary bombs, which, like incandescent gold ingots, sparked and crackled, continuously setting off numerous new fires. The only way to counteract them was to cover them with sand. Then I looked up at the sky and saw hundreds of rising columns of smoke, dust, and fire. When I looked back inside the crater for the woman, she had disappeared.

The efficiency of the RAF bombings had intensified once the British discovered that the shortwave radios of the German antiaircraft batteries emitted signals that bounced off the metal of their airplanes, thereby revealing their exact location. To foil this system, the RAF pilots threw sheets of tinfoil out of their planes. Often after a ferocious bombardment, scraps of tinfoil would rain down on our heads.

Another vivid memory I have of Berlin is the visit I made, with about half a dozen directors of Hochtief, to the office of Albert Speer, then minister for weaponry and munitions of the Third Reich and after the war condemned to twenty years of prison for crimes against humanity and war crimes by the Nuremberg Tribunal. When I met him he was already a defeated and troubled man who had just received news of the destruction of the Peenemünde air base, one of the German army's most important centers for rocket development.

During that meeting, we discussed building a new bunker for the Führer, in addition to the antiaircraft bunker in the gardens of the Old Reich Chancellery. No one would have dared say so outright, but this was clearly another sign that the Nazis knew they were losing the war.

Although I never saw the finished plans, I did have the opportunity to look over some of the designs and was even consulted on certain technical aspects of the project. In this way I found out they were talking about building a bunker fifteen meters underground, with two floors, each one about twenty by eleven meters, and connected to the original 1936 bunker through a staircase, with an emergency exit and a conical turret for ventilation and protection. The walls would be two and a half meters thick, with a roof of reinforced concrete and steel between three and five meters wide.

But it was the model of Germania that drew my attention more powerfully than anything else in Speer's office. It showed a city built around a cross formed by two enormous avenues, one running north-south and the other east-west; from it radiated streets and boulevards in concentric circles like a dense spiderweb 50 kilometers in diameter. The avenues—some as wide as 120 meters and as long as 7 kilometers—symbolized the attainment of the lebensraum, or vital space. The heart of this imaginary city was the Volkshalle, or People's Hall, the largest building ever designed: 290 meters high and weighing 9 million tons, with a holding capacity of between 150,000 and 180,000 people.

Anyone wishing to study the evolution of war today has only to take a look at the trajectory of Speer's architectural work; he began by designing a utopian city on an extraordinary scale and ended up building fortresses such as his "Riese," a huge underground refuge constructed with 257,000 cubic meters of concrete and steel and 100 kilometers of pipes in the Góry Sowie Mountains. Certainly, by 1944, the Third Reich was buried, condemned to live out its days in ever-deeper passageways. In a way, Himmler's dream of finding an underground world became a reality, and if the war had been prolonged, I am sure the Nazis would have continued digging into the bowels of the earth until they reached Hell itself.

There was nothing more for me to do in Berlin, but leaving was not easily accomplished; I needed an exit visa from the police, but only the so-called *Ausgebombte*, or victims of the bombings, were given them. I had to turn to Junio, and he to Colonel Eugen Dollmann.

As the airplane traced an arc over the skies of Berlin, I contemplated the city below me sinking into its own rubble. Throughout the four long months I had been there, I had had many opportunities to see the face of destruction; but now, from the air, for the first time in my life, I saw it all at once: a dying city surrounded by snowy fields that looked like shrouds.

9.

I RETURNED TO ROME in the middle of February 1944, and although
the city was still standing, the Romans were despairing. The Four-
teenth German Army had come to Kesselring's aid from the north of
Italy, which had so far prevented the Allied troops from landing on the
beaches of Anzio and Nettuno. The Romans' disappointment at the
delay in being liberated when the Allies were already so close could be
summed up in the irony expressed in the graffiti along Viale Trastevere
that read: "Americans, don't despair! We'll liberate you soon!" In addition, the Allied bombing raids had become more and more frequent; a
clear, windless day became known as *una giornata da B-17*, the name of
the American Flying Fortresses. Hunger gnawed away at the population,
infectious diseases had begun to spread, and there was potable water
only in neighborhoods where Germans were living. Wehrmacht para-
troopers stood guard day and night on the other side of the white line
that separated the Vatican City State from occupied Rome. There were
more and more roundups of forced labor to work on the Reich's projects,
and operations intent on ending the resistance intensified. Telephone
lines were often cut, and the authorities listened in on private calls.
Speaking in English on the phone was considered a crime. Helping the
"evaders" or the "refugees" was punishable by death. Rome, in short, had
become a frontier city, wild and lawless, situated in a no-man's-land

between two enemy armies and two worlds in conflict. Suspicion, contraband, terror, intimidation, and jockeying for advantage were the norm during those months of the German occupation. Herbert Kappler himself and his second in command, Captain Erich Priebke, personally took charge of interrogations, and the Gestapo headquarters on Via Tasso turned into the city's cruelest, most sophisticated torture center. Rumor had it that Kappler and Priebke used brass knuckles, barbed clubs, whips, blowtorches, nails driven into flesh and under fingernails, and even chemical injections to get information out of the prisoners. And as if what the Germans were doing wasn't enough, the Italian Fascists created a special police unit, known as the Koch Gang. Its leader, Pietro Koch, who wanted to be addressed as "Doctor," was an Italian of German parentage whose specialty was hunting down partisans. The chief of police, Tamburini, set up his headquarters at the Pensione Oltremare on Via Principe Amadeo, near the Termini Station. The torture techniques used by the Koch Gang were even more refined than those used by the Germans, and included iron bars, wooden maces, presses for breaking bones, sharp objects driven into the prisoners' temples, the pulling out of nails and teeth, as well as filling prisoners' mouths with ash or pubic hair. By the end of April, needing a larger space to carry out their activities (for the Oltremare Hotel occupied only one floor and the neighbors were complaining about the noise), Koch and his men took over the Pensione Jaccarino, a beautiful Tuscan-style manor house on Via Romagna, which was converted into a residence and center for torture, kidnapping, and interrogations. Among the many macabre anecdotes told about Koch's Gang was that one of its members was a Benedictine monk known as "Epaminonda"; his job was to play Schubert on the piano while the prisoners were being tortured so that their shouts would not be heard outside the building. At the same time, dozens of clandestine Communist, Socialist, and monarchist organizations were operating, not to mention the secret services of the Allied powers. While before, Rome had gone from being a *città aperta* to being a *città colpita* due to the bombings, it had now become a *città esplosiva*, on the verge of erupting.

The SS stopped me twice at random when I was in the tram on my way to work. In both cases, I was exempted from forced labor because of my services to the Reich in southern Italy and Berlin. But all of this was about to change.

One afternoon, when I got home, I found Junio there. His face was grave, and the fact that he was wearing his Fascist uniform lent a certain official nature to his visit. Montse was sitting next to him, but she seemed upset, and she quickly stood up as soon as I entered the room. Junio spoke first.

"They have arrested the leader of an illegal organization named "Smith." Among the documents they confiscated were some plans of the German lines of defense. They have proven that it is your handwriting on the papers. Tonight Kappler will sign an order for your arrest. I've been telling Montse that you should go into hiding."

I didn't even attempt to defend myself.

"I suppose this had to happen sooner or later," I said with resignation.

"The Germans are taking the issue of clandestine organizations very seriously," Junio responded flatly. "They want to finish off the resistance at all costs."

"What happened to Smith?" I asked.

"He did not survive the Gestapo's interrogations. But he did not give your name. As I said, the Germans got to you by other means."

Realizing that Smith also hadn't given Montse's name to the Germans reassured me.

I looked at Montse and sat down. "What should I do?" I asked her helplessly.

"Remember the apartment on Via dei Coronari?" Junio asked. "You'll be safe there until things get back to normal."

"I'm to remain in hiding until the Germans have left Rome?"

"You will need a lot of patience."

"Why are you helping me?" I asked point-blank.

Junio returned my gaze. "Because I don't care what you might have done," he said, finally. "It doesn't matter anymore. And," he added, "there's Montse to consider."

"I'm not going to leave her alone. If the Germans don't find me, they'll take her."

"I'll protect her. She'll be safe with me."

That was precisely what I was trying to avoid. I didn't want to leave her in his hands. I didn't want to be indebted to him for saving both our lives. The job I had I owed to Junio; if we needed food or medicine, he got them for us. He had too much power over our lives; things had gone too far.

"Maybe you don't understand," I stated firmly. "I want to be the one to protect her."

We were speaking about Montse as if she wasn't there, though she was following our conversation with close attention.

"I'm afraid that won't be possible in your current situation," Junio stated bluntly.

"Can you leave us alone for a few minutes?" Montse interrupted, turning to Junio. "I need to talk to José María alone."

"Of course," said the prince. "I'll wait downstairs in the car."

"Thank you."

The minute Junio closed the door behind him, I said, "I don't want to put you in danger, but I don't want to be apart from you ever again."

"I think it is too late for that," she said flatly.

I suddenly realized that something profound had changed in our marriage during my absence in Berlin. "What do you mean?"

Montse turned to one of the bookshelves in the room and leafed through the pages of a book until she found a pamphlet with the title "The Rules of Partisan Struggle." She handed it to me and I read a random paragraph, which recommended beginning with the simplest actions, like throwing four-pointed nails along roads most frequently used by enemy vehicles or spreading wires from one side of a road to the other to "saw off" the heads of drivers and passengers of enemy motorcycles.

"What the hell is this?" I asked her.

"I've met some people . . ." she stammered.

"What people?" I asked.

"Members of the resistance, of the Patriotic Action Groups," Montse said.

"You mean murderers! What they are recommending isn't very different from what the Germans are doing."

"Yes, it is!" she shot back. "They are struggling for a just cause!"

"Cutting off heads?" I emphasized my words by waving the paper in front of her face.

"It's necessary," she said automatically, as if she were praying.

"I still remember how you reacted when your father and Secretary Olarra justified the killing of German Jews on Kristallnacht."

"The circumstances are totally different," she said, defending herself. "I've promised I would help, and nothing will make me change my mind."

"You also promised to remain by my side, in sickness and in health," I reminded her.

"My decision has nothing to do with our marriage," she retorted.

"Then who does it have to do with?"

"With me, José María. It has to do with my conscience."

I began to feel like a blackmailer trying to force an honorable person to trust me. "And now your conscience tells you to abandon me and devote yourself to murdering Germans?"

"You are being terribly unfair. I think this simply isn't the best time for you to be asking me to be a model wife."

The truth was that after the long months I had spent first on the Gustav Line and then in Berlin, that was precisely what I wanted. But by then Montse, like a large segment of the Roman population, had imbibed the inexhaustible spirit of resistance, which was wholly at odds with a peaceful domestic life.

"Can I know where you met those people?" I asked, continuing the interrogation.

"You really want to know?"

I nodded.

"They came looking for you."

"Looking for me?"

"They were going to kill you. They believed you were a collaborator, that we were traitors. I had to tell them the truth, about Smith and your drawings. We are now all fighting the same enemy."

I felt she still didn't understand the dangers she was facing.

"You heard Junio. Smith died in the hands of the Gestapo. God knows I'll never forgive myself if you end up like him."

As I feared, this outburst did not have the intended effect.

"If I go into hiding with you, I would have to live the rest of my life with the feeling that I didn't do enough."

"We've already done enough. If we hadn't, the Germans wouldn't be after me."

"The war is being fought on the streets of Rome, and I have no intention of going into hiding," she said, unwavering.

"Have you been assigned a particular mission?" I asked, resigned to her once again gaining the upper hand.

"Tomorrow I have to go pick up a box of four-pointed nails at a hardware store in Trastevere, and the next day I may have to pass out some clandestine literature."

Few things upset the Germans as much as those four-pointed nails, a stroke of genius the partisans had resurrected from the era of Caesar's Rome, which had shown itself to be incredibly effective at puncturing the tires of the Nazi army's motorized vehicles.

"Have your friends told you that if they catch you in possession of those nails, they'll shoot you?"

"I know. It's a risk I have to take. Delivering nails or passing out leaflets that call for an uprising are part of the training. I will be assigned a more important mission as soon as I've finished my training," Montse said.

"What kind of mission?"

Montse paused for a few seconds. Then she said, "To kill Junio."

For a moment I thought she was joking, but the tense expression on her face made me understand that she spoke in deadly earnest.

"Are you going to do it?" I asked her.

"That's precisely what I was talking to him about when you arrived. I've told him to leave Rome, because if it's not me, it will be another comrade who will take his life."

I ignored her use of the word *comrade*. "What did Junio say?"

"That I shouldn't worry about his safety, that he knows how to protect himself, and that if I promise not to make any attempts on his life, he promises to save yours."

"And, naturally, you agreed."

"Yes."

"So, you have pardoned him in exchange for his saving my life."

"More or less."

"I'm going to pack."

"I gave away some of your clothes," she said.

"You what?"

"Only what you didn't need."

"Can I know to whom?"

"Refugees, some Jews who are hiding in the house of some friends, soldiers who have deserted the Italian army and refused to take orders from the German military authorities. Anybody who needs them."

"I don't recognize you, Montse."

"Did you really think I was going to sit here twiddling my thumbs while you were risking your life in Berlin? I had absolutely no guarantee that I would ever see you again. Anyway, I needed to give my life some meaning."

"Your life has meaning."

"No life has meaning under the cruelest dictatorship humanity has ever seen," she answered.

What more could I say? Nobody can argue with fanaticism, and Montse had gone from being an idealist to being a fanatic; she was now cold and calculating rather than passionate and vehement. I had yet to find out how far she was willing to go.

IO.

WHEN I FINALLY GOT INTO Junio's car I was determined to retain some shred of dignity despite the conversation I had just had with Montse. I didn't want his compassion, and, moreover, I wasn't willing to acknowledge what he was about to do for me. But a moment later, when I found myself alone with him after such a long time, I changed my mind. There were many things I wished to tell him, and many doubts I hoped he could allay.

"Everything okay?" he asked me as we drove off.

"More or less. May I ask you a question?"

"Of course."

"Would you have offered to help me without Montse?"

Junio subjected me to a thorough scrutiny, then offered me an inscrutable smile. "Of course I would have. Believe me, I have always held you in high esteem."

At that moment I realized that he was driving in a slightly erratic manner, as if he didn't know how to handle the pedals, the steering wheel, and the gears at the same time.

"Where's Gabor?"

"I've given him the day off. Let's say it's better for him not to know certain things."

"Like your betrayal of the Reich?"

"It's not a betrayal."

"So what is it?"

"A bit of humanitarianism. Having a little common sense in the middle of this collective insanity. Respect for the lives of individuals must always be above ideologies, don't you agree?"

I was about to ask him when and why he had changed his opinion.

"Anyway, if I allowed Kappler to torture and execute you, I would have to carry the burden of your death for the rest of my life," he continued.

"But then you could also 'carry the burden' of the widow," I said.

Junio took this additional blow with exemplary chivalry. After all, perhaps he really was a gentleman, no matter how often he dressed up as a Nazi.

"Montse is a strong woman, she always has been. No man will 'carry' her if she is left a widow. You, on the other hand . . . just look at you."

"What about me?"

"You'd make a terrible widower. You'd take to drink or something of the kind."

"Suicide's always an option," I said.

"No, not for you."

"How can you be so sure?"

"Because if you kill yourself, you'll miss out on the pleasure of feeling guilty. It would put an end to your self-pity, and without Montse, the only reason for your existence would be precisely that: to exacerbate your own suffering, sink into the dark hole of despair, lift yourself up, then fall again, endlessly. This is the only way some people can tolerate life, wallowing in their own misery."

A gang of Fascists making truculent gestures and shouting in high-pitched voices greeted the prince as we drove by Palazzo Braschi.

"Long live princes Junio Valerio Cima Vivarini and Junio Valerio Borghese!" shouted the youngest member of the group.

Prince Borghese was the leader of the Decima MAS, a unit of the Italian army that had always been loyal to Mussolini and the Germans, even at the most difficult moments.

"Those, on the other hand . . . they enjoy making others suffer," Junio continued, returning their greeting without enthusiasm.

"They hail you as a hero."

"He who flatters you today will shoot you tomorrow. I assure you, the day I have to flee, I'll be sure not to do so in the company of such individuals. I don't even plan to let Gabor come with me."

"No? I thought you two were very close."

"Merely comrades in arms. Gabor is the price I've had to pay to earn the Nazis' trust. He is in charge of watching me, though he thinks I don't know, and in exchange I let him do the dirty work. It might seem like I've tamed him, but that's only a façade. When he was chosen to fornicate for the Reich, I thought I'd gotten rid of him forever. But his semen wasn't as good as he and the Germans had thought, so they sent him back to me 'with his tail between his legs,' so to speak. In other words, I have kept my antipathy for him well hidden for many years. No, I'll escape alone, that's why I've decided to learn to drive, once and for all."

Junio's tone of voice was as unexpected as the words themselves. It was as if he were rehearsing a strategy out loud, practicing for when things got even more twisted.

"Where do you plan to go?"

"I still don't know, maybe some remote spot in Africa or Asia. The important thing is to find a place where I don't understand the natives and they don't understand me. And no matter how long I stay there, I don't plan on learning the native language or adapting to their local customs, because what I want is precisely to be isolated. I feel nothing but disdain for the world we have created, even now that we have destroyed it."

A new group of Fascists lifted their arms to salute us as our car drove by.

"*Porci, carogne fasciste!*" I shouted.

"If shouting makes you feel better, go right ahead, just make sure none of those madmen hears you, because then not even I could stop them from stringing you up on a lamppost. And if something should happen to you, I'm sure Montse would carry out her threat."

"What did you think when she told you she had orders to kill you?"

"I didn't think anything. I only felt. I felt . . . deeply discomfited. Once I had overcome the first shock, I did manage to formulate a few thoughts."

"Such as?"

"Such as if I had to die, there would be nobody better than she to press the trigger. It's not the same to be shot by an angel as by a devil, don't you agree? Then I thought that I've never known anybody as brave as she is. Finally, I thought of you . . . and I felt deeply envious, because your wife was granting me a pardon in exchange for my saving you, and I think that is a reflection of the love she has for you."

"Why, then, doesn't she want to go into hiding with me until all this blows over?"

"Precisely because she is such a brave woman."

It occurred to me then to ask him for an unusual favor.

"If Montse is arrested . . ." I said hesitantly, "I'd like her not to suffer, to have a sweet death. . . ."

Junio looked at me in surprise. "Are you asking *me* to kill her if she falls into German hands?"

"You are the only person I know who would have access to her if she were arrested. I don't want that monster Kappler to get his hands on her. I couldn't bear it if her last experience of this world was a blowtorch burning the soles of her feet."

There was now deep reproach in Junio's eyes as he looked at me. "I have the feeling you care less about what might happen to her than about the suffering her suffering would cause you."

"It's not that complicated," I said.

"Oh, really? Let's see: Montse grants me a pardon in exchange for my saving your life, and now that the two of us are safe, you suggest that it be I who kills your wife. I'm afraid that sounds pretty complicated."

"Forget it."

"Of course I'm going to forget it, and this whole conversation, and for your own good I hope you do, too. You're going to have to spend a while shut up in a house, alone, and I don't think you'll be able to stand it for long with that attitude."

"Can I have visitors?"

"One person will bring you food once a week."

"Must it be one person in particular?"

"Yes, it must be one particular individual. They will have to follow certain safety protocols."

"Couldn't Montse be that person? We've just spent more than four months apart, and many more months might pass before the Allies take over the city."

"I'm surprised they haven't done so yet," Junio said. "But—okay, I'll work things out so that Montse is the one to bring your food."

"I am very grateful."

"You don't have to be grateful to me for anything; I'm only thinking of my own future! The warrant for your arrest signed by Kappler will open many doors for you once the city changes management, and the same for Montse now that she 'works' for the resistance. If I'm arrested trying to escape, I'll count on both of you to intercede on my behalf."

"Is there anything else I should know?"

"There's a radio and a few books in the house. Read and relax. Keep the shutters closed, and if for any reason you feel the need to open them, try not to show yourself at the window. And, needless to say, don't open the door to anybody you don't know and trust. If somebody you don't know comes to the door, look carefully through the peephole and wait for the password: *casalinga*. As soon as there is any news, I'll let you know. There's a set of keys in the glove compartment. Take them."

We drove the rest of the way in silence.

When we arrived, I waited in the car until the street was empty. We then said good-bye with a long, firm handshake. I expected never to see him again.

Once on the pavement, I became aware of the effect Junio's driving had had on my stomach. I vomited right in front of the door to 23 Via dei Coronari. Then I climbed the stairs, two at a time, hoping I had not been seen.

II.

I F MARCH, the first month of my confinement, was characterized by a series of dramatic events, April and May brought hunger and exhaustion. Rome had become little more than a trophy of war the Allies wanted to claim and the Nazis wanted to retain at any cost. As usual, the first victims were the people, who watched as the Allied bombings destroyed convoys of supplies regardless of whether they were being escorted by the Red Cross or the Vatican. If Rome was hungry, there was more chance that the Romans would rise up against their occupiers, or so the Allies thought. The Germans, however, believed that hunger, in combination with the Allied bombings, played against the Allies. Both sides strangled the city, and when the scarcity of food became desperate and there was not enough left to feed the population for more than a few days, the Nazis reinitiated their roundups of forced labor, though this time they had a secondary purpose: by deporting thousands to the north of Italy or Germany, they had that many fewer mouths to feed.

Meanwhile, the resistance was active and Montse was in its ranks. I suppose the fact that I was truly in love with my wife complicated matters, for what made my confinement most trying was not knowing where she was and whom she was with at every minute, and whether or not her life was in danger. To make matters worse, when I settled into the apartment on Via dei Coronari, I saw I had enough food for a whole week; I knew that this was how long I would have to wait for Montse's first visit.

When she finally came, she looked thinner, maybe because she was wearing my raincoat and was carrying a knapsack full of food.

"The Germans came looking for you the same night you left. You've escaped by the skin of your teeth," she told me after rewarding me with a kiss on the lips.

The thought occurred to me that if I had been arrested and tortured, the only name I could have given the Germans, now that the second Smith and Father Sansovino were dead, was hers.

"Did they harass you?" I asked her.

"I told them I hadn't heard from you since you'd been back from Germany, and I pretended I didn't care about you anymore. Then I showed them there weren't any men's clothes in the house. Junio was with me, so they did only a routine check."

"I see."

"Junio told me that Kappler has placed a price on your head, and Koch has made it his business to capture you, no matter what it takes."

"How much am I worth for Kappler?"

"A million lire."

"Koch must be taking his job very seriously. How did you manage to get all this food?"

"Junio knows a *corsaro della fame*." Those who sold food on the black market were called "pirates of hunger."

I rifled through the knapsack and found a pistol and a hand grenade under the food. "What are these for?" I asked her, surprised.

"I want you to have them, just in case," she answered.

"I've never fired a gun. And I don't plan on starting now."

Montse ignored my protests. "It's simple," she began, giving me a lesson. "First you remove the safety clip, then you take aim, keeping your hand very steady, then you press the trigger. The grenade is even easier, but you have to be more careful. You just pull the ring and throw it. If somebody tries to force their way in, you should throw it against the door, run into the bathroom, lock the door, and jump into the bathtub. You have fifteen seconds. Nothing on either side of the door will remain standing. Then, leave the house immediately and climb up to the roof. You can jump from there onto the roof next door. Never run toward the street, because there's usually somebody standing guard at the entrance to the building."

"Is this what your new friends have taught you?" I asked, quite taken aback by her didacticism.

"It's all theoretical," she assured me. "I haven't fired a single shot, not yet. They've assigned me to collect information on the German troops. And Junio is passing me the information, voluntarily. I explained the situation to my comrades and they realized that he is worth more to us alive than dead. So now we go together to dinners and parties organized by the Nazis at the Hotel Flora and the Excelsior. Yesterday, for example, I dined at the same table as Erich Priebke. He was with the actress Laura Nucci."

Imagining Montse dressed in an evening gown walking along the plush carpets of the luxury hotels on Via Veneto hanging from Junio's arm opened a bitter and cavernous pit in my stomach.

"And Priebke, he didn't ask you about me?"

"Junio introduced me as Miss Fábregas."

"Oh, so you've gone back to being single."

"Only temporarily. It's all part of the plan. We want it to appear that he's courting me."

"Junio is quite astute. Now he wants to collect points for when the city is liberated by the Allies. The other day he told me as much. Well, I don't plan on moving a finger for him if that happens." I was speaking out of spite, but what else was left to me?

"Naturally, Junio will have to pay for the crimes he has committed, but that doesn't mean that the tribunal that judges him shouldn't take into account that he is helping the resistance. Maybe they will reduce his sentence," Montse said.

"Is that how this story will end: 'The murderer managed to have his sentence reduced, they ate quail, and lived happily ever after'?"

"Why do you make such an effort to be so paranoid? Maybe I should try to get you out of Rome, take you to the mountains. You'd be more relaxed."

"I don't want you treating me like I've got tuberculosis or something! I'm just a damned prisoner."

"You are an 'evader,' and that's the same as saying you are privileged. Prisoners are the ones in jail in Regina Coeli, in the dungeons of Villa Tasso, and in the Pensione Oltremare. And most are tortured before being shot."

"Well, if I'm so privileged, tonight I would like to have the privilege of your company," I said.

"Sorry, but I have instructions not to stay in the apartment more time than is absolutely necessary."

"And how much time would that be? A minute, an hour, two, three? How many?"

"At least not the whole night. The first rule is to not arouse any suspicions in the neighbors. German agents have infiltrated everywhere."

"You have a date with Junio?"

"I have a dinner date with the Germans at the Excelsior. General Mältzer will be there."

"Well, well, the king of Rome!" I exclaimed cynically.

Lieutenant General Kurt Mältzer, after succeeding General Stahel as the highest military authority in the capital, had settled into a luxurious suite in the Excelsior and proclaimed himself "the king of Rome." In reality he was nothing more than a belligerent, arrogant alcoholic.

"I'll be back next week to bring you more food. Take care of yourself."

When we embraced, I could feel a large, hard object in one of the pockets of her raincoat.

"What do you have there?" I asked her.

"A pistol, like the one I gave you," she said nonchalantly. "To defend myself if necessary."

"Don't forget to leave it at home tonight. I wouldn't want the Germans to discover it and shoot you at dawn next to the prince. I wouldn't be able to stand so much romanticism," I said in an awkward attempt to relieve the tension.

"Don't worry. If they shoot me one day, I'll do everything in my power to make sure it happens with you at my side," she said.

THAT NIGHT I DREAMED I had been arrested by members of Koch's Gang and taken to Pensione Jaccarino. There, "Doctor" Koch awaited me. He was a young man, around twenty-five, who looked a little like Junio.

"So you're the man who's worth a million lire," he said. "Kappler is very, very disappointed in your behavior. I, on the other hand, told him that I believe in your repentance and your predisposition to confess everything. I'm right, am I not?"

Before I even had a chance to answer, he jabbed an iron bar into my kidneys and I doubled over in pain. He then began to bash my knees with terrible ferocity until my legs collapsed under me.

"You know what I need to do to make you talk?" he continued. "I need to discover your pain threshold, that's all, and I have all the time in the world to do so. This means that the duration and intensity of this show depends entirely on you. What do you say?"

For some strange reason, something prevented me from speaking, even though I was willing to do so. I wanted to be able to scream in this monster's face, tell him he could go straight to hell. But my vocal cords didn't respond, as if my throat were suddenly paralyzed. My silence spent Koch's small store of patience, and he ordered his henchmen to tie my feet and hands to the legs and back of a wooden chair. Next, he applied a dozen electric charges to my genitals to the accompaniment of some piano chords of a Schubert piece. After the shocks came blows and kicks. Then I lost consciousness.

When I came around, one of the henchmen was holding my mouth open with some pliers while Koch himself was stuffing in pubic hair that he was picking up from a porcelain plate with some tongs. He was doing it carefully, meticulously.

I gagged.

"Does this disgust you? It shouldn't, because it's hair from your wife's cunt. We bit it off in mouthfuls before we fucked her. You don't believe me, do you? You don't think I'd be capable of something like . . ."

Koch opened a door that led into the adjoining room and there, hanging from a beam, was Montse. She seemed dead or unconscious, and the pubic hair had been torn from her flesh.

With that horrific sight, I recovered my voice.

After letting out a deep, agonizing scream of fury and pain, I woke up.

PROHIBITED FROM OPENING the shutters or looking outside, I lost all sense of time and reality. And without time or space to contain me, tedium and despair took over. Sometimes I felt like I was hibernating, living underground, where the only approved activity was inactivity. Just like my windows, all options, all roads, were shut.

To avoid worrying inordinately about what was happening on the streets, I decided to spend my time reading rather than listening obsessively to the radio. The books Junio had talked about were the complete works of Emilio Salgari. There I was, a pistol in one hand and a grenade in the other, reading the suicidal Salgari. Perhaps I managed to survive thanks precisely to his simple and enthusiastic style, which had little in common with my image of him as a person. Grappling with this discovery—that the life and the work of the author pertained to different people, as if there were a schism between the two—lasted several days and through it I gained a better understanding of Montse. Sometimes, in response to the demands of a historic moment—and there was no doubt we were living through extraordinary times—a person is forced to do extraordinary things. This does not mean that the person has changed for the worse, or that their former life has been erased forever. Yes, you could act in one way and live in another for a certain period of time, and then return to normal life, I thought, trying to reassure myself.

At times I attempted to accompany these reflections with some form of physical exercise, for I feared my muscles would become atrophied from prolonged periods of inactivity. Even prisoners have access to a courtyard where they can stretch their legs. I had to try to make as little noise as possible; to become, as far as possible, evanescent.

But when I finished reading all the books, I had no choice but to plug in the radio and listen to a voice other than my own conscience.

It was around noon on March 25, and I was about to complete three weeks in hiding. When I tuned in to Radio Roma, I heard the following report recorded the night before by the German High Command:

On the afternoon of March 23, 1944, criminal elements bombed a column of German police on Via Rasella. As a result, thirty-two members of the German police force were killed and several were wounded. This vile ambush was perpetuated by *comunisti-badogliani*. An investigation is ongoing to discover to what degree this act can be attributed to Anglo–North American forces. The German command is resolved to stop the activities of these deranged hooligans. Nobody must be allowed to sabotage with impunity the newly executed Italian-German agreement for cooperation. The German command, as a result, has ordered the execution of ten *comunisti-badogliani* for every murdered German. This order has already been carried out.

This meant that the Nazis had executed 320 *comunisti-badogliani*, that is, Communist and monarchist partisans. Badoglio had been the leader of the last monarchist government before he and the king had fled Rome in the dead of night and left it in the hands of the Germans. Dividing the number of victims between the two factions, each had lost 160 people. And since Montse belonged to the Patriotic Action Group, or GAP, associated with the clandestine Communist Party, the possibility that she had been among the executed seemed to me to be very high.

Condemned as I was to total isolation, I had no way of knowing that the German report was far from reliable. My despair was so great that I was on the verge of leaving my hiding place and going out to look for her.

But I decided that if something had happened to Montse, Junio would have let me know.

When Montse visited me a few days later, she told me that the attack on Via Rasella had been carried out by a dozen members of the GAP, who had planted a powerful bomb in a street sweeper's cart that had been stolen and placed in the path of the Eleventh Company of the Third Bozen Battalion of the SS. Their barracks were on the Viminal Hill, at a site given to them by the Italian Ministry of the Interior, but every day they marched through Rome's *centro storico* to conduct training exercises near Ponte Milvio. Worst of all, they walked in formation, more than 150 of them, all singing a ridiculous song called "Hupf, mein Mädel," which means something like "Jump, my little girl." The large number of soldiers, the amount of equipment they carried with them through the city, as well as their unvarying schedule, turned them into an easy target.

The problem was that on this occasion, and given the magnitude of the attack, the Germans were determined not simply to absorb the high losses and pretend as if nothing had happened, as they seemed to have done on other occasions, but to use the opportunity to teach a lesson. Things could have been even worse.

Among the hodgepodge of reports the attack and its aftermath generated, I read that Hitler asked for the heads of thirty-five Italians for every German victim. It must have been Kesselring, fearing a popular uprising if the Führer's wishes were carried out, who managed to lower the figure to ten Italians for every German killed. The Todeskandidaten, or "candidates for death" operation, was led and carried out completely by Kappler, and his intention was to summarily execute all prisoners who either had already been given a death sentence or were strong candidates for getting one, but he soon realized that there weren't enough of them, so he asked for help from Koch's Gang and the police *questore*, an arriviste named Pietro Caruso. Together they drew up a combined list that included members of the resistance, Jews, workers, common criminals, and even a priest. The place chosen for the execution was the so-called Ardeatine Caves between the San Calisto and Domitilla catacombs. I knew the spot well from my days building bunkers; this was the quarry where we obtained sand to make concrete. It was a gigantic cave with many rooms and long corridors. The original announcement said that there were to be 320 Italian victims, but when Rome was liberated and the caves reopened, 335 cadavers were found. Apparently a wounded member of the Eleventh Company had died while they were organizing the reprisal, so Kappler added ten more to the list, as ordered. The other five were executed by mistake. Somebody—Koch, Caruso, or Kappler himself—had counted incorrectly. Once there, however, they had become involuntary witnesses to the massacre and had to be executed. The 335 victims were taken inside the cave in groups of five, and each received a bullet in the neck. That, at least, was the plan. Because the blood orgy took so long, many of the soldiers carrying out the executions had to get drunk in order to be able to kill so many in cold blood. And because of the soldiers' drunkenness, some prisoners were literally decapitated by their executioners' barrage of bullets and their bad aim. When it was all over, Kappler ordered the entrance sealed with dynamite. But there was one thing Kappler couldn't control: a few days later, a bad smell began to permeate the area, and the locals began to complain and ask uncomfortable questions. Kappler's solution was to turn the entrance to the Ardeatine Caves into a public garbage dump so that its stench would cover up that of the corpses buried inside.

But life in Rome carried on, even after those terrible events. One of the first measures the Germans adopted after the attack on Via Rasella was to ration bread to one hundred grams a day and intensify the struggle against the resistance. Montse could explain this more fully, but as far as I remember, the presence of a traitor among the GAP threw the organization into disarray and forced many of its members to go into hiding for weeks.

Montse had no choice but to take refuge in the apartment where I was living.

When she burst in, her face was pale, her hair down, her eyes burning with anxiety. She was gasping for breath. I assumed she had had an accident. Without giving me a chance to ask her what had happened, she cried out:

"Please forgive me."

"For what?" I asked, surprised.

"For not being the wife—the person—you deserve."

"What do you mean?"

Montse sought refuge in my arms before making her confession. "I just killed a man."

I hugged her with all my strength, pressing my body against hers. I felt the pistol in one of her pockets, digging into me. It was still warm.

"Calm down. I'm sure it was in self-defense," I said, willing to say anything to offer her solace. "We'll sort everything out soon enough."

"Everything happened so quickly . . ." she continued, breathlessly "I was on my way here, near the Palazzo Braschi, and a young Fascist approached me. I was lost in my thoughts, trying not to call attention to myself, and the young man spoke in dialect, maybe in Sicilian. So I didn't pay any attention to him. Then he started following me and kept talking to me. At first his voice sounded friendly, but the longer he tried to get my attention, the more it changed; he started making frightening gestures, and his tone became rude. Then he told me to stop and asked for my documents. I don't know if he just wanted to impress me or if he was really angry, but I got very nervous. I thought that if I showed him my documents, he would want to search me, because for some reason I was convinced that the only thing he wanted to do was get his hands on me. So I grabbed my pistol and turned around and, without saying a word, I shot him twice at point-blank range. Lots of people turned around when the shots rang out, and when he realized what had happened, with two bullets in his stomach, he shouted, 'The bitch shot me! The bitch killed me!' Then I ran."

Montse had murdered the young man out of fear. By imposing a state of terror, the Germans had turned fear into a reason as legitimate as any other to kill.

"Maybe he'll live," I said.

"Do you really think so?"

"Many people survive two bullets in the stomach."

I knew nothing about bullet wounds, but I was sure that as soon as Montse had gotten past the adrenaline of the moment, she would collapse. I had had the foresight to stuff a couple of bottles of *amaro* in my luggage, so I forced her to drink several glasses. After about half an hour, her voice got thick, she stopped speaking clearly, and the stern mask her face had become gave way, first to exhaustion, then to sleep.

But the next morning, Montse acted as if nothing had happened. I was disappointed by her behavior because it showed me that the changes she had undergone were deeper than I had imagined. I had expected at the very least some words of regret from her, a nod of empathy toward her victim, but Montse said nothing; she only carried her hand repeatedly to the base of her neck, as if she could make her anxiety vanish through this gesture. Then, after listening to Colonel Stevens, the BBC newscaster, report on new attacks by the resistance in the Quadraro district, next to Via Tuscolana, Montse swelled with pride and said, "The comrades in Zone VIII have attacked again. I should have joined them. I've heard the Germans don't dare even enter Quadraro. Hiding here was a mistake."

"Maybe," I said.

With those words we put an end to an episode in Montse's life that—had it been me—would have scarred me forever. In the hundreds of conversations we had about the war after it was over, she never once mentioned the incident. Not even when talking with other members of the GAP, her "comrades." Nonetheless, I suspect Montse carries that weight in some corner of her conscience. She shot that young man in the Piazza di Pasquino, and she has never stepped foot there again.

The "war of bread" began on the first of April and ended a few days later when a mob of hungry women and children attacked a bakery distributing bread to the SS in the Ostiense neighborhood. The Nazis arrested ten of the women, led them to Ponte di Ferro, had them face the river, then riddled them with machine-gun bullets.

Even though it would be another two months before the city was finally liberated, I have no clear memories of how I felt as the time approached. I do, however, retain a clear memory of the atrocities the Germans committed before they left. Maybe they stick in my mind because they were so futile. Once the *goumiers* of the French Marshal Juin broke through the Gustav Line, it was the beginning of the end. On that night, on the steep cliffs in the province of Frosinone, the German dream of Rome and the legend that Marshal Kesselring was invincible collapsed. People still wonder today why they didn't blow it up as they retreated, as they had in Naples. Some claim they actually took into account what a loss it would mean for humanity. In my opinion, they spared Rome in order to keep alive the dream of conquering it in the future.

When, eventually, it was safe to open the windows, the light hurt my eyes.

We found a note from Prince Cima Vivarini in the mailbox. It read, "I'm fleeing with the barbarians to the north. Adieu, Junio."

It's odd how the human mind works, but after three months of being shut in, I noticed only one thing missing on my first walk through the liberated city: the cats, at other times swarming the streets, had disappeared. *Not a cat or a prince*, I thought.

12.

AFTER LIBERATION, I opened my own architectural studio. I have designed dozens of houses that have been built over the ruins left by the Allied bombs, and the government has given me Italian citizenship in recognition of my services before and during the German occupation. As Junio predicted, the arrest warrant signed by Kappler opened many doors for me. The maps I drew of the German lines of defense were found among the documents seized at Gestapo headquarters on Via Tasso, and the government now wants to include them, together with many other "memorabilia" of the war, in an exhibit of "the weapons used by the resistance."

Montse turned into a minor celebrity when her name appeared in the press together with her nom de guerre, "Liberty." Seven years later she continues to be treated as a heroine at the beauty salon and the neighborhood grocery store. As soon as the war ended, she joined the Italian Communist Party. She too was given Italian citizenship, and went back to her work as a librarian.

On September 18, 1944, the trial began against the ex-*questore* Pietro Caruso, accused of handing fifty prisoners over to Kappler from the Regina Coeli prison to fill out the roster for the Ardeatine Caves. A furious crowd burst into the courtroom demanding vengeance, but since Caruso had not yet arrived, they threw themselves on Donato Carretta, the warden of Regina Coeli during the occupation and the main prosecution witness, and lynched him. Two days later, the verdict was delivered: Caruso was sentenced to death by firing squad the following day in Forte Bravetta.

On April 20, 1945, Mussolini dismantled the offices of his puppet government and attempted to flee to Switzerland. He was arrested a week later by the Masso partisans and shot the following day in the Giulino quarter of Mezzegra. Hours later, his body and that of his lover, Claretta Petacci, were hung facedown over a gas station in the Piazza Loreto in Milan, where they were desecrated by one and all.

By then, Hitler had decided to kill himself in his Berlin bunker, and had ordered that his body be incinerated. He had seen the pictures of Mussolini hanging like a slaughtered pig, and he must have been terrified of meeting the same fate.

The exact same hour as Hitler's suicide, Colonel William Horn entered the strong room in the city of Nuremberg where the Nazis stored the Hapsburg treasures, and took possession of the Holy Lance of Longinus in the name of the United States of America.

On June 4, 1945, on the first anniversary of the liberation of Rome, Pietro Koch was charged with numerous crimes, including torture, against the Italian people. He was found guilty and condemned to death. Before he was executed—wearing a rosary Pius XII had given him around his head but without touching it so as not to dirty it with the blood of his victims—he asked for God's forgiveness for the suffering he had caused.

"My country damns me and is in the right; justice has sent me to my death and is in the right; the Pope has forgiven me, and that is even better. If I had always been blessed with the guidance of such forgiveness in the school of goodness, you, my dear sirs, would not be here now wasting your time, and above all, I would not be here awaiting the wagon of death," he said, moments before he was executed.

In November 1946, all of Rome rejoiced at the prosecution of generals Eberhard von Mackensen and Kurt Mältzer, though their trials were held in a British tribunal rather than an Italian one, for they were prisoners of war subject to the protocols of international justice. Both were sentenced to death by firing squad. The sentences, however, were never carried out.

The next one to sit in the dock was Field Marshal Kesselring, who, like the others, was sentenced to death. In the end, his sentence was reduced to imprisonment and he has recently been freed. Many in Rome and all over the world have protested this measure.

Finally, Herbert Kappler was tried by an Italian tribunal in May 1948. He was found guilty of the massacre of the Ardeatine Caves and condemned to *ergastolo*, the maximum sentence permitted under the new Italian constitution. He is currently serving his sentence in Gaeta prison.

As for Eugen Dollmann, after his arrest he confessed to being a spy for the North American OSS during the war, and in 1949 he published a book entitled *Roma Nazista*. I haven't read it yet. After all, what could Dollmann tell me that I didn't already know?

Little by little, the wounds left by the war began to heal. The city recovered its former vitality, and the Romans began to overcome their sorrow and look toward the future. It was then that the old idea of EUR as an extension of Rome toward the sea and a residential and business center was resuscitated, and I came to work on that project.

In March 1950 Montse attended a conference on systems of library categorization held in the city of Como. Naturally, the program included a visit to Triangolo Lariano, formed by the city of Como and the two neighboring towns of Lecco and Bellagio. After exploring the area, the librarians made their way to the terrace of the Villa Serbelloni to have some refreshments. There, sitting at a table with a view of the lake, sat Junio.

When she returned, she told me she had found him much changed. He was wearing an elegant Prince of Wales suit and had gained a few kilos. Incipient baldness was beginning to appear on the crown of his head. He went by the name of Warburg, which was his mother's surname, and said he lived in the Swiss city of Lugano, working in real estate. He told her he often thought of me because they needed so many architects to rebuild the cities of Germany and other European countries, and he never gave up hope that one day we could work together again. Even though Junio looked like the personification of prosperity, he told Montse that his life was in danger. And when she asked him what he was talking about, he answered, "If I told you, your life would also be in danger. I will, perhaps, need your help later, after I am dead. Then you will have to take my place. There's nobody else left." It was a sunny day, the perfect temperature for that time of year, and the beauty of the surroundings was matchless, so Montse thought that Junio was joking, that this was some kind of attempt to bring back the good old days. There weren't even any charges hanging over him from the Italian courts that he needed to worry about. Thanks to his contacts he had been spared (mysteriously, the Italian courts had been unable to reconstruct his whereabouts or come up with any kind of evidence that would incriminate him in any crime whatsoever), though he did have to place a national border or two in between. Thus he was able to live in peace and quiet. "Everything you're talking about, Junio, is over," Montse told him. He replied, "Maximilian. Call me Maximilian. And if you think that everything is as it was before the war, you are wrong. Or you could say that's exactly what is happening. Nothing has changed. Everything is the same as it was before Poland was invaded, and this will lead us back into a disaster," Junio replied. Montse thought he was raving, and she was pressed for time. When the moment came to say good-bye— the group had planned a visit to the gardens of azaleas and rhododendrons in the neighboring Villa Melzi D'Eril—Junio, after kissing Montse on the cheeks, whispered in her ear: "If something happens to me, you may re-ceive some papers. If so, I beg you to read them and act according to your conscience."

There was no question that this conversation was very disturbing. I even wondered whether Junio had lost his mind, or perhaps that he had not made the psychological transition from war to peace, the way many adolescents struggle against accepting adulthood. Imagining him as a bourgeois made me feel almost sorry for him, for it was a clear sign that his world had collapsed. The Europe of the great families had given way to the Europe of the great companies, and to be part of that new elite you had to unbutton your shirt collar and roll up your sleeves. The war had not only swept away cities, towns, villages, and fields, it had also destroyed a way of life. In this new world order, Junio had ceased to be a favored son.

My hands, clutching that newspaper, had grown stiff and numb; as I unclenched and stretched them, I glanced back over the towers and domes I could see from our apartment terrace. I felt as if I was comtemplating a new city, a renovated city, as if the Rome of Junio and men like him had vanished forever with his death. I carefully closed the newspaper, conscious that I was, in fact, closing the most important chapter of my past. As I entered the house, Montse's perfume, floating in the air like a harrowing trace of life, enveloped me, a sign from a future that could be smelled, brushed with the tips of the fingers. Finally, I turned toward the kitchen to prepare lunch.

EPILOGUE

Dear José María:

If you are reading this letter, I am dead. Forgive me if my words seem detached and awkward, but I have little time and many things to explain to you. It is best for me to get straight to the point.

It all began in the year 1922, when Count Richard Coudenhove-Kalergi proposed the formation of a Pan-European Union at a conference attended by two thousand delegates (more or less, the exact number doesn't matter). The Austrian aristocrat called for the dissolution of all nation states in Western Europe, and at the same time warned against the Bolshevik threat. The launching of this Union would be financed by the German-Venetian Warburgs, my mother's family. Max Warburg, head of the German branch of the family, gave Coudenhove-Kalergi sixty thousand gold marks. The intellectual inspirations for the movement were Immanuel Kant, Napoleon Bonaparte, Giuseppe Manzini, and Friedrich Nietzsche. But Coudenhove-Kalergi's pan-Europeanism was really looking to establish control over the financial world and finally the political one. The economic crisis of 1929 and the rise of Mussolini and then Hitler transformed it into a universal Fascist movement whose goal was the creation of a feudal European state.

My father opposed the movement from the outset, though he had to do so with great caution. Let us just say that he established contacts with influential people in England and France who opposed pan-Europeanism after Mussolini's and Hitler's rise to power. Obviously, taking a stand against the pan-Europeanism that emerged from the economic crisis of 1929 was the same as opposing Fascism and National Socialism. This was how my father became involved in a secret organization named "Smith." I was a teenager at the time, and it took me a few years to realize what was going on around me, for my mother, like a good Warburg, had allowed herself to be hypnotized by the Nazis' siren song. Greater Germany was to be the epicenter of the new Europe, whose strength and determination would prevent the advance of the Bolshevik hordes across the rest of the continent. My father, on the contrary, always believed that Europe's best hope after the First World War was for Germany to keep its head down.

So it was that the salons of the family *palazzo* were filled with the illustrious members of the Nazi party, whom my mother feted and my father spied on. Nazis of the stature of Alfred Rosenberg, Karl Haushofer, Rudolf Hess, Dietrich Eckart, and Rudolf Von Sebottendorff spent time there. Von Sebottendorff was always talking about Cairo, the city where he had lived for a long time, and where he had come into contact with mystic Islam and the teachings of the Mevlevi dervishes. He had even been a member of a Masonic lodge, which was where he first heard about the Creator's Map. Imbued with these esoteric beliefs, Von Sebottendorff had founded the Thule Society in August 1918.

At that time, my father owned an estate seventy kilometers from Venice. With its many lakes it was the perfect place for duck hunting, and my father went there often and took me with him. My memories of it are among the happiest of my entire childhood. I can still recall the sound of the rushes brushing against the boat, the sudden flapping of wings when the ducks saw us, the iridescent brilliance of the water—blinding and hypnotic—the smell of spring, the tame calm of summer, the buzzing of the bluebottle flies. We often met up with other hunters, friends of my father who were also members of Smith. It was in this innocent way that I met those men and first heard about Von Sebottendorff and his map.

At this point in my story I would like to say, to explain my father and myself, that among men of our class, working had always been frowned upon—the world of work was thought to be controlled by ambitious and unscrupulous men. In exchange for being exempted from that sphere, people in my position had to engage in other activities that were useful to society in order to justify our privilege. That is why philanthropy was the true vocation of many of us, whether by collecting works of art that were then donated to the community or by financing the construction of a university or a hospital. The point is that when the time came to decide which of these activities to devote his life to, my father chose spying as a way of redeeming himself to the world. As I'm sure you can imagine the importance of the weight of tradition in families like ours, you can understand that I didn't have much choice about carrying on what my father had begun and fulfilling the commitments he had made. Considering my background, my contacts, my knowledge of languages, it would have been unforgivable for me not to take advantage of "my predilection" for spying. Rather than carry on in this cynical vein, I will continue with the much more important confessions I still must make.

Once my father died and I took his place in the secret organization, I had no difficulty at all passing myself off as a fervent Fascist and one of Hitler's most enthusiastic followers. Thanks to the relations my mother maintained with some of the most prominent German leaders, I was able to meet Heinrich Himmler. He was known to be extremely reserved, someone who opened up only to his most intimate circle, the dozen SS officers he shared residency with in Wewelsburg Castle. Undoubtedly, one of the Reichsführer's weak points was his esoteric beliefs, which always seemed rather absurd. But precisely because they were absurd, they opened up unlimited opportunities for those willing to take advantage of them. After all, what is superstition, if not a branch of faith? Yes, in his way, Himmler was nothing more than a believer, a man of faith, someone awaiting a miracle—and that's just what we gave him.

As I already said, I had heard my father talk about the legend of the Creator's Map; and soon all our efforts at "Smith" centered around devising a plan that would culminate in my "discovery" of that document, which I could serve up to Himmler on a silver platter and thereby win his trust and gain access to the heart of the Third Reich.

Carrying out a plan of such magnitude meant spinning a very fine web that involved a large number of people; we also needed people with specialized knowledge in unusual areas, such as paleography, library sciences, the restoration of cultural artifacts, and falsifications. To that end we established contact with the Occult Bureau of the British MI5, which had been created precisely to keep abreast of the "occult" activities of the Nazis. Their technical-esoteric consultant was a man by the name of Aleister Crowley. It is no easy task to describe a person like Crowley. Suffice it to say that in my entire life I have never known anybody so conniving, so monstrous, and so wholly devoid of respect for others. As it was, his consultations weren't of much help. He convinced the British authorities to use as the symbol of victory, later popularized by Churchill, an ancient magic symbol of destruction from the Egyptian culture. He proposed distributing on German soil pamphlets with false occultist information, and he printed up some quartets by Nostradamus that predicted the defeat of Germany in the war, all with the goal of undermining the enemy's morale.

Nor was it easy to find a copy of *Hieroglyphica, or a Commentary on the Sacred Alphabet of the Egyptians and Other Peoples* by Pierus Valerianus on the international secondhand book market. Once we did, we sent it to England, where an expert falsifier added a short appendix that refers to the Creator's Map. The next step was to invent a believable trajectory the map had taken. You already know what we came up with: it went from Persia to Egypt, then Germania, to the Pyramid of Caius Cestius, and ended up with Keats. But we still didn't have a place to "deposit" the map in such a way that neither Von Sebottendorff nor Himmler would doubt its authenticity. Obviously, there was no better place than the Vatican Library.

As a citizen of the Sovereign Military Order of Malta, I was able to study paleography at the Vatican School, where, as you know, I met Father Giordano Sansovino. You also know, because I mentioned this to you on several occasions, that Sansovino was a member of the Holy Alliance, the secret service of the Vatican City State. But Pius XII's tepid resistance to the Nazis was not to Father Sansovino's liking; thus it was not difficult to convince him to join our organization. Once Father Sansovino was a member of Smith, we were able to introduce the Creator's Map into the Vatican Library. Then all we had to do was wait for the right moment to give it to Himmler.

I must move quickly now to 1934, when the entire world was hanging on the events in Spain, whose government seemed to be losing control of the situation. The possibilities of an armed conflict increased by the day, forcing us to focus our attention on your country. "Spain was the problem; Europe the solution," as someone has recently written.

I arrived in Barcelona at the beginning of that year. Awaiting me there was a person who had been recruited into the organization. His name was Jaime Fábregas. And through Señor Fábregas I met his niece Montserrat, an idealistic and beautiful young woman who had just turned seventeen, and who had taken sides against her family in the lawsuit they were bringing against her beloved uncle. You must believe me when I tell you that I still blush when I remember that I fell in love with Montse one second after meeting her, and she with me. Much happened during those months I spent in Barcelona with her. As a result of our relationship, Montse grew from a child into a responsible adult, with the ability to discern good from evil. I think that if I can be proud of anything it is that I taught Montse that commitment stands above and beyond anything else, even personal feelings. What I am trying to say is that Montse understood that the strength of our love was built on the firmness of our convictions and the fulfillment of our obligations, and that betraying those principles would be the same as burying our love forever. Ironically, I believe that this is why our love died—first because of distance, and later because of the political commitments we both had to make.

But let us return to Rome and the winter of 1937. As luck would have it, the Fábregas family was forced to take refuge in the Spanish Academy, and with Montse in charge of the institution's library, we saw our opportunity to carry out our plan for the Creator's Map once and for all. We had the map, the book, and the librarian who would find it on the shelves of an ancient institution in economic crisis due to the war raging in Spain. All that remained to put the first part of our plan in motion was to find a bookseller willing to collaborate with us—which we soon did.

The Pierus Valerianus left the academy and came to me through Signor Tasso; I then gave the book and the information about the existence of the Creator's Map to Himmler, just as we had planned.

In order to take the next step, it was absolutely necessary to establish a safe means of communication between the members of the organization. The information I obtained had to reach "Smith" without raising any suspicions—and that is when we thought of you. I am certain that by this point, you must be overwhelmed by anger and bewilderment, but believe me when I tell you that security was the only reason for keeping you in the dark. Organizations such as ours must function as much as possible like a submarine, with separate watertight compartments; if there is a breach in one, the ship's integrity will not be compromised. The equation was very simple: if you were unaware that I was part of "Smith," there was no risk that you could expose me. Moreover, it was vital for you to believe in the existence of the map, for you to have heard it spoken about and even to have been present when its authenticity was discussed. All this was to ensure that if you were captured by the Germans and tortured, your words would be truthful and reveal little.

In spite of taking all possible precautions, we suffered several casualties: the two Smiths, Father Sansovino, and the *scriptor* of the Vatican Library, who supposedly sold me the Creator's Map. I did indeed order the *scriptor's* murder, may God forgive me. Gabor did the dirty work. Let us just say it was a necessary "sacrifice," though to qualify the death of a man with such a euphemism is repugnant from any point of view. Let me assure you, however, that the *scriptor* knew from the very beginning the fate that awaited him. I think I told you once about the secret organizations that operate within the Church but are marginal to it. Father Sansovino was in charge of keeping them together and assigning them missions. In this way groups like the Assassini and the Octagonus Circle, whose collaboration was crucial, took part. They were true and brave soldiers and martyrs, guided by their unbreakable faith. I assure you that in many circumstances faith is the greatest ally of an organization such as ours.

But let's move forward. Since the Creator's Map was obviously a fake, we had to make it impossible for the Germans to open it once it was turned over to them. It was then that we thought of having the map undergo some kind of chemical process whereby its contents would be erased when it came into contact with the air, and to permeate its pages with anthrax.

The plan was to open the map when Hitler or Himmler was within range of the anthrax, but once I saw myself surrounded by the Nazis' top brass in the Führer's carriage, my courage failed me. Perhaps at the moment of truth, I was unable to fully grasp the consequences of my action, or inaction. I thought only of my own life, and not of those I could have saved. The brave agents of the secret Vatican organizations I mentioned above would not have hesitated for an instant to sacrifice their own lives in order to liberate the world from Hitler, from Himmler, or from any other Nazi official. Yes, José María, I was afraid, and to this day I continue to wonder if the possibility of changing the course of history had been in my hands. Unfortunately, I didn't have Nicolás Estorzi or any other assassini with me. Do you remember I once mentioned Estorzi, a spy the Germans called "The Messenger"? We met in Venice, and thanks to his participation in the "Taras Borodajkewycz" case, we managed to get hold of the three million marks in gold ingots the Nazis had hoped to use to buy the election of the new pope when Pius XI died. That money allowed us to buy a couple of buildings, among these the apartment at 23 Via dei Coronari, which you know so well, and to collaborate with the Delegazione Assistenza Emigranti Ebrei, an organization that helped emigrant Jews who had managed to escape from the Nazi regime, something that we had previously done on our own. You probably haven't forgotten the first job I assigned you. The package you delivered from Don Oreste's pharmacy to the apartment on Via dei Coronari contained morphine, and its destination was an old rabbi from Hamburg with a serious stomach ailment.

After Germany's defeat on the Russian front, the war took a decisive turn. Himmler's response was to create a secret organization whose goal was to rescue the high Nazi functionaries and their treasures in case of defeat. Escape routes were sought and numerous businesses were founded in countries such as Spain (where the Sofindus Consortium was already operational), Argentina (where between three and four hundred companies were formed), Chile, and Paraguay. In 1944, Himmler sent secret agents to Madrid to set up an escape route for defeated Nazis. The first such route was established between Berlin and Barcelona on Lufthansa's regular flights between the two cities. A year later, in March 1945, an agent of the Foreign Intelligence Service of the SS named Carlos Fuldner (born in Argentina of German parentage) landed in Madrid on an airplane loaded with valuable paintings and a huge quantity of cash. He was ostensibly opening an art gallery, but behind that façade hid an organization devoted to facilitating the entry of prominent Nazis into Spain.

Once the Third Reich was defeated, the Allies began Operation Safehaven, whose purpose was to guarantee that German wealth be used in the reconstruction of Europe and the payment of compensation to the Allies, to restore property confiscated by the Germans to their legitimate owners, and to prevent the escape of prominent Nazis to neutral countries. These measures were also intended to prevent the Nazis from using their resources abroad to set up a Fourth Reich. For the first few months after the war ended, Operation Safehaven showed some positive results, but toward the end of 1946, customs regulations were relaxed and a large number of Nazi leaders, who had remained hidden with false identification, took the opportunity to come out of hiding and seek refuge in South America. That is how the so-called ratlines were established between

Germany and South America through Italy; the so-called B-B route between Bremen and the Italian port of Bari; the Vatican Corridor the Holy
See controlled through Father Krunoslav Draganovic (don't they say that
all roads lead to Rome?); and the northern escape route from Copenhagen
to Bilbao or San Sebastian.

In 1947, the Perón government, through the Argentine Immigration
Delegation in Europe, devised a plan to rescue Nazis who had intellectual
or scientific training that might prove useful to the development of that
country. The people in charge of carrying out this operation were the spy
Reinhard Koops and the Austrian archbishop Alois Hudel, rector of
Santa Maria dell'Anima and spiritual director of the German colony in
Rome. Koops had the support of the Argentinean consulate in Genoa,
and Hudel had the support of numerous Catholic organizations (one of
the largest centers receiving Nazis in Rome was the Franciscan convent
on Via Sicilia). Permits were granted by the Migration Department in
Buenos Aires, and passports were issued by the International Red Cross
(whose mission was to "documentally" help refugees who had lost their
identification documents during the war). That was how, for example,
Klaus Barbie, the Butcher of Lyon, escaped: he took a boat from Genoa
to Buenos Aires and, once in safe territory, he continued from there to
Bolivia. I have also discovered that Martin Bormann, Hitler's powerful
personal secretary, who was condemned to death in absentia by the
Nuremberg Tribunal, managed to reach Spain with false documents provided to him by the Vatican; once there, a Spanish spy of the Gestapo
with the last name of Alcázar de Velasco took him in a submarine to
Argentina. Something similar happened with Josef Mengele, the so-
called Angel of Death of the Auschwitz-Birkenau concentration camps.
After hiding out in a farm in Bavaria and practicing veterinary medicine,
he crossed the Austro-Italian border and made it to Bolzano, where the
Vatican provided him with false documents; after a brief sojourn in
Spain, he took a boat to South America. The same thing happened to
Adolf Eichmann, one of the ideologues of the "Final Solution" against

the Jews, who, after undergoing plastic surgery, has been living in Argentina since 1950 under the name of Ricardo Klement. But the list doesn't end there. Erich Priebke, one of the men responsible for the Ardeatine Caves massacre, escaped from the Rimini prison camp and found refuge in the city of Bariloche in Argentina. He had the help of a Catholic organization in Rome, which intervened on his behalf with the Argentinean authorities so they would accept the passport the International Red Cross had given him. Priebke and his family sailed from Genoa on the *San Giorgio* transatlantic cruiser, and after working as a waiter, he now manages a sausage shop. Reinhard Spitzy, Von Ribbentrop's assistant, has been living in Argentina since 1948. That same year SS General Ludolf von Alvensleben also arrived in Argentina. Believe me, tens of thousands of Nazis have managed to elude justice by using the Vatican Corridor and other escape routes. But the story doesn't end there.

When the war ended, the Allies were facing two urgent problems. The first was the need to hunt down the Nazis responsible for the war. The second had to do with the rise of Communism in Europe, which had turned into a danger as great as the Third Reich had once been. Or at least that's how the government of the United States saw it. As a result, Section X2 of the OSS (after 1947, the CIA) was assigned the task of finding Nazi agents who had scattered around the world after Germany's defeat. Those agents, known as "stay-behinds," that is, those who remain behind enemy lines, were not sought in order to be arrested or shot but rather so they could be used in case of a new war, this time against the Communists. The first one to benefit from this measure was Prince Junio Valerio Borghese, the chief of the Decima MAS, Mussolini's death squads, who had no qualms about revealing the names of his agents in order to save them. The next was René Bourguet, secretary general of the collaborationist French police, who also identified the French stay-behinds. And after the surrender, General Reinhard Gehlen, chief of the secret service of the German army on the Eastern front, was "recycled" into active service. Gehlen's organization has among its members SS intelligence officers such as Alfred Sies, Emil Augsburg, Klaus Barbie, Otto von

Bolschwing, and Otto Skorzeny, the soldier who freed Mussolini. The point is that many of these agents have been sent to South America, awaiting the moment when they will be "recycled." And much of this has been made possible thanks to the Holy See.

This first measure has been followed by others, no less worrisome, such as Operation Paperclip, which has consisted of recruiting Nazi scientists who specialize in aeronautics, biological and chemical warfare, and nuclear research to work in the United States. In many cases, their military records were falsified to free them from prosecution by the international tribunals held on German soil after the war.

Thus, after dedicating several years of my life to finding the whereabouts of dangerous Nazis, I have discovered that many of them work for those who are hunting them, and that they are living under the protection of those governments that fought them. Can you imagine a greater expression of cynicism? I wonder what has come of the Moscow Declaration of 1943, when Roosevelt, Churchill, and Stalin solemnly agreed that war criminals would not escape justice, that they would be pursued to the ends of the earth and returned to the scene of their crimes to be judged by the persons against whom they had acted. That has turned out to be an enormous lie. Europe has blamed everything that happened on Germany, the Germans in turn blame the Nazis, who in turn blame Hitler, who is dead . . . .

At this point, I can't even count on the collaboration of "Smith," whose members accept this new understanding of international relations, so to speak. So I have remained alone. Yes, José María, I am at a dead end, in a blind alley. I know too much and I'm afraid it will soon cost me my life. Yesterday a man asked for me at the reception desk of the hotel while I was out. According to the owner of the establishment, himself a Hungarian who has been living in this part of Austria for fifteen years, the person spoke German with a Hungarian accent. Naturally, I thought of Gabor, whom I have not seen since we escaped from Rome. I am afraid that he is an assassin who now works for the Allied powers. That is why I must ask you one last favor. I want you to give this letter to Montse.

She is the only person I can trust. She will know what to do with this information.

I think the time has come for me to say farewell.

Forgive me.

With deep affection,

Smith.

I DON'T KNOW HOW LONG it took me to pull myself together after reading that letter, but I felt as if I had endured the anguish of crossing an entire ocean during a fierce storm. Though I tried to hang on to the railing with all my strength, every word shook me, buffeted me about like a violent wave, again and again, word by word, paragraph by paragraph, page by page, until I felt myself rolling headlong across the deck. When I finally got to my feet, my head was bursting, my cheeks burned with humiliation, and the world ceased to contain discernible shapes and colors. Only every once in a while could I make out a flash of lightning, small shimmers of light that reached my eyes in bursts, carrying images of the past that corroborated Junio's words: Montse's and Junio's playacting that they didn't know each other in Signor Tasso's bookstore; the first Smith "baptizing" Montse with the code name "Liberty" when that name existed long before that meeting; Montse telling me the sad story of her Uncle Jaime, her abortion, and her passionate romance with a "young foreigner," who was Junio all along; Father Sansovino asking me to inform him about the prince's activities, and Smith asking me to do the same about the priest, when what both of them were doing was using me as a go-between. I thought of Montse's pained reaction after she read the news of Junio's death. I now understood her misery, her deep, extended lament, which I, in my blindness, interpreted as a simple expression of grief.

The storm finally abated and I could look up and see the horizon spreading out in front of me, but it wasn't clear and I had no hope I would ever reach it. I felt exhausted, drained, and profoundly disoriented.

Then I realized that I had in fact been waiting for that storm for years. That letter simply spelled out what my conscious mind had refused to admit but subconsciously I had always suspected. And yet, in the end, the only thing that really mattered was that I had achieved my goal of marrying the woman I loved, independently of whether my love was or was not reciprocated.

Ten years earlier Junio's letter would have destroyed me, but things were different now. I had learned that sacrifice is born of love, and I was willing to sacrifice myself in order to preserve our relationship. For a few seconds I debated with myself about what to do with the letter, then decided I would not give it to Montse. I made that decision not because I considered Junio's information unimportant but because I considered my love to be more so: I was now certain that my relationship with Montse had been built upon an enormous lie; clearly, the truth would destroy it. I decided it was best, at least for the time being, to leave things as they were, pretend I knew nothing, and wait for the wound in my heart to heal.

I went out to the terrace, found an empty flowerpot, placed the pages in it, and lit them with a match. Two minutes later, Junio's letter had been transformed into a sheet of ash so light that one puff was enough to make it fall apart. When the last wisps of smoke had cleared, I became aware of the cold damp of sweat on my chest and in the folds of my flesh.

I sat down to wait, as I did every day, for Montse to come home for lunch. I turned on the radio and tried to focus my attention on the noon news, on a report about the country's reconstruction efforts and the unseasonably cold autumn.

I wondered if the shock had left any visible signs on my face; apparently it had, for as soon as Montse arrived, she told me I looked awful. "Breakfast didn't sit right with me. I've been vomiting for the last half hour," I lied.

"Do you want me to make you some rice, peel you an apple?" she offered.

"No, thanks, I don't think I should eat anything."

"Your eyelids are swollen, as if you'd been crying," she added.

Had I cried? I wasn't even conscious of having done so. Maybe the redness in my eyes was due to the length of time I had held them open, without blinking, paralyzed by shock and incredulity.

"I've never been much good at vomiting, so it takes a lot of effort. But I'm already feeling better."

I went to wash up, and when I looked at myself in the mirror I saw that my face showed more tension than illness.

"Do you smell something burning?" Montse asked when I returned to the living room.

For a moment I had the impression that she was trying to trap me into revealing whatever it was I was keeping hidden. I even wondered if she had been waiting for that letter, whose contents she would have already known.

"I've burned some papers on the terrace," I admitted.

"You've burned some papers? What kinds of papers?"

"Old documents, unimportant letters."

"I hope not the ones I sent you from Barcelona," she joked.

I couldn't resist, and took advantage of that concession. I wanted to make it clear that I knew more than it seemed, but without giving myself away.

"No, they were letters I wrote to you and never sent you because I didn't know your address."

"I don't believe a word of it. You never spoke to me about any such letters."

"Let's just say they were letters written to you but meant for myself. They weren't letters that were meant to be sent."

"What did they say?" she asked.

"Things I'm ashamed of now. That's why I burned them."

"You have never been ashamed of showing your love in public or private. That's one of the things I've always liked about you."

"I'm not ashamed of my feelings but rather of the past," I replied.

"You're ashamed of your past?"

"That's right. After reading those letters I realized how cowardly I've been. I've always been good at registering the facts, but I've never known how to interpret emotions. To put it in other words, my life has been led too properly."

"And that bothers you?"

"Considering that the world is in large part improper, yes. Many people have taken advantage of me."

"Is this an underhanded reproach?"

It wasn't. I just wanted to give my wounded pride a touch of satisfaction.

"You seem strange," she added.

"I'm just tired."

And it was true. I was exhausted, incapable of thinking even moments ahead.

ON JANUARY 6, we decided to join in the celebration of the Epiphany, which in Italy has come to be personified by a good witch named Befana. Befana wears striped robes, worn-out shoes, and travels on a broomstick, which allows her to move through the air at great speed, land on rooftops, and slip down chimneys to leave presents for children. Befana's operational center in Rome is Piazza Navona, where everybody, including street vendors and musicians, gathers each year on that day.

The rain, which had been falling incessantly all night, let up at the first light of dawn, allowing the humidity to penetrate the bones more deeply than the cold. From the Gianicolo came the penetrating fragrance of fallen leaves on wet earth. The muddy waters of the Tiber were churning, causing a deafening roar as they smashed against the dam on the Isola Tiberina, which looked like a ship tossing helplessly upon the waves. The streets were empty, increasing the sense of solitude. Montse and I walked in silence, our arms linked, trying to spot the nuances of winter—a slippery *sanpietrino*, or black cobblestone, or an icicle hanging precariously from a cornice, as if they were strangers we were seeing for the first time. We crossed Piazza Farnese and Campo dei Fiori, and when we reached Palazzo Braschi, Montse, as usual, led us the long way around to Piazza Navona.

Once in the plaza, everything suddenly changed: the solid mass of human warmth dispersed the cold. Solitude was replaced by a crowd pulsating with a single heartbeat, and the sounds of piccolos and bagpipes banished the silence.

We were quickly absorbed into the crowd, which carried us toward a group of Abruzzo shepherds, whose music accompanied a Befana who frightened the children with her grimaces and gestures.

"*Se qualcuno è stato disubbidiente, troverà carbone, cenere, cipolle, e aglio!*" she shouted. ("The naughty ones get only charcoal, ashes, onions, and garlic!")

But it seemed that all the children had been obedient and therefore received chocolates and sweets. This was the highlight of the celebration, and it was repeated over and over with new groups of children. It had been a long time since I had felt surrounded by happiness, but it did nothing but make me sad. In fact, disaster seemed imminent and had been approaching us with the implacability of a gathering storm ever since Junio's letter had arrived. Our relationship had taken a nosedive, and I was making no effort to set us right. Although the damage seemed irreparable, there might still have been some way to save our love by tying together all the loose strands of the story, but we didn't. Or, rather, I didn't. I preferred to build a wall of silence between us.

I hadn't said anything that directly revealed my feelings, but my spirits failed to rally, and I was despondent most of the time. Such erratic moods and a noticeable decrease in my appetite and energy couldn't help but alert Montse to that fact that something was profoundly wrong, and she began to be defensive. It was as if we had taken up positions for the coming assault, but so far had remained passive though vigilant.

On many occasions I was on the verge of confessing the truth—holding on to that secret served no purpose other than to accentuate my sense that the past was more alive than ever—but I couldn't muster the courage. Whenever the moment approached, my heart began to beat furiously, my lungs shut down, and the words wouldn't come out of my mouth.

We made our way through the crowd and found a chestnut seller. We bought a bag and stood in a doorway, out of the cold and away from the crowds. As had been the case recently, we hardly exchanged any words. But at that moment, surrounded by so much noise, there grew within each of us an awareness of everything not said. Then, as if my subconscious had made a decision all on its own to initiate the liberation process, I heard myself saying the following words:

"The papers I told you I burned were really a letter from Junio. I know everything."

I think I even had a surprised look on my face.

Montse looked at me with profound disdain before she said, "You don't know anything," and immediately walked away.

I followed her through the crowd, pushing people aside so I could remain near her.

"Maybe I don't know everything, but I know enough," I shouted.

"You think so? Not even if I explained it to you from the very beginning would you manage to understand."

"Maybe not, but at least it would help me to comprehend what has been, and continues to be, my role in this charade. Maybe if you could simply explain one or two things, I could stand to live with myself."

"That's really what you think it's been, then, a charade? I may have done some horrible things, I've even killed a man, but the greatest mistake of my life has been to love two men at the same time!"

It was as if we were dancing and there was no music, no rhythm, no tune, a formless dance that reflected all the sad circumstances surrounding our relationship: a divided love and a shared life.

The parade of passersby grew and the faces in the crowd blurred into an incomprehensible mass. I was afraid of losing Montse, who continued to plow her way through that human maze, so I placed my hands on her shoulders and tried to direct her to a less crowded spot.

"Let's get out of here. Let's go somewhere quieter where we can talk," I suggested.

"Don't touch me."

"There's one thing I can't make out. If the purpose of that letter was for you to have all that information about the Nazis, why did he address it to me?" I asked.

"I don't know! But I assure you there was a different plan. When the letter reached me, I was supposed to hand it over to the leadership of the Italian Communist Party. Junio promised me he would keep you out of it," she answered.

"So your meeting in Bellagio wasn't fortuitous."

"We took advantage of a librarians' conference in Como to meet. Junio wanted to bring me up to date on his latest discoveries. It wasn't a lie when I told you he was considering sending me some sensitive information because his life was in danger."

"But, at the hour of truth, he sent me the letter. Maybe he wanted to clear his conscience at the last moment," I said.

"As I did. . . . In Bellagio he told me there was a possibility we wouldn't see each other again, that 'Smith' was spreading a net around him. And when I heard that, I decided he had the right to know what had happened in Barcelona."

"Are you talking about your pregnancy and the abortion?"

Montse didn't respond. She kept walking aimlessly through the crowd.

"Well, that explains Junio's reaction, don't you think? Sending me the letter was his way of getting back at you," I suggested.

"You shouldn't have burned it. You've ruined everything. You've both ruined everything," she said with a look of such total dejection I knew I was witnessing something I hadn't thought possible: Montse, defeated.

A loud noise sounded right in front of us, an explosion that made the crowd instantly disperse. At the next instant, Montse turned toward me, the entire weight of her body falling into my arms. The suddenness of the movement made me think it was a gesture of reconciliation, but I soon realized that her limbs were completely limp.

"What's wrong? Are you okay?" I asked, my voice mounting in panic as I held up her body.

In the midst of all the confusion, she cried out with astonishment, "Gabor!"

Holding her body pressed up against mine, I felt the struggle in her chest as she tried to breathe, the beginning of the death rattle, as blood streamed from her chest. I tried to staunch the flow with my fingers, and could feel her heart beating more faintly with each pulse.

I knelt down so she wouldn't fall to the ground, and I looked up at the people surrounding us. A familiar face stood out: a man with cold blue eyes, wearing a hunter's cap with earflaps and a chin strap. As our eyes met, he smiled at me as if in greeting, stretched out his arm, and fired again.

THE DOCTORS COULD DO nothing to save Montse's life; I, on the contrary, posed less of a problem. The shot had gone through my neck and caused several tears in muscles and tissue, but miraculously had hit no arteries. My vocal cords, however, were affected, and I couldn't speak for three months. My forced silence was a serious inconvenience for the police, who had to make do with a written declaration of what had happened. I told them what I knew about Gabor and his ties to Prince Cima Vivarini. I mentioned Junio's letter, though I don't think it did much good. After all, I don't remember many of the names he mentioned, and none of the details. Or better said, the only details I remember clearly are those having to do with me and Montse.

When I asked the doctor where my wife's lifeless body was, he told me that after two days in the morgue, they had done an autopsy and had buried her according to the law. Because of the gravity of my situation for the first forty-eight hours, I had been fully sedated, and the decision about where to bury Montse had fallen to her comrades in the Italian Communist Party. They had chosen to bury her in the Protestant Cemetery in Rome, next to Antonio Gramsci. The decision seemed to me fitting.

Today, finally, I was able to visit Montse's grave, accompanied by a strange feeling that hovers between guilt and shame. I have been unable to shed a single tear. The gravestone, devoid of any adornment (though covered with numerous bouquets of flowers from many public and private organizations), lends her grave an anonymous and even soulless appearance. After thinking about it for some time, I ordered the following inscription:

LIBERTY

1917–1953

I then went to sit on the bench in front of the graves of John Keats and his faithful friend, the painter Severn. From the trees hung icicles shaped like tears, and the ground was covered with a fine sprinkling of snow. I felt the cold January air slowly enveloping my body and focused my attention on how little mountains of snow framed some of the graves, giving them a romantic air. The sadness that has weighed so heavily upon me has given way to a strange sense of peace. I am now certain that death brings a kind of liberation. Without it, life would lack symmetry, balance. I know that Gabor will likely make another attempt on my life. There is even the possibility that he has followed me here today and will appear at any moment from behind a gravestone. If that should happen, I have no intention of moving. All that is left is for me to wait. But, then again, isn't that what I have been doing all this time?

I turn to look at Keats's grave. Inside me I hear the echo of Montse's voice, her voice from one long-ago day when she read me the poet's epitaph: "Here lies one whose name was writ in water."

Acknowledgments

The Creator's Map is a work of fiction. The idea came from a mysterious stone tablet of undetermined antiquity found in Dasha, in the Russian region of Bashkortostan, that was given the name the "Creator's Map" because it showed the remains of a relief map of the Urals. I have turned the stone from Dasha into a papyrus map and transferred its source to a different region of the planet. I have also played with time and space, situating the action of the novel in Rome during the government of Mussolini. Nevertheless, many of the characters who pass through the pages of this novel were real people. Such is the case with Don José Olarra, whose character is based on documents I found at the Spanish Ministry of Foreign Affairs and in Juan María Montijano's book *La Academia de España en Roma (The Spanish Academy in Rome)*. Those sources substantiate accusations of his being an informer. At the same time, I have endeavored to be as loyal as possible to the historical events narrated in this novel, even reproducing real situations and dialogues. Of course it is not easy to write about a historical period, especially one as complex as that which includes the Spanish Civil War and the Second World War, but I have tried to do my best and have read many accounts, political chronicles, and historic essays in the course of my research. Among them, I would like to mention the book *Los cien últimos días de Berlín (The Last Hundred Days in Berlin)* by Antonio Ansuátegui, a civil engineering student at the Royal Technical College of Charlottenburg in Berlin. Mr. Ansuátegui had the advantage of arriving in Berlin in 1943, when the Second World War was in its final throes. His eyewitness report gave me a more precise idea of what life was like in the German capital in the autumn of 1943 and the winter of 1944, when the Allied air attacks intensified. Unfortunately, his book has been out of print since 1973 (when it was last published in Mexico), and as far as I know, there are only three copies of it in the Biblioteca Nacional in Madrid. I was also guided by a book by Robert Katz, *The Battle for Rome: The Germans, the Allies, the Partisans, and the Pope, September 1943–June 1944*. Highly readable and rigorously researched, this book tells of the German occupation of the Italian capital and the Allied attempts to liberate it from the Nazi noose.

The characters of SS Colonel Eugen Dollmann and the paramilitary Fascist Pietro Koch, both real historical figures, would not have appeared as they have in this novel without Mr. Katz's information and analysis. I would also like to mention Eric Frattini's magnificent book *La Santa Alianza: Cinco Siglos de Espionaie Vaticano (The Holy Alliance: Five Centuries of Vatican Espionage)*. Without it, I would never have been able to understand the role Pius XII played in relation to the Nazis and the Jewish "question," as well as the intervention of the Holy Alliance, that is, the secret services of the Vatican City State, in the events that took place before and during the war and once it was over. Thanks to that book I have been able to include in my novel controversial and enigmatic characters such as Nicolás Estorzi and Taras Borodajkewycz, two infamous spies with ties to the Holy See, who functioned in Rome before the Second World War. In a spy novel, which this pretends to be, one needs characters whose identities are doubtful and whose actions are unclear.

Since the mid-1970s, some have asserted that Martin Bormann, Adolf Hitler's personal secretary, died in the Führer's bunker. This was based on forensic analysis done on an unidentified skull, which was believed to belong to a member of the Nazi High Command. In this novel it is stated that Bormann managed to escape and found refuge in South America. This is not the case. This does not negate, however, the Holy

See's decisive participation in the escape of famous Nazis (not only Germans, but also Croatians, Hungarians, and those of other nationalities) to countries such as Spain, Argentina, Paraguay, and Bolivia.

I wish to extend my gratitude to the Spanish Academy in Rome, which awarded me a fellowship in 2004; it was within those old walls that this story was born and grew.